A SENTIMENTAL JOURNEY
WITH
THE JOURNAL TO ELIZA
AND
A POLITICAL ROMANCE

LAURENCE STERNE was born in 1713 at Clonmel in Ireland, the son of an army ensign, Roger Sterne, and his wife Agnes. In 1723 or 1724, he left Ireland for school near Halifax, proceeding in 1733 to Jesus College, Cambridge. He graduated B.A. in 1737 and entered the Church of England as a deacon, being appointed curate at St. Ives and obtaining the living of Sutton-on-the-Forest in Yorkshire the following year. In 1741, Sterne married Elizabeth Lumley. In 1759 he published the first two volumes of *The Life and Opinions of Tristram Shandy, Gentleman* in York, and found himself immediately famous. Extravagantly praised for its humour and roundly condemned for its indecency, *Tristram Shandy* was an enormous literary success and Sterne was lionized both in London and Paris. Seven subsequent volumes of *Tristram Shandy* appeared between 1761 and 1767. In 1760, Sterne published two volumes of his sermons under the title *The Sermons of Mr. Yorick*, adding two further volumes in 1766. In 1767, he met Mrs. Elizabeth Draper, twenty-three-year-old wife of an East India Company official with whom he enjoyed a brief but intense sentimental friendship which bore literary fruit in *The Journal to Eliza*. In February 1768 he published the two volumes of *A Sentimental Journey through France and Italy*. Sterne died in London of consumption on 18 March 1768.

IAN JACK is Professor of English at the University of Cambridge, and General Editor of the Clarendon Edition of the Novels of the Brontës. Among his books are *Augustan Satire*, *English Literature 1815–1832*, and *Browning's Major Poetry*.

THE WORLD'S CLASSICS

LAURENCE STERNE

A Sentimental Journey
through France and Italy
By Mr. Yorick
with
The Journal to Eliza
and
A Political Romance

EDITED WITH INTRODUCTIONS BY
IAN JACK

Oxford   New York
OXFORD UNIVERSITY PRESS

Oxford University Press, Walton Street, Oxford OX2 6DP

Oxford New York Toronto
Delhi Bombay Calcutta Madras Karachi
Kuala Lumpur Singapore Hong Kong Tokyo
Nairobi Dar es Salaam Cape Town
Melbourne Auckland Madrid

and associated companies in
Berlin Ibadan

Oxford is a trade mark of Oxford University Press

British Library Cataloguing in Publication Data

Data available

Library of Congress Cataloging in Publication Data
Sterne, Laurence, 1713-1768.
A sentimental journey through France and Italy.
(The World's classics)
Originally published: London: 1968
Bibliography: p.
I. Jack, Ian Robert James. II. Title. III. Title:
Journal to Eliza. IV. Title: Political romance.
PR3712.J3 1984 823'.6 83-26757
ISBN 0-19-281685-3 (pbk.)

7 9 10 8

Printed in Great Britain by
BPCC Paperbacks Ltd
Aylesbury, Bucks

CONTENTS

CONTENTS

ACKNOWLEDGEMENTS

In preparing this revised version of my Oxford English Novels edition, first published in 1968, I have been helped by two friends: Mr John Oates, of Cambridge University Library, and Professor Arthur H. Cash, now acknowledged as the leading authority on Sterne.

INTRODUCTION TO
A Sentimental Journey

WHEN one is speculating about the nature of originality in literature, it is as well to remember the strange case of Laurence Sterne. If ever there was an original work, it was *Tristram Shandy*. To this day it remains in a category of its own, an odd unclassifiable sort of book, an irrelevance to sociological critics and a perpetual embarrassment to historians of the novel.

And yet in fact *Tristram Shandy* is as much part of the tradition of the eighteenth-century novel as *Tom Jones* or *Humphry Clinker*. If Defoe and Richardson and Fielding and Smollett had not written their books, Sterne could not have written his. As its title reminds us—'The Life *and Opinions* of Tristram Shandy, Gentleman'—the book is among other things an oblique commentary on the conventional eighteenth-century novel. Whereas the average novel of the period deals with the life of a young man or woman in the months immediately preceding marriage and settling-down—a period (most often) of travel, adventure, and cheerful wild oats, or of virginity heroically defended—*Tristram Shandy* is the story of the begetting, the birth, and the early education of a misnamed child. Its principal characters, far from being young and attractive, are irredeemably middle-aged. Instead of an account of adventure and sexual licence, we are treated to interminable conversations between people who seldom listen to each other, and about each of whom—as about the hero himself—there hangs a strong suggestion of sexual impotence. *Tristram Shandy* stands to the eighteenth-century novel much as *Waiting for Godot* stands to the well-written play.

A Sentimental Journey makes fun of the conventional book

of travels, as *Tristram Shandy* makes fun of the conventional novel. Throughout the eighteenth century the English passion for travelling was frequently commented on. The English, wrote the Abbé Le Blanc in 1745, 'look on their isle as a prison; and the first use they make of their love of liberty is to get out of it'. As the century wore on the habit of travelling grew more widespread. In 1772 we find the author of *Letters Concerning the Present State of England* estimating that where 'one Englishman travelled in the reigns of the first two Georges, ten now go on a grand tour'. Fifteen years earlier Dean Tucker had produced his *Instructions for Travellers*, in which he divides 'persons who propose to themselves a Scheme for Travelling' into five classes, of which the most highly approved consists of travellers who wish to 'rub off local Prejudices . . . and to acquire that impartial view of Men and Things, which no single Country can afford'. It is not surprising that travel-books appeared in ever-increasing numbers. On one occasion Dr. Johnson gave it as his opinion that travel writers as a class 'were more defective than any other writers'. In a more tolerant mood he remarked to Boswell that Twiss's *Travels in Spain* was 'as good as the first book of travels that you will take up', adding: 'I have not, indeed, cut the leaves yet; but I have read in them where the pages are open, and I do not suppose that what is in the pages which are closed is worse than what is in the open pages.' Perhaps his most memorable observation on travel-writers is to be found in the *Idler*, where he complains that the typical writer of travels 'conducts his reader through wet and dry, over rough and smooth, without incidents, without reflection; and, if he obtains his company for another day, will dismiss him again at night, equally fatigued with a like succession of rocks and streams, mountains and ruins. . . . He that would travel for the entertainment of others, should remember that the great object of remark is human life.' On that matter, at least, Sterne would cordially have agreed with him.

The idea of writing some sort of travel-book had been in Sterne's mind ever since the winter of 1762-3, which he had spent in Toulouse. In November 1764 we find him promising to send his friend Robert Foley the seventh and eighth volumes of *Tristram Shandy*, in which he

will read as odd a Tour thro' france, as ever was projected or executed by traveller or travel Writer, since the world began—
—tis a laughing good temperd Satyr against Traveling (as puppies travel)—

A brief specimen of this odd Tour, in which Sterne makes fun of the *Nouveau Voyage de France*, by Piganiol de la Force, and other Baedekers of the period, may be in place here: it comes from chapter iv of Volume VII:

'Now before I quit *Calais*,' a travel-writer would say, 'it would not be amiss to give some account of it.'—Now I think it very much amiss—that a man cannot go quietly through a town, and let it alone, when it does not meddle with him.... For my own part, as heaven is my judge ... I know no more of *Calais*, (except the little my barber told me of it, as he was whetting his razor) than I do this moment of *Grand Cairo*; for it was dusky in the evening when I landed, and dark as pitch in the morning when I set out, and yet by merely knowing what is what, and by drawing this from that in one part of the town, and by spelling and putting this and that together in another—I would lay any travelling odds, that I this moment write a chapter upon *Calais* as long as my arm ...

The satirical tour is one of the better episodes in this instalment of *Tristram Shandy*, but it has the unmistakable air of an interpolation made by an author whose inspiration is beginning to flag. The public noticed this, and so did the reviewers. In the *Monthly Review* for February 1765 Ralph Griffiths wrote:

The Public, if I guess right, will have *had enough*, by the time they get to the end of your eighth volume.... One of our gentlemen once remarked ... that he thought your excellence lay in the PATHETIC. I think so too. In my opinion, the little story of LE

FEVRE has done you more honour than every thing else you have wrote, except your Sermons. Suppose you were to strike out a new plan? Give us none but amiable or worthy, or exemplary characters; or, if you will, to enliven the drama, throw in the *innocently humourous*. . . . Paint Nature in her loveliest dress—her native simplicity. Draw natural scenes, and interesting situations—In fine, Mr. Shandy . . . excite our passions to *laudable* purposes. . . . Let morality, let the cultivation of virtue be your aim—let wit, humour, elegance and pathos be the means.

This was sound advice, not only because many readers had in fact had enough of *Tristram Shandy*, but also because 'the PATHETIC' was now exercising an increasing influence. In England people were reading Goldsmith and Shenstone and Gray: in France they were reading the *Contes moraux* of Marmontel and the *Nouvelle Héloïse* of Rousseau.

In October 1765 Sterne went abroad again, travelling from Calais to Paris and on to Italy in search of inspiration for a new book. Although he remained abroad for some eight months it is a paradoxical fact that the event which gave him most help in the composition of his book occurred in England a month or so before his return. Early in May, R. Baldwin published two volumes with the following rather pompous legend on their title-page: 'Travels through France and Italy. Containing Observations on Character, Customs, Religion, Government, Police, Commerce, Arts, and Antiquities. With a particular Description of the Town, Territory, and Climate of Nice: To which is added, A Register of the Weather, kept during a Residence of Eighteen Months in that City. By T. Smollett, M. D.' There followed a motto from Ennius:

> Ut Homo qui erranti comiter monstrat viam,
> Quasi lumen de suo lumine accendat, facit;
> Nihilominus ipsi luceat, cum illi accenderit.

Sterne knew that Smollett had been writing his travels, and when the book came into his hands he must have felt a mischievous gratification. Remembering (perhaps) Dean Tucker's categories of travellers he decided to offer a classification of his own, featuring Smollett as a Splenetic Traveller and Samuel Sharp (another medical man who published a travel-book in the same year) as a Proud Traveller. 'The learned SMELFUNGUS', Sterne writes in his *Journey* ('Smeldungus' had been the original nickname), 'travelled from Boulogne to Paris—from Paris to Rome—and so on—but he set out with the spleen and jaundice, and every object he pass'd by was discoloured or distorted—He wrote an account of them, but 'twas nothing but the account of his miserable feelings.' Grossly unfair, of course: Smollett's *Travels* have a great deal of merit, and if they contain more complaints than is altogether becoming, Smollett had travelled as a seriously sick man. Sterne was not concerned to give a true account of Smollett and his *Travels*, but to promote Yorick and *his*. Smollett's book helped Sterne to define a *persona* for himself, as a traveller. He would be the Sentimental Traveller, and his observations would be 'altogether of a different sort from any of my forerunners'.

It is interesting to trace the composition of the book, as recorded in Sterne's letters. In July 1766, about a month after his return from abroad, we find him assuring a correspondent that next year he will 'begin a new work of four volumes, which when finish'd, I shall continue Tristram with fresh spirit'. By 20 February in the following year the work has acquired its title:

Im going to publish a *Sentimental Journey* through *France & Italy*—the undertaking is protected & highly encouraged by all our *Noblesse*—& at the rate tis subscribed-for, will bring me a thousand guineas (au moins)—twil be an Original—in large Quarto—the Subscription half a Guinea—if you can procure me the honour of a few names of men of Science or Fashion—I shall thank you.

Three days later he tells his daughter that he will not begin the book until he reaches Coxwould, adding: 'I have laid a plan for something new, quite out of the beaten track.' In March he wishes that Eliza Draper could be by him as he writes: in June he complains that he cannot get on with his book because of thinking of Eliza, and then brings her in.[1] When he sets out for Crazy Castle, on 21 June, he takes his 'sentimental Voyage' and his *Journal* with him, 'as certain as the two first Wheels of my Chariot'. On the last day of the month he writes to Ignatius Sancho about his health and his new book:

> I left town very poorly—and with an idea I was taking leave of it for ever. . . . I shall live this year at least, I hope, be it but to give the world, before I quit it, as good impressions of me, as you have, Sancho. I would only covenant for just so much health and spirits, as are sufficient to carry my pen thro' the task I have set it this summer.

Three days later he tells Eliza that he is able to 'steal something every day from my sentimental Journey—to obey a more sentimental impulse' in writing to her; while a letter to Mr. and Mrs. James on the 6th records that he is now 'beginning to be truly busy' on his new book: 'the pains and sorrows of this life having retarded its progress—but I shall make up my lee-way, and overtake every body in a very short time.' On 3 September he assures Thomas Becket that *A Sentimental Journey* 'goes on well—and some Geniuses in the North declare it an Original work, and likely to take in all Kinds of Readers', concluding this ambiguous observation with the proverb that 'the proof of the pudding is in the eating'. A week or two later a minor writer called Richard Griffith met Sterne at the home of the Bishop of Cork and Ross, and wrote of *A Sentimental Journey* as follows:

> It has all the Humour and Address of the best Parts of Tristram, and is quite free from the Grossness of the worst. There is but about

Half a Volume wrote of it yet. He promises to spin the Idea through several Volumes, in the same chaste way, and calls it his *Work of Redemption*.

On 27 September Sterne tells a friend that he hopes to see him in London in the spring:

and then my Sentimental Journey will, I dare say, convince you that my feelings are from the heart, and that that heart is not of the worst of molds—praised be God for my sensibility! Though it has often made me wretched, yet I would not exchange it for all the pleasures the grossest sensualist ever felt.

A week later he writes to tell Mr. and Mrs. James that he has been 'hard writing' ever since he left Scarborough, and hopes to be able to visit them by Christmas:

I assure you I spur on my Pegasus more violently upon that account, and am now determined not to draw bit, till I have finish'd this Sentimental Journey.

On 12 November he says that he is certain that the book will please Mrs. James and his daughter:

—I can answer for those two. It is a subject which works well, and suits the frame of mind I have been in for some time past—I told you my design in it was to teach us to love the world and our fellow creatures better than we do—so it runs most upon those gentler passions and affections, which aid so much to it.

Three days later he writes as follows to a certain mysterious 'Hannah':

I have something else for you, which I am fabricating at a great rate, & that is my Journey, which shall make you cry as much as ever it made me laugh—or I'll give up the Business of sentimental writing—& write to the Body . . .

On the 28th he tells an unidentified Earl that Yorick

has worn out both his spirits and body with the Sentimental Journey—'tis true that an author must feel himself, or his reader will not—but I have torn my whole frame into pieces by my feelings. . . . I have long been a sentimental being—whatever your Lordship may think to the contrary.—The world has imagined, because I wrote Tristram Shandy, that I was myself more Shandean than I really ever was. . . . If it is not thought a chaste book, mercy on them that read it, for they must have warm imaginations indeed!

On 3 December he is nearing the end of his patience, and of the book:

In three weeks I shall kiss your hand [he writes to Sir George Macartney]—and sooner, if I can finish my Sentimental Journey. —The duce take all sentiments! I wish there was not one in the world! . . . Unless what I shall bring forth is not *press'd* to death by these devils of printers, I shall have the honour of presenting to you a *couple of as clean brats* as ever chaste brain conceiv'd—they are frolicksome too, *mais cela n'empeche pas* . . .

On 26 February we find him presenting Mrs. Montagu with 'a set upon Imp¹ Paper before the publication', and the book appeared a day or two later.

The idea of *A Sentimental Journey* is simple enough. 'When once you have thought of big men and little men', as Johnson observed of *Gulliver's Travels*, 'it is easy to do all the rest.' Once Sterne had thought of a Sentimental Traveller, his main task was that of selection and elimination. The book may be compared to a portfolio of sketches made by an artist who knows his own subject-matter, and who ignores everything else. Here is Yorick's comment on his journey from Paris to Versailles:

As there was nothing in this road, or rather nothing which I look for in travelling, I cannot fill up the blank better than with a short history of this self-same bird, which became the subject of the last chapter.

There is no attempt at all to conform to the importance attached to things by more conventional travellers:

I have not seen the Palais royal—nor the Luxembourg—nor the Façade of the Louvre—nor have attempted to swell the catalogues we have of pictures, statues, and churches—I conceive every fair being as a temple, and would rather enter in, and see the original drawings and loose sketches hung up in it, than the transfiguration of Raphael itself.

When he visits a place that offers nothing to his Sensibility, he will say nothing of it. When (on the other hand) a great deal happens, he need not worry at all about keeping conventional proportions. As in *Tristram Shandy*, what concerns Sterne is not time as measured by watches and calendars, but time as measured by the beating of his own heart:

Lord! said I, hearing the town clock strike four, and recollecting that I had been little more than a single hour in Calais—

—What a large volume of adventures may be grasped within this little span of life by him who interests his heart in every thing, and who, having eyes to see, what time and chance are perpetually holding out to him as he journeyeth on his way, misses nothing he can *fairly* lay his hands on—

Which raises the question of the Fille de Chambre on the last page.

Since we know that Sterne travelled in search of inspiration, it is natural to look for autobiographical elements in *A Sentimental Journey*. Yet while Yorick has a good deal in common with his creator, only a simple-minded reader will identify the two. Such incidents as we can check seldom seem to correspond to actual events. The adventure of the shared bedroom did not happen to Sterne himself, but to an acquaintance; and the reality was much less piquant than the fiction was to be. Sterne's manipulation of his memories is constantly crossing the line that divides fiction and fact. The description of his encounter with Smollett in 'the grand portico of the Pantheon' at Rome, with the latter's remark that it was '*nothing but a huge cock-pit*', is a story based on an actual remark in Smollett's *Travels*. It is true that Mrs. Thrale claimed to have met the original of Father Lorenzo in 1775, when she was at Calais with her husband and Dr. Johnson; but against this must be set the statement attributed to M. Dessin, 'that no monk any way answering that description, ever in his time, lived at Calais'. It is true that an account of Sterne supposedly based on the reminiscences of 'La Fleur' appeared in the *European Magazine* in the year 1790; but one does not have to be very suspicious to doubt its veracity. It is true that Sterne had to wait upon the comte de Choiseul at Versailles to solicit help in the matter of a passport; but one cannot possibly tell whether the 'great Indulgence' shown him took the form with which we are familiar in the pages of his book. It is something of a relief to come on the reassuring fact that M. Dessin was in fact the name of the proprietor of an inn in Calais.

One difficulty is that Sterne travelled in France on two occasions, and that *A Sentimental Journey* seems to owe more to his visit of 1762-4 than to that of 1765-6. But a more fundamental difficulty is that the experiences which matter to a Sentimental Traveller are precisely of the sort which leaves no record in the history books. Sterne may well have seen or heard of real beggars who suggested to him the aristocratic beggar whom he describes at Versailles, or the flattering beggar who occurs in his description of Paris. How are we ever to know? Was there a dead ass lying on the road between Montreuil and Nampont, one day in 1765—or in 1762? Was there a starling in a cage at Sterne's hotel in Paris which had been taught to say 'I can't get out—I can't get out'? How many little milliners did Sterne talk to, during his various visits to Paris, and what precisely did he say to them?

Faced with such tantalizing problems, we do well to remember what the Sentimental Traveller does with the love-letter so obligingly provided by the warm-hearted 'La Fleur'. First of all he changes the Corporal into the Count: then he says 'nothing about mounting guard on Wednesday': and then—

realizing that further treatment is required—he goes on to take the cream 'gently off it' and to whip it up 'in my own way'. Whatever facts there may be in *A Sentimental Journey*, they have been whipped up in Sterne's own manner into a confection of remarkable lightness, and the result is closer to fiction than to rapportage, closer to the novel than to a travel-book. It may in fact be regarded as yet another offshoot from the picaresque stock which bore such varied fruit throughout the seventeenth and eighteenth centuries and which remains unpredictably alive to the present day. Yorick is not (after all) the first amorous traveller to be met with in European fiction; nor is he the first protagonist of a novel to be accompanied by a resourceful servant whose character is admirably suited to his own. The fact that the name 'La Fleur' is that of a servant in a well-known play by Philippe Néricault (Destouches)—*Le Glorieux*—is itself suggestive. Sterne is not the first wanderer to describe the hardships and the strokes of good fortune that have come his way, or to entertain us with wise reflections, inset stories, *doubles entendres*, and accounts of remarkable coincidences. He is not the first eighteenth-century novelist to describe an encounter with a strange lady in the bedroom of an inn.

'*C'est le ton qui fait la chanson*', and one is tempted to say that the tone of *A Sentimental Journey* is given by the amorous encounters which begin when the Traveller meets the fair Flemish lady as he negotiates to buy a carriage, and terminate so tantalizingly when volume ii breaks off. The completed work is very different from the book suggested by Ralph Griffiths, a study in 'the PATHETIC' full of exemplary characters enlivened only by 'the *innocently humourous*'. We do not know how far Sterne's intentions developed as he wrote, but it may be significant that the only references in the letters which suggest anything 'frolicksome' in the book are the last three, which come from letters written shortly before the manuscript was dispatched to the printers. The main theme of the book is the connection between sexual attraction and the finer feelings in man and woman—a theme first suggested by the way in which the Traveller refuses alms to the Franciscan when he is alone, and then makes amends because he is anxious to give the Flemish lady a favourable impression of his own character. 'If ever I do a mean action', the Traveller comments elsewhere, 'it must be in some interval betwixt one passion and another; whilst this interregnum lasts, I always perceive my heart locked up.' It is the combination of Sentiment with a sophisticated eroticism which saves the book from insipidity and makes it still a living classic in an age when Mackenzie's *The Man of Feeling*, the most celebrated of all the imitations, has become a mere historical curiosity. '*Qu'en pensez-vous?*', as M. Dessin asked Frederic Reynolds, 'in a voice lowered almost to a whisper'.

NOTE ON THE TEXTS

THE text of *A Sentimental Journey* is based on that of the first edition (*A*), which appeared about 27 February 1768. In the second edition, which appeared on 29 March (eleven days after the death of Sterne), a number of misprints and other obvious errors were corrected, but there are no signs of authorial revision. I depart from the text of the first edition only in the following instances:

Page and line
of present edition

11, 12–14
The simple Traveller, and last of all (if you please) The Sentimental Traveller (meaning thereby myself)]

The simple Traveller, And last of all (if you please) The Sentimental Traveller (meaning thereby myself) *A*

17, 20 attached] which attached *A*
32, 11 ill off] ill of *A*
37, 4 well be,] be well, *A*
45, 6 *fille de chambre*,] *fille dè chambre*, *A*
46, 15 angry:] angry· *A*
50, 21 to think] of thinking *A*
64, 13 he loves] he love *A*
65, 5 if it is] if is *A*
65, 19 one] one one *A*
65, 35 together.] together *A*
68, 6 set out;] sat out; *A*
68, 18, 20, and 26–7 La Fleur] Le Fleur *A*
70, 21 I could not] that I could not *A*
71, 35 nor do I remember] or do I remember *A*
72, 31 multitude of] multitude of of *A*
73, 34 by myself] by himself *A*
74, 15 a livre] a a livre *A*
74, 29 Lord C's gentleman] Lord's C's gentleman *A*
78, 11 coachman] coachmen *A*
85, 21 *Me Voici!*] Me, *Voici! A*
87, 3 moments!—] moments!— — *A*
89, 19 *polis.*] *poli.s A*
90, 4 the heart] the the heart *A*

90, 10 refinements,] resentments, *A*
90, 21 rubbing] ribbing *A*
91, 15 WHEN] WHEY *A*
92, 4-5 the same colour as] the same colour of *A*
93, 16 into the left—] into into the left— *A*
99, 19 Montriul] Montreal *A*
104, 29 where am I] where I am *A*
105, 21 be read] me read *A*
106, 16 prithee,] pritheé, *A*
109, 3 the morning] the the morning *A*
113, 17-18 neighbourhood] neighbouthood *A*
116, 1 too much] to much *A*
117, 5 sufferings had] sufferings has *A*
121, 3 his road up.] his up road. *A*
121, 19 beds in it,] beds, in it *A*
121, 34 a look] alook *A*
123, 33 inasmuch as] inasmuch *A*
124, 34 by way of asseveration—] by way asseveration— *A*

In the first edition open inverted commas are renewed at the beginning of each new line of a speech or other quotation: no attempt has been made to follow this practice. Nor have the full-stops after the heading of each chapter been reproduced.

The text of *The Journal to Eliza* is based on that in *Letters of Laurence Sterne*, edited by Lewis Perry Curtis, but it has been collated throughout with the manuscript in the British Museum. Fuller annotation (to which the brief notes in the present edition are indebted) may be found in Curtis. Whereas Curtis presents an exact transcript, I have omitted almost all the numerous deletions in the manuscript, and expanded most of the abbreviations. Like Curtis, I retain Sterne's spelling and punctuation. On several occasions Sterne's original doubling of words has been retained.

A Political Romance is reprinted from the copy in the Library of Trinity College, Cambridge, in strict observance of Sterne's injunction to the original printer: 'at your Peril, ... do not presume to alter or transpose one Word, nor rectify one false Spelling, nor so much as add or diminish one Comma or Tittle, in or to my *Romance*.'

SELECT BIBLIOGRAPHY

STERNE'S principal publications are listed in the Chronology on pp. xxv–vi. The most comprehensive edition of the *Works* is still that edited by Wilbur L. Cross (12 vols., New York, 1904), but it is being slowly replaced by the Florida Edition. The Shakespeare Head Edition was published in seven volumes at Oxford in 1926–7. *A Political Romance* has been reprinted for The Club of Odd Volumes (by Bruce Rogers, with an introduction by Cross, Boston, Mass., Oct. 1914), and in facsimile by the Scolar Press (Menston, Yorkshire, 1971). The 1769 text was reprinted for the Georgian Society (London) in 1902, along with *Yorick's Sentimental Journey Continued . . . by Eugenius*. There is a useful edition of *Tristram Shandy* by James Aiken Work (Odyssey Press, New York, 1940), and another by Ian Campbell Ross (World's Classics, 1983). The edition of the *Letters* by L. P. Curtis (Oxford, 1935), which includes a careful transcription of *The Journal to Eliza*, is indispensable.

Little need be said of early criticism. *Illustrations of Sterne*, by John Ferriar (1798; second ed., 2 vols., 1812), is notable as the first source-study of an English novelist. Hazlitt described My Uncle Toby as 'one of the finest compliments ever paid to human nature' (*Lectures on the English Comic Writers*, 1819, Lecture vi). Thackeray was much less complimentary in *The English Humourists of the Eighteenth Century* (1853). Leslie Stephen's essay in *Hours in a Library* (vol. iii, 1879) is of great interest.

The most important modern study is *Laurence Sterne: The Early & Middle Years*, by Arthur H. Cash (1975), now complemented by *The Later Years* (1986), by the same author. *The Life and Times of Laurence Sterne*, by Wilbur L. Cross (3rd ed., New Haven and London, 1929), is still worth consulting. Other important studies include: L. P. Curtis, *The Politicks of Laurence Sterne* (Oxford and London, 1929); John Traugott, *Tristram Shandy's World: Sterne's Philosophical Rhetoric* (Berkeley and Los Angeles, 1954); Stuart Tave, *The Amiable Humorist* (Chicago, 1960); Henri Fluchère, *Laurence Sterne: de l'homme à l'œuvre* (Paris, 1961; trans. and abridged by Barbara Bray, London, 1965); Melvyn New, *Laurence Sterne as Satirist* (Gainesville, Florida, 1965); Arthur H. Cash, *Sterne's Comedy of Moral Sentiments: The Ethical Dimension of the 'Journey'* (Pittsburgh, Pennsylvania, 1966); John M. Stedmond, *The Comic Art of Laurence Sterne: Convention and Innovation in 'Tristram Shandy' and 'A Sentimental Journey'* (Toronto and London, 1967); Ronald Paulson, *Satire and the Novel in Eighteenth-Century England* (New Haven and London, 1967); Arthur H. Cash and John M. Stedmond (eds.), *The Wingèd Skull* (London and Kent, Ohio, 1971); Richard A. Lanham, *Tristram Shandy: the Games of Pleasure* (Berkeley, California U. P., 1973); and *Sterne: The Critical Heritage*, ed. Alan B. Howes (London and Boston, 1974).

Articles cannot be listed here, but mention must be made of important treatments of Sterne in *To the Palace of Wisdom*, by Martin Price (New York, 1965), and in four notable books on the novel: A. A. Mendilow, *Time and the Novel* (London, 1952); Dorothy Van Ghent, *The English Novel, Form and Function* (New York, 1953); A. D. McKillop, *The Early Masters of English Fiction* (Lawrence, Kansas, 1956); and Wayne C. Booth, *The Rhetoric of Fiction* (Chicago, 1961).

The standard edition of *A Sentimental Journey* is that edited by Gardner D. Stout (Berkeley and Los Angeles, 1967). Stout's text and apparatus are of a high order, but the text given here corrects a handful of misprints from the first edition, while the notes deal with one or two matters passed over by him, notably the meaning of the opening of the book.

A CHRONOLOGY OF
LAURENCE STERNE

A
SENTIMENTAL JOURNEY
THROUGH
FRANCE AND ITALY
BY
MR. YORICK

VOLUME I

A SENTIMENTAL JOURNEY
&c. &c.

——T H E Y order, said I, this matter[1] better in France—
——You have been in France? said my gentleman,[2] turning
quick upon me with the most civil triumph in the world.—
Strange! quoth I, debating the matter with myself, That one
and twenty miles sailing, for 'tis absolutely no further from
Dover to Calais, should give a man these rights—I'll look into
them: so giving up the argument—I went straight to my
lodgings, put up half a dozen shirts and a black pair of silk
breeches—'the coat I have on, said I, looking at the sleeve,
will do'—took a place in the Dover stage; and the packet
sailing at nine the next morning—by three I had got sat down
to my dinner upon a fricassee'd chicken so incontestably in
France, that had I died that night of an indigestion, the whole
world could not have suspended the effects of the *Droits
d'aubaine*—my shirts, and black pair of silk breeches—portmanteau and all must have gone to the King of France—even
the little picture which I have so long worn, and so often have
told thee, Eliza, I would carry with me into my grave, would
have been torn from my neck.—Ungenerous!—to seize upon
the wreck of an unwary passenger, whom your subjects had
beckon'd to their coast—by heaven! SIRE, it is not well done;
and much does it grieve me, 'tis the monarch of a people so
civilized and courteous, and so renown'd for sentiment and
fine feelings, that I have to reason with——

But I have scarce set foot in your dominions——

* All the effects of strangers (Swiss and Scotch excepted) dying in France, are
seized by virtue of this law, tho' the heir be upon the spot——the profit of these
contingencies being farm'd, there is no redress.[3]

CALAIS

When I had finish'd my dinner, and drank the King of France's health, to satisfy my mind that I bore him no spleen, but, on the contrary, high honour for the humanity of his temper—I rose up an inch taller for the accommodation.[1]

—No—said I—the Bourbon is by no means a cruel race: they may be misled like other people; but there is a mildness in their blood. As I acknowledged this, I felt a suffusion of a finer kind upon my cheek—more warm and friendly to man, than what Burgundy (at least of two livres a bottle, which was such as I had been drinking) could have produced.

—Just God! said I, kicking my portmanteau aside, what is there in this world's goods which should sharpen our spirits, and make so many kind-hearted brethren of us, fall out so cruelly as we do by the way?

When man is at peace with man, how much lighter than a feather is the heaviest of metals in his hand! he pulls out his purse, and holding it airily and uncompress'd, looks round him, as if he sought for an object to share it with—In doing this, I felt every vessel in my frame dilate—the arteries beat all chearily together, and every power which sustained life, perform'd it with so little friction, that 'twould have confounded the most *physical precieuse*[2] in France: with all her materialism, she could scarce have called me a machine—

I'm confident, said I to myself, I should have overset her creed.

The accession of that idea, carried nature, at that time, as high as she could go—I was at peace with the world before, and this finish'd the treaty with myself—

—Now, was I a King of France, cried I—what a moment for an orphan to have begg'd his father's portmanteau of me!

THE MONK
CALAIS

I HAD scarce utter'd the words, when a poor monk of the order of St. Francis came into the room to beg something for his convent. No man cares to have his virtues the sport of contingencies—or one man may be generous, as another man is puissant[1]—*sed non, quo ad hanc*—or be it as it may—for there is no regular reasoning upon the ebbs and flows of our humours; they may depend upon the same causes, for ought I know, which influence the tides themselves—'twould oft be no discredit to us, to suppose it was so: I'm sure at least for myself, that in many a case I should be more highly satisfied, to have it said by the world, 'I had had an affair with the moon, in which there was neither sin nor shame,' than have it pass altogether as my own act and deed, wherein there was so much of both.

—But be this as it may. The moment I cast my eyes upon him, I was predetermined not to give him a single sous; and accordingly I put my purse into my pocket—button'd it up—set myself a little more upon my centre, and advanced up gravely to him: there was something, I fear, forbidding in my look: I have his figure this moment before my eyes, and think there was that in it which deserved better.

The monk, as I judged from the break in his tonsure, a few scatter'd white hairs upon his temples, being all that remained of it, might be about seventy—but from his eyes, and that sort of fire which was in them, which seemed more temper'd by courtesy than years, could be no more than sixty—Truth might lie between—He was certainly sixty-five; and the general air of his countenance, notwithstanding something seem'd to have been planting wrinkles in it before their time, agreed to the account.

It was one of those heads, which Guido[2] has often painted—

mild, pale—penetrating, free from all common-place ideas of
fat contented ignorance looking downwards upon the earth—
it look'd forwards; but look'd, as if it look'd at something
beyond this world. How one of his order came by it, heaven
above, who let it fall upon a monk's shoulders, best knows:
but it would have suited a Bramin[1], and had I met it upon the
plains of Indostan, I had reverenced it.

The rest of his outline may be given in a few strokes; one
might put it into the hands of any one to design, for 'twas
neither elegant or otherwise, but as character and expression
made it so: it was a thin, spare form, something above the
common size, if it lost not the distinction by a bend forwards
in the figure—but it was the attitude of Intreaty[2]; and as it
now stands presented to my imagination, it gain'd more than
it lost by it.

When he had enter'd the room three paces, he stood still;
and laying his left hand upon his breast, (a slender white
staff with which he journey'd being in his right)—when I had
got close up to him, he introduced himself with the little story
of the wants of his convent, and the poverty of his order—
and did it with so simple a grace—and such an air of depreca-
tion was there in the whole cast of his look and figure—I was
bewitch'd not to have been struck with it—

—A better reason was, I had predetermined not to give him
a single sous.

THE MONK
CALAIS

—'Tis very true, said I, replying to a cast upwards with his
eyes, with which he had concluded his address—'tis very
true—and heaven be their resource who have no other but

the charity of the world, the stock of which, I fear, is no way sufficient for the many *great claims* which are hourly made upon it.

As I pronounced the words *great claims*, he gave a slight glance with his eye downwards upon the sleeve of his tunick— I felt the full force of the appeal—I acknowledge it, said I— a coarse habit, and that but once in three years, with meagre diet—are no great matters; and the true point of pity is, as they can be earn'd in the world with so little industry, that your order should wish to procure them by pressing upon a fund which is the property of the lame, the blind, the aged and the infirm—the captive who lies down counting over and over again the days of his afflictions, languishes also for his share of it; and had you been of the *order of mercy*, instead of the order of St. Francis[1], poor as I am, continued I, pointing at my portmanteau, full chearfully should it have been open'd to you, for the ransom of the unfortunate—The monk made me a bow—but of all others, resumed I, the unfortunate of our own country, surely, have the first rights; and I have left thousands in distress upon our own shore—The monk gave a cordial wave with his head—as much as to say, No doubt, there is misery enough in every corner of the world, as well as within our convent—But we distinguish, said I, laying my hand upon the sleeve of his tunick, in return for his appeal— we distinguish, my good Father! betwixt those who wish only to eat the bread of their own labour—and those who eat the bread of other people's, and have no other plan in life, but to get through it in sloth and ignorance, *for the love of God*.

The poor Franciscan made no reply: a hectic of a moment pass'd across his cheek, but could not tarry—Nature seemed to have had done with her resentments in him; he shewed none—but letting his staff fall within his arm, he press'd both his hands with resignation upon his breast, and retired.

THE MONK
CALAIS

My heart smote me the moment he shut the door—Psha! said I with an air of carelessness, three several times—but it would not do: every ungracious syllable I had utter'd, crouded back into my imagination: I reflected, I had no right over the poor Franciscan, but to deny him; and that the punishment of that was enough to the disappointed without the addition of unkind language—I consider'd his grey hairs —his courteous figure seem'd to re-enter and gently ask me what injury he had done me?—and why I could use him thus—I would have given twenty livres for an advocate—I have behaved very ill; said I within myself; but I have only just set out upon my travels; and shall learn better manners as I get along.

THE DESOBLIGEANT
CALAIS

When a man is discontented with himself, it has one advantage however, that it puts him into an excellent frame of mind for making a bargain. Now there being no travelling through France and Italy without a chaise—and nature generally prompting us to the thing we are fittest for, I walk'd out into the coach yard to buy or hire something of that kind to my purpose: an old *Desobligeant in the furthest corner of the court, hit my fancy at first sight, so I instantly got into it, and finding it in tolerable harmony with my feelings, I ordered the waiter to call Monsieur Dessein the master of the hôtel—

* A chaise, so called in France, from its holding but one person.

but Monsieur Dessein being gone to vespers, and not caring to face the Franciscan whom I saw on the opposite side of the court, in conference with a lady just arrived, at the inn—I drew the taffeta curtain betwixt us, and being determined to write my journey, I took out my pen and ink, and wrote the preface to it in the *Disobligeant*.

PREFACE
IN THE DESOBLIGEANT

I T must have been observed by many a peripatetic philosopher[1], That nature has set up by her own unquestionable authority certain boundaries and fences to circumscribe the discontent of man: she has effected her purpose in the quietest and easiest manner by laying him under almost insuperable obligations to work out his ease, and to sustain his sufferings at home. It is there only that she has provided him with the most suitable objects to partake of his happiness, and bear a part of that burden which in all countries and ages, has ever been too heavy for one pair of shoulders. 'Tis true we are endued with an imperfect power of spreading our happiness sometimes beyond *her* limits, but 'tiş so ordered, that from the want of languages, connections, and dependencies, and from the difference in education, customs and habits, we lie under so many impediments in communicating our sensations out of our own sphere, as often amount to a total impossibility.

It will always follow from hence, that the balance of sentimental commerce is always against the expatriated adventurer: he must buy what he has little occasion for at their own price—his conversation will seldom be taken in exchange for theirs without a large discount—and this, by the by, eternally driving him into the hands of more equitable brokers for such conversation as he can find, it requires no great spirit of divination to guess at his party—

This brings me to my point; and naturally leads me (if the see-saw of this *Desobligeant* will but let me get on) into the efficient as well as the final causes of travelling—

Your idle people that leave their native country and go abroad for some reason or reasons which may be derived from one of these general causes—

> Infirmity of body,
> Imbecility of mind, or
> Inevitable necessity.

The first two include all those who travel by land or by water, labouring with pride, curiosity, vanity or spleen, subdivided and combined *in infinitum*.

The third class includes the whole army of peregrine martyrs; more especially those travellers who set out upon their travels with the benefit of the clergy[1], either as delinquents travelling under the direction of governors recommended by the magistrate—or young gentlemen transported by the cruelty of parents and guardians, and travelling under the direction of governors recommended by Oxford, Aberdeen and Glasgow.

There is a fourth class, but their number is so small that they would not deserve a distinction, was it not necessary in a work of this nature to observe the greatest precision and nicety, to avoid a confusion of character. And these men I speak of, are such as cross the seas and sojourn in a land of strangers with a view of saving money for various reasons and upon various pretences: but as they might also save themselves and others a great deal of unnecessary trouble by saving their money at home—and as their reasons for travelling are the least complex of any other species of emigrants, I shall distinguish these gentlemen by the name of
Simple Travellers.

Thus the whole circle of travellers may be reduced to the following *Heads*.

Idle Travellers,[1]
Inquisitive Travellers,
Lying Travellers,
Proud Travellers,
Vain Travellers,
Splenetic Travellers.

Then follow the Travellers of Necessity.

The delinquent and felonious Traveller,
The unfortunate and innocent Traveller,
The simple Traveller,

and last of all (if you please) The Sentimental Traveller (meaning thereby myself) who have travell'd, and of which I am now sitting down to give an account—as much out of *Necessity*, and the *besoin de* Voyager, as any one in the class.

I am well aware, at the same time, as both my travels and observations will be altogether of a different cast from any of my fore-runners; that I might have insisted upon a whole nitch entirely to myself—but I should break in upon the confines of the *Vain* Traveller, in wishing to draw attention towards me, till I have some better grounds for it, than the mere *Novelty of my Vehicle*.

It is sufficient for my reader, if he has been a traveller himself, that with study and reflection hereupon he may be able to determine his own place and rank in the catalogue—it will be one step towards knowing himself; as it is great odds, but he retains some tincture and resemblance, of what he imbibed or carried out, to the present hour.

The man who first transplanted the grape of Burgundy to the Cape of Good Hope (observe he was a Dutch man) never dreamt of drinking the same wine at the Cape, that the same grape produced upon the French mountains—he was too phlegmatic for that—but undoubtedly he expected to drink some sort of vinous liquor; but whether good, bad, or indifferent—he knew enough of this world to know, that it did not depend upon his choice, but that what is generally called *chance* was to decide his success: however, he hoped for the best; and in these hopes, by an intemperate confidence in the fortitude of his head, and the depth of his discretion, *Mynheer* might possibly overset both in his new vineyard; and by discovering his nakedness[1], become a laughing-stock to his people.

Even so it fares with the poor Traveller, sailing and posting through the politer kingdoms of the globe in pursuit of knowledge and improvements.

Knowledge and improvements are to be got by sailing and posting for that purpose; but whether useful knowledge and real improvements, is all a lottery—and even where the adventurer is successful, the acquired stock must be used with caution and sobriety to turn to any profit—but as the chances run prodigiously the other way both as to the acquisition and application, I am of opinion, That a man would act as wisely, if he could prevail upon himself, to live contented without foreign knowledge or foreign improvements, especially if he lives in a country that has no absolute want of either—and indeed, much grief of heart has it oft and many a time cost me, when I have observed how many a foul step the inquisitive Traveller has measured to see sights and look into discoveries; all which, as Sancho Pança said to Don Quixote,[2] they might have seen dry-shod at home. It is an age so full of light, that there is scarce a country or corner of Europe whose beams are not crossed and interchanged with others—Knowledge in most of its branches, and in most affairs, is like music in an Italian street, whereof those may partake, who pay nothing—But there is no nation under heaven—and God is my record, (before whose tribunal I must one day come and give an account of this work)—that I do not speak it vauntingly

—But there is no nation under heaven abounding with more variety of learning—where the sciences may be more fitly woo'd, or more surely won than here—where art is encouraged, and will so soon rise high[1]—where Nature (take her all together) has so little to answer for—and, to close all, where there is more wit and variety of character to feed the mind with—Where then, my dear countrymen, are you going—

—We are only looking at this chaise, said they—Your most obedient servant, said I, skipping out of it, and pulling off my hat—We were wondering, said one of them, who, I found, was an *inquisitive traveller*—what could occasion its motion.— —'Twas the agitation, said I coolly, of writing a preface—I never heard, said the other, who was a *simple traveller*, of a preface wrote in a *Desobligeant*.—It would have been better, said I, in a *Vis a Vis*.

—*As an English man does not travel to see English men*, I retired to my room.

CALAIS

I PERCEIVED that something darken'd the passage more than myself, as I stepp'd along it to my room; it was effectually[2] Mons. Dessein, the master of the hôtel, who had just return'd from vespers, and, with his hat under his arm, was most complaisantly following me, to put me in mind of my wants. I had wrote myself pretty well out of conceit with the *Des-obligeant*; and Mons. Dessein speaking of it, with a shrug, as if it would no way suit me, it immediately struck my fancy that it belong'd to some *innocent traveller*, who, on his return home, had left it to Mons. Dessein's honour to make the most of. Four months had elapsed since it had finish'd its career of Europe in the corner of Mons. Dessein's coach-yard; and having sallied out from thence but a vampt-up business at the first, though it had been twice taken to pieces on Mount Sennis, it had not profited much by its adventures—but by none so little as the standing so many months unpitied in the corner of Mons. Dessein's coach-yard. Much indeed was not to be said for it—but something might—and when a few words will rescue misery out of her distress, I hate the man who can be a churl of them.

—Now was I the master of this hôtel, said I, laying the point of my fore-finger on Mons. Dessein's breast, I would inevitably make a point of getting rid of this unfortunate *Desobligeant*—it stands swinging reproaches at you every time you pass by it—

Mon Dieu! said Mons. Dessein—I have no interest—Except the interest, said I, which men of a certain turn of mind take, Mons. Dessein, in their own sensations—I'm persuaded, to a man who feels for others as well as for himself, every rainy night, disguise it as you will, must cast a damp upon your spirits—You suffer, Mons. Dessein, as much as the machine—

I have always observed, when there is as much *sour* as *sweet* in a compliment, that an Englishman is eternally at a loss within himself, whether to take it, or let it alone: a Frenchman never is: Mons. Dessein made me a bow.

C'est bien vrai, said he—But in this case I should only exchange one disquietude for another, and with loss: figure to yourself, my dear Sir, that in giving you a chaise which would fall to pieces before you had got half way to Paris—figure to yourself how much I should suffer, in giving an ill impression of myself to a man of honour, and lying at the mercy, as I must do, *d'un homme d'esprit*.

The dose was made up exactly after my own prescription; so I could not help taking it—and returning Mons. Dessein his bow, without more casuistry we walk'd together towards his Remise[1], to take a view of his magazine of chaises.

IN THE STREET
CALAIS

IT must needs be a hostile kind of a world, when the buyer (if it be but of a sorry post-chaise) cannot go forth with the seller thereof into the street to terminate the difference betwixt them, but he instantly falls into the same frame of mind and views his conventionist with the same sort of eye, as if he was going along with him to Hyde-park corner to fight a duel. For my own part, being but a poor sword's-man, and no way a match for Monsieur *Dessein*, I felt the rotation of all the movements within me, to which the situation is incident—I looked at Monsieur *Dessein* through and through—ey'd him as he walked along in profile—then, *en face*—thought he look'd like a Jew—then a Turk—disliked his wig—cursed him by my gods—wished him at the devil—

—And is all this to be lighted up in the heart for a beggarly account of three or four louisd'ors, which is the most I can be over-reach'd in?—Base passion! said I, turning myself about, as a man naturally does upon a sudden reverse of sentiment—base, ungentle passion! thy hand is against every man, and every man's hand against thee—heaven forbid! said she, raising her hand up to her forehead, for I had turned full in front upon the lady whom I had seen in conference with the monk—she had followed us unperceived—Heaven forbid indeed! said I, offering her my own—she had a black pair of silk gloves open only at the thumb and two fore-fingers, so accepted it without reserve—and I led her up to the door of the Remise.

Monsieur *Dessein* had *diabled* the key above fifty times before he found out he had come with a wrong one in his hand: we were as impatient as himself to have it open'd; and so attentive to the obstacle, that I continued holding her hand almost without knowing it; so that Monsieur *Dessein* left us together with her hand in mine, and with our faces turned towards the door of the Remise, and said he would be back in five minutes.

Now a colloquy of five minutes, in such a situation, is worth one of as many ages, with your faces turned towards the street: in the latter case, 'tis drawn from the objects and occurrences without—when your eyes are fixed upon a dead blank—you draw purely from yourselves. A silence of a single moment upon Monsieur *Dessein*'s leaving us, had been fatal to the situation—she had infallibly turned about—so I begun the conversation instantly.—

—But what were the temptations, (as I write not to apologize for the weaknesses of my heart in this tour,—but to give an account of them)—shall be described with the same simplicity, with which I felt them.

THE REMISE DOOR
CALAIS

WHEN I told the reader that I did not care to get out of the *Desobligeant*, because I saw the monk in close conference with a lady just arrived at the inn—I told him the truth; but I did not tell him the whole truth; for I was full as much restrained by the appearance and figure of the lady he was talking to. Suspicion crossed my brain, and said, he was telling her what had passed: something jarred upon it within me—I wished him at his convent.

When the heart flies out before the understanding, it saves the judgment a world of pains—I was certain she was of a better order of beings—however, I thought no more of her, but went on and wrote my preface.

The impression returned, upon my encounter with her in the street; a guarded frankness with which she gave me her hand, shewed, I thought, her good education and her good sense; and as I led her on, I felt a pleasurable ductility about her, which spread a calmness over all my spirits—

—Good God! how a man might lead such a creature as this round the world with him!—

I had not yet seen her face—'twas not material; for the drawing was instantly set about, and long before we had got to the door of the Remise, *Fancy* had finished the whole head, and pleased herself as much with its fitting her goddess, as if she had dived into the TIBER for it[1]—but thou art a seduced, and a seducing slut; and albeit thou cheatest us seven times a day with thy pictures and images, yet with so many charms dost thou do it, and thou deckest out thy pictures in the shapes of so many angels of light, 'tis a shame to break with thee.

When we had got to the door of the Remise, she withdrew her hand from across her forehead, and let me see the original —it was a face of about six and twenty—of a clear transparent brown, simply set off without rouge or powder—it was not critically handsome, but there was that in it, which in the frame of mind I was in, attached me much more to it—it was interesting; I fancied it wore the characters of a widow'd look, and in that state of its declension, which had passed the two first paroxysms of sorrow, and was quietly beginning to reconcile itself to its loss—but a thousand other distresses might have traced the same lines; I wish'd to know what they had been—and was ready to enquire, (had the same *bon ton* of conversation permitted, as in the days of Esdras)—'*What aileth thee? and why art thou disquieted? and why is thy understanding troubled?*'[2]—In a word, I felt benevolence for her; and resolved some way or other to throw in my mite of courtesy—if not of service.

Such were my temptations—and in this disposition to give way to them, was I left alone with the lady with her hand in mine, and with our faces both turned closer to the door of the Remise than what was absolutely necessary.

THE REMISE DOOR
CALAIS

THIS certainly, fair lady! said I, raising her hand up a little lightly as I began, must be one of Fortune's whimsical doings: to take two utter strangers by their hands—of different sexes, and perhaps from different corners of the globe, and in one moment place them together in such a cordial situation, as Friendship herself could scarce have atchieved for them, had she projected it for a month—

—And your reflection upon it, shews how much, Monsieur, she has embarassed you by the adventure.—

When the situation is, what we would wish, nothing is so ill-timed as to hint at the circumstances which make it so: you thank Fortune, continued she—you had reason—the heart knew it, and was satisfied; and who but an English philosopher would have sent notices of it to the brain to reverse the judgment?

In saying this, she disengaged her hand with a look which I thought a sufficient commentary upon the text.

It is a miserable picture which I am going to give of the weakness of my heart, by owning, that it suffered a pain, which worthier occasions could not have inflicted.—I was mortified with the loss of her hand, and the manner in which I had lost it carried neither oil nor wine to the wound: I never felt the pain of a sheepish inferiority so miserably in my life.

The triumphs of a true feminine heart are short upon these discomfitures. In a very few seconds she laid her hand upon the cuff of my coat, in order to finish her reply; so some way or other, God knows how, I regained my situation.

—She had nothing to add.

I forthwith began to model a different conversation for the lady, thinking from the spirit as well as moral of this, that I had been mistaken in her character; but upon turning her face

towards me, the spirit which had animated the reply was fled
—the muscles relaxed, and I beheld the same unprotected look
of distress which first won me to her interest—melancholy!
to see such sprightliness the prey of sorrow.—I pitied her
from my soul; and though it may seem ridiculous enough
to a torpid heart,—I could have taken her into my arms, and
cherished her, though it was in the open street, without
blushing.

The pulsations of the arteries along my fingers pressing
across hers, told her what was passing within me: she looked
down—a silence of some moments followed.

I fear, in this interval, I must have made some slight efforts
towards a closer compression of her hand, from a subtle
sensation I felt in the palm of my own—not as if she was
going to withdraw hers—but, as if she thought about it—
and I had infallibly lost it a second time, had not instinct more
than reason directed me to the last resource in these dangers—
to hold it loosely, and in a manner as if I was every moment
going to release it, of myself; so she let it continue, till Monsieur *Dessein* returned with the key; and in the mean time I set
myself to consider how I should undo the ill impressions
which the poor monk's story, in case he had told it her, must
have planted in her breast against me.

THE SNUFF-BOX
CALAIS

THE good old monk was within six paces of us, as the idea of
him cross'd my mind; and was advancing towards us a little
out of the line, as if uncertain whether he should break in
upon us or no.—He stopp'd, however, as soon as he came up to
us, with a world of frankness; and having a horn snuff-box

in his hand, he presented it open to me—You shall taste mine
—said I, pulling out my box (which was a small tortoise one)
and putting it into his hand—'Tis most excellent, said the
monk; Then do me the favour, I replied, to accept of the box
and all, and when you take a pinch out of it, sometimes
recollect it was the peace-offering of a man who once used
you unkindly, but not from his heart.

The poor monk blush'd as red as scarlet. *Mon Dieu!* said
he, pressing his hands together—you never used me unkindly.
—I should think, said the lady, he is not likely. I blush'd in
my turn; but from what movements, I leave to the few
who feel to analyse—Excuse me, Madame, replied I—I
treated him most unkindly; and from no provocations—'Tis
impossible, said the lady.—My God! cried the monk, with a
warmth of asseveration which seemed not to belong to him—
the fault was in me, and in the indiscretion of my zeal—the
lady opposed it, and I joined with her in maintaining it was
impossible, that a spirit so regulated as his, could give offence
to any.

I knew not that contention could be rendered so sweet and
pleasurable a thing to the nerves as I then felt it.—We
remained silent, without any sensation of that foolish pain
which takes place, when in such a circle you look for ten minutes
in one another's faces without saying a word. Whilst this
lasted, the monk rubb'd his horn box upon the sleeve of his
tunick; and as soon as it had acquired a little air of brightness
by the friction—he made a low bow, and said, 'twas too late to
say whether it was the weakness or goodness of our tempers
which had involved us in this contest—but be it as it would—
he begg'd we might exchange boxes—In saying this, he
presented his to me with one hand, as he took mine from me
in the other; and having kiss'd it—with a stream of good
nature in his eyes he put it into his bosom—and took his leave.

I guard this box, as I would the instrumental parts of my
religion, to help my mind on to something better: in truth,

I seldom go abroad without it; and oft and many a time have I called up by it the courteous spirit of its owner to regulate my own, in the justlings of the world; they had found full employment for his, as I learnt from his story, till about the forty-fifth year of his age, when upon some military services ill requited, and meeting at the same time with a disappointment in the tenderest of passions, he abandon'd the sword and the sex together, and took sanctuary, not so much in his convent as in himself.

I feel a damp upon my spirits, as I am going to add, that in my last return through Calais, upon inquiring after Father Lorenzo, I heard he had been dead near three months, and was buried, not in his convent, but, according to his desire, in a little cimetiery belonging to it, about two leagues off: I had a strong desire to see where they had laid him—when, upon pulling out his little horn box, as I sat by his grave, and plucking up a nettle or two at the head of it, which had no business to grow there, they all struck together so forcibly upon my affections, that I burst into a flood of tears—but I am as weak as a woman; and I beg the world not to smile, but pity me.

THE REMISE DOOR
CALAIS

I HAD never quitted the lady's hand all this time; and had held it so long, that it would have been indecent to have let it go, without first pressing it to my lips: the blood and spirits, which had suffer'd a revulsion from her, crouded back to her, as I did it.

Now the two travellers who had spoke to me in the coach-yard, happening at that crisis to be passing by, and observing our communications, naturally took it into their heads that we must be *man and wife* at least; so stopping as soon as they came up to the door of the Remise, the one of them, who was the inquisitive traveller, ask'd us, if we set out for Paris the next morning?—I could only answer for myself, I said; and the lady added, she was for Amiens.—We dined there yesterday, said the simple traveller—You go directly through the town, added the other, in your road to Paris. I was going to return a thousand thanks for the intelligence, *that Amiens was in the road to Paris*; but, upon pulling out my poor monk's little horn box to take a pinch of snuff—I made them a quiet bow, and wishing them a good passage to Dover—they left us alone—

—Now where would be the harm, said I to myself, if I was to beg of this distressed lady to accept of half of my chaise?—and what mighty mischief could ensue?

Every dirty passion, and bad propensity in my nature, took the alarm, as I stated the proposition—It will oblige you to have a third horse, said AVARICE, which will put twenty livres out of your pocket.—You know not who she is, said CAUTION —or what scrapes the affair may draw you into, whisper'd COWARDICE—

Depend upon it, Yorick! said DISCRETION, 'twill be said you went off with a mistress, and came by assignation to Calais for that purpose—

—You can never after, cried HYPOCRISY aloud, shew your face in the world—or rise, quoth MEANNESS, in the church— or be any thing in it, said PRIDE, but a lousy prebendary.

—But 'tis a civil thing, said I—and as I generally act from the first impulse, and therefore seldom listen to these cabals, which serve no purpose, that I know of, but to encompass the heart with adamant—I turn'd instantly about to the lady—

—But she had glided off unperceived, as the cause was pleading, and had made ten or a dozen paces down the street, by the time I had made the determination; so I set off after her with a long stride, to make her the proposal with the best address I was master of; but observing she walk'd with her cheek half resting upon the palm of her hand—with the slow, short-measur'd step of thoughtfulness, and with her eyes, as she went step by step, fix'd upon the ground, it struck me, she was trying the same cause herself.—God help her! said I, she has some mother-in-law, or tartufish[1] aunt, or nonsensical old woman, to consult upon the occasion, as well as myself: so not caring to interrupt the processe, and deeming it more gallant to take her at discretion than by surprize, I faced about, and took a short turn or two before the door of the Remise, whilst she walk'd musing on one side.

IN THE STREET
CALAIS

HAVING, on first sight of the lady, settled the affair in my fancy, 'that she was of the better order of beings'—and then laid it down as a second axiom, as indisputable as the first, That she was a widow, and wore a character of distress— I went no further; I got ground enough for the situation which pleased me—and had she remained close beside my elbow till midnight, I should have held true to my system, and considered her only under that general idea.

She had scarce got twenty paces distant from me, ere something within me called out for a more particular inquiry—it brought on the idea of a further separation—I might possibly never see her more—the heart is for saving what it can; and I wanted the traces thro' which my wishes might find their way to her, in case I should never rejoin her myself: in a word, I wish'd to know her name—her family's—her condition; and as I knew the place to which she was going, I wanted to know from whence she came: but there was no coming at all this intelligence: a hundred little delicacies stood in the way. I form'd a score different plans—There was no such thing as a man's asking her directly—the thing was impossible.

A little French *debonaire* captain, who came dancing down the street, shewed me, it was the easiest thing in the world; for popping in betwixt us, just as the lady was returning back to the door of the Remise, he introduced himself to my acquaintance, and before he had well got announced, begg'd I would do him the honour to present him to the lady—I had not been presented myself—so turning about to her, he did it just as well by asking her, if she had come from Paris?— No: she was going that rout, she said.—*Vous n'etez pas de Londre?*—She was not, she replied.—Then Madame must have come 'thro' Flanders.—*Apparamment vous etez Flammande?* said the French captain.—The lady answered, she was.—*Peutetre, de Lisle?* added he—She said, she was not of Lisle.—Nor Arras?—nor Cambray?—nor Ghent?—nor Brussels? She answered, she was of Brussels.

He had had the honour, he said, to be at the bombardment of it last war—that it was finely situated, *pour cela*—and full of noblesse when the Imperialists were driven out by the French (the lady made a slight curtsy)—so giving her an account of the affair, and of the share he had had in it—he begg'd the honour to know her name—so made his bow.

—*Et Madame a son Mari?*—said he, looking back when he had made two steps—and without staying for an answer— danced down the street.

Had I served seven years apprenticeship to good breeding, I could not have done as much.

THE REMISE
CALAIS

As the little French captain left us, Mons. Dessein came up with the key of the Remise in his hand, and forthwith let us into his magazine of chaises.

The first object which caught my eye, as Mons. Dessein open'd the door of the Remise, was another old tatter'd *Desobligeant*: and notwithstanding it was the exact picture of that which had hit my fancy so much in the coach-yard but an hour before—the very sight of it stirr'd up a disagreeable sensation within me now; and I thought 'twas a churlish beast into whose heart the idea could first enter, to construct such a machine; nor had I much more charity for the man who could think of using it.

I observed the lady was as little taken with it as myself: so Mons. Dessein led us on to a couple of chaises which stood abreast, telling us as he recommended them, that they had been purchased by my Lord A. and B. to go the *grand tour*, but had gone no further than Paris, so were in all respects as good as new—They were too good—so I pass'd on to a third, which stood behind, and forthwith began to chaffer for the price—But 'twill scarce hold two, said I, opening the door and getting in—Have the goodness, Madam, said Mons. Dessein, offering his arm, to step in—The lady hesitated half a second, and stepp'd in; and the waiter that moment beckoning to speak to Mons. Dessein, he shut the door of the chaise upon us, and left us.

C'EST bien comique, 'tis very droll, said the lady smiling, from the reflection that this was the second time we had been left together by a parcel of nonsensical contingencies—*c'est bien comique*, said she—

—There wants nothing, said I, to make it so, but the comick use which the gallantry of a Frenchman would put it to—to make love the first moment, and an offer of his person the second.

'Tis their *fort*: replied the lady.

It is supposed so at least—and how it has come to pass, continued I, I know not; but they have certainly got the credit of understanding more of love, and making it better than any other nation upon earth: but for my own part I think them errant bunglers, and in truth the worst set of marksmen that ever tried Cupid's patience.

—To think of making love by *sentiments*!

I should as soon think of making a genteel suit of cloaths out of remnants:—and to do it—pop—at first sight by declaration—is submitting the offer and themselves with it, to be sifted, with all their *pours* and *contres*, by an unheated mind.

The lady attended as if she expected I should go on.

Consider then, madam, continued I, laying my hand upon hers—

That grave people hate Love for the name's sake—

That selfish people hate it for their own—

Hypocrites for heaven's—

And that all of us both old and young, being ten times worse frighten'd than hurt by the very *report*—What a want of knowledge in this branch of commerce a man betrays, whoever lets the word come out of his lips, till an hour or two at least after the time, that his silence upon it becomes tormenting.

A course of small, quiet attentions, not so pointed as to alarm—nor so vague as to be misunderstood,—with now and then a look of kindness, and little or nothing said upon it—leaves Nature for your mistress, and she fashions it to her mind.—

Then I solemnly declare, said the lady, blushing—you have been making love to me all this while.

THE REMISE
CALAIS

Monsieur *Dessein* came back to let us out of the chaise, and acquaint the lady, the Count de L—— her brother was just arrived at the hotel. Though I had infinite good will for the lady, I cannot say, that I rejoiced in my heart at the event—and could not help telling her so—for it is fatal to a proposal, Madam, said I, that I was going to make you—

—You need not tell me what the proposal was, said she, laying her hand upon both mine, as she interrupted me.—A man, my good Sir, has seldom an offer of kindness to make to a woman, but she has a presentiment of it some moments before—

Nature arms her with it, said I, for immediate preservation—But I think, said she, looking in my face, I had no evil to apprehend—and to deal frankly with you, had determined to accept it.—If I had—(she stopped a moment)—I believe your good will would have drawn a story from me, which would have made pity the only dangerous thing in the journey.

In saying this, she suffered me to kiss her hand twice, and with a look of sensibility mixed with a concern she got out of the chaise—and bid adieu.

IN THE STREET

CALAIS

I NEVER finished a twelve-guinea bargain so expeditiously
in my life: my time seemed heavy upon the loss of the lady,
and knowing every moment of it would be as two, till I put
myself into motion—I ordered post horses directly, and
walked towards the hotel.

Lord! said I, hearing the town clock strike four, and recollecting that I had been little more than a single hour in Calais—

—What a large volume of adventures may be grasped
within this little span of life by him who interests his heart in
every thing, and who, having eyes to see, what time and chance
are perpetually holding out to him as he journeyeth on his way,
misses nothing he can *fairly* lay his hands on.—

—If this won't turn out something—another will—no
matter—'tis an assay upon human nature—I get my labour for
my pains—'tis enough—the pleasure of the experiment has
kept my senses, and the best part of my blood awake, and laid
the gross to sleep.

I pity the man who can travel from *Dan* to *Beersheba*,[1] and
cry, 'Tis all barren—and so it is; and so is all the world to him
who will not cultivate the fruits it offers. I declare, said I,
clapping my hands chearily together, that was I in a desart,
I would find out wherewith in it to call forth my affections—
If I could not do better, I would fasten them upon some sweet
myrtle, or seek some melancholy cypress to connect myself
to—I would court their shade, and greet them kindly for their
protection—I would cut my name upon them, and swear they
were the loveliest trees throughout the desert: if their leaves
wither'd, I would teach myself to mourn, and when they
rejoiced, I would rejoice along with them.

The learned SMELFUNGUS[2] travelled from Boulogne to
Paris—from Paris to Rome—and so on—but he set out with

the spleen and jaundice, and every object he pass'd by was discoloured or distorted—He wrote an account of them, but 'twas nothing but the account of his miserable feelings.

I met Smelfungus in the grand portico of the Pantheon—he was just coming out of it—'*Tis nothing but a huge cock-pit**, said he—I wish you had said nothing worse of the Venus of Medicis, replied I—for in passing through Florence, I had heard he had fallen foul upon the goddess, and used her worse than a common strumpet, without the least provocation in nature.

I popp'd upon Smelfungus again at Turin, in his return home; and a sad tale of sorrowful adventures had he to tell, 'wherein he spoke of moving accidents by flood and field, and of the cannibals which each other eat: the Anthropophagi'[1]—he had been flea'd alive, and bedevil'd, and used worse than St. Bartholomew, at every stage he had come at—

—I'll tell it, cried Smelfungus, to the world. You had better tell it, said I, to your physician.

Mundungus,[2] with an immense fortune, made the whole tour; going on from Rome to Naples—from Naples to Venice—from Venice to Vienna—to Dresden, to Berlin, without one generous connection or pleasurable anecdote to tell of; but he had travell'd straight on looking neither to his right hand or his left, lest Love or Pity should seduce him out of his road.

Peace be to them! if it is to be found; but heaven itself, was it possible to get there with such tempers, would want objects to give it— every gentle spirit would come flying upon the wings of Love to hail their arrival—Nothing would the souls of Smelfungus and Mundungus hear of, but fresh anthems of joy, fresh raptures of love, and fresh congratulations of their common felicity—I heartily pity them: they have brought up no faculties for this work; and was the happiest mansion in heaven to be allotted to Smelfungus and Mundungus, they would be so far from being happy, that the souls of Smelfungus and Mundungus would do penance there to all eternity.

* Vide S——'s Travels.[3]

I HAD once lost my portmanteau from behind my chaise, and twice got out in the rain, and one of the times up to the knees in dirt, to help the postilion to tie it on, without being able to find out what was wanting—Nor was it till I got to Montriul, upon the landlord's asking me if I wanted not a servant, that it occurred to me, that that was the very thing.

A servant! That I do most sadly, quoth I—Because, Monsieur, said the landlord, there is a clever young fellow, who would be very proud of the honour to serve an Englishman—But why an English one, more than any other?—They are so generous, said the landlord—I'll be shot if this is not a livre out of my pocket, quoth I to myself, this very night—But they have wherewithal to be so, Monsieur, added he—Set down one livre more for that, quoth I—It was but last night, said the landlord, *qu'un my Lord Anglois presentoit un ecu a la fille de chambre—Tant pis, pour Mad^{lle} Janatone,*[1] said I.

Now Janatone being the landlord's daughter, and the landlord supposing I was young in French, took the liberty to inform me, I should not have said *tant pis*—but, *tant mieux*. *Tant mieux, toujours, Monsieur,* said he, when there is any thing to be got—*tant pis*, when there is nothing. It comes to the same thing, said I. *Pardonnez moi*, said the landlord.

I cannot take a fitter opportunity to observe once for all, that *tant pis* and *tant mieux* being two of the great hinges in French conversation, a stranger would do well to set himself right in the use of them, before he gets to Paris.

A prompt French Marquis at our ambassador's table demanded of Mr. H——[2], if he was H—— the poet? No, said H—— mildly—*Tant pis*, replied the Marquis.

It is H—— the historian, said another—*Tant mieux*, said the Marquis. And Mr. H——, who is a man of an excellent heart, return'd thanks for both.

When the landlord had set me right in this matter, he called in La Fleur, which was the name of the young man he had spoke of—saying only first, That as for his talents, he would presume to say nothing—Monsieur was the best judge what would suit him; but for the fidelity of La Fleur, he would stand responsible in all he was worth.

The landlord deliver'd this in a manner which instantly set my mind to the business I was upon—and La Fleur, who stood waiting without, in that breathless expectation which every son of nature of us have felt in our turns, came in.

MONTRIUL

I AM apt to be taken with all kinds of people at first sight; but never more so, than when a poor devil comes to offer his service to so poor a devil as myself; and as I know this weakness, I always suffer my judgment to draw back something on that very account—and this more or less, according to the mood I am in, and the case—and I may add the gender too, of the person I am to govern.[1]

When La Fleur enter'd the room, after every discount I could make for my soul, the genuine look and air of the fellow determined the matter at once in his favour; so I hired him first—and then began to inquire what he could do: But I shall find out his talents, quoth I, as I want them—besides, a Frenchman can do every thing.

Now poor La Fleur could do nothing in the world but beat a drum, and play a march or two upon the fife. I was determined to make his talents do; and can't say my weakness was ever so insulted by my wisdom, as in the attempt.

La Fleur had set out early in life, as gallantly as most Frenchmen do, with *serving* for a few years; at the end of which, having satisfied the sentiment, and found moreover,

That the honour of beating a drum was likely to be its own reward, as it open'd no further track of glory to him—he retired *a ses terres*, and lived *comme il plaisoit a Dieu*—that is to say, upon nothing.

—And so, quoth *Wisdome*, you have hired a drummer to attend you in this tour of your's thro' France and Italy! Psha! said I, and do not one half of our gentry go with a hum-drum *compagnon du voiage* the same round, and have the piper and the devil and all to pay besides? When man can extricate himself with an *equivoque* in such an unequal match—he is not ill off—But you can do something else, La Fleur? said I— —*O qu'oui!*—he could make spatterdashes,[1] and play a little upon the fiddle—Bravo! said Wisdome—Why, I play a bass myself, said I—we shall do very well.—You can shave, and dress a wig a little, La Fleur?—He had all the dispositions in the world—It is enough for heaven! said I, interrupting him —and ought to be enough for me—So supper coming in, and having a frisky English spaniel on one side of my chair, and a French valet, with as much hilarity in his countenance as ever nature painted in one, on the other—I was satisfied to my heart's content with my empire; and if monarchs knew what they would be at, they might be as satisfied as I was.

MONTRIUL

As La Fleur went the whole tour of France and Italy with me, and will be often upon the stage, I must interest the reader a little further in his behalf, by saying, that I had never less reason to repent of the impulses which generally do determine me, than in regard to this fellow—he was a faithful, affectionate, simple soul as ever trudged after the heels of a philosopher; and notwithstanding his talents of drum-beating and spatter-dash-making, which, tho' very good in themselves, happen'd

to be of no great service to me, yet was I hourly recompenced
by the festivity of his temper—it supplied all defects—I had a
constant resource in his looks in all difficulties and distresses
of my own—I was going to have added, of his too; but La
Fleur was out of the reach of every thing; for whether 'twas
hunger or thirst, or cold or nakedness, or watchings, or whatever stripes of ill luck La Fleur met with in our journeyings,
there was no index in his physiognomy to point them out by—
he was eternally the same; so that if I am a piece of a philosopher, which Satan now and then puts it into my head I
am—it always mortifies the pride of the conceit, by reflecting
how much I owe to the complexional[1] philosophy of this poor
fellow, for shaming me into one of a better kind. With all this,
La Fleur had a small cast of the coxcomb—but he seemed at
first sight to be more a coxcomb of nature than of art; and
before I had been three days in Paris with him—he seemed to
be no coxcomb at all.

MONTRIUL

THE next morning La Fleur entering upon his employment,
I delivered to him the key of my portmanteau with an in-
ventory of my half a dozen shirts and silk pair of breeches;
and bid him fasten all upon the chaise—get the horses put to
—and desire the landlord to come in with his bill.

C'est un garçon de bonne fortune, said the landlord, pointing
through the window to half a dozen wenches who had got
round about La Fleur, and were most kindly taking their leave
of him, as the postilion was leading out the horses. La Fleur
kissed all their hands round and round again, and thrice he
wiped his eyes, and thrice he promised he would bring them
all pardons from Rome.

The young fellow, said the landlord, is beloved by all the

town, and there is scarce a corner in Montriul where the want of him will not be felt: he has but one misfortune in the world, continued he, 'He is always in love.'—I am heartily glad of it, said I,—'twill save me the trouble every night of putting my breeches under my head. In saying this, I was making not so much La Fleur's eloge[1], as my own, having been in love with one princess or another almost all my life, and I hope I shall go on so, till I die, being firmly persuaded, that if ever I do a mean action, it must be in some interval betwixt one passion and another: whilst this interregnum lasts, I always perceive my heart locked up—I can scarce find in it, to give Misery a sixpence; and therefore I always get out of it as fast as I can, and the moment I am re-kindled, I am all generosity and good will again; and would do any thing in the world either for, or with any one, if they will but satisfy me there is no sin in it.

—But in saying this—surely I am commending the passion—not myself.

A FRAGMENT[2]

——THE town of Abdera, notwithstanding Democritus lived there trying all the powers of irony and laughter to reclaim it, was the vilest and most profligate town in all Thrace. What for poisons, conspiracies and assassinations—libels, pasquinades and tumults, there was no going there by day—'twas worse by night.

Now, when things were at the worst, it came to pass, that the Andromeda of Euripides[3] being represented at Abdera, the whole orchestra[4] was delighted with it: but of all the passages which delighted them, nothing operated more upon their imaginations, than the tender strokes of nature which the poet had wrought up in that pathetic speech of Perseus,
        O Cupid, prince of God and men, &c.

Every man almost spoke pure iambics the next day, and talk'd of nothing but Perseus his pathetic address—'O Cupid! prince of God and men'—in every street of Abdera, in every house—'O Cupid! Cupid!'—in every mouth, like the natural notes of some sweet melody which drops from it whether it will or no—nothing but 'Cupid! Cupid! prince of God and men'—The fire caught—and the whole city, like the heart of one man, open'd itself to Love.

No pharmacopolist could sell one grain of helebore—not a single armourer had a heart to forge one instrument of death—Friendship and Virtue met together, and kiss'd each other in the street—the golden age return'd, and hung o'er the town of Abdera—every Abderite took his oaten pipe, and every Abderitish woman left her purple web, and chastly sat her down and listen'd to the song—

'Twas only in the power, says the Fragment, of the God whose empire extendeth from heaven to earth, and even to the depths of the sea, to have done this.

MONTRIUL

WHEN all is ready, and every article is disputed and paid for in the inn, unless you are a little sour'd by the adventure, there is always a matter to compound at the door, before you can get into your chaise; and that is with the sons and daughters of poverty, who surround you. Let no man say, 'let them go to the devil'—'tis a cruel journey to send a few miserables, and they have had sufferings enow without it: I always think it better to take a few sous out in my hand; and I would counsel every gentle traveller to do so likewise: he need not be so exact in setting down his motives for giving them—they will be register'd elsewhere.

For my own part, there is no man gives so little as I do

for few that I know have so little to give: but as this was the first publick act of my charity in France, I took the more notice of it.

A well-a-way! said I. I have but eight sous in the world, shewing them in my hand, and there are eight poor men and eight poor women for 'em.

A poor tatter'd soul without a shirt on instantly withdrew his claim, by retiring two steps out of the circle, and making a disqualifying bow on his part. Had the whole parterre[1] cried out, *Place aux dames*, with one voice, it would not have conveyed the sentiment of a deference for the sex with half the effect.

Just heaven! for what wise reasons hast thou order'd it, that beggary and urbanity, which are at such variance in other countries, should find a way to be at unity in this?

—I insisted upon presenting him with a single sous, merely for his *politesse*.

A poor little dwarfish brisk fellow, who stood over-against me in the circle, putting something first under his arm, which had once been a hat, took his snuff-box out of his pocket, and generously offer'd a pinch on both sides of him: it was a gift of consequence, and modestly declined—The poor little fellow press'd it upon them with a nod of welcomeness—*Prenez en—prenez*, said he, looking another way; so they each took a pinch—Pity thy box should ever want one! said I to myself; so I put a couple of sous into it—taking a small pinch out of his box, to enhance their value, as I did it—He felt the weight of the second obligation more than that of the first—'twas doing him an honour—the other was only doing him a charity—and he made me a bow down to the ground for it.

—Here! said I to an old soldier with one hand, who had been campaign'd and worn out to death in the service—here's a couple of sous for thee—*Vive le Roi!* said the old soldier.

I had then but three sous left: so I gave one, simply *pour l'amour de Dieu*, which was the footing on which it was begg'd—The poor woman had a dislocated hip; so it could not well be, upon any other motive.

Mon cher et tres charitable Monsieur—There's no opposing this, said I.

My Lord Anglois—the very sound was worth the money—so I gave *my last sous for it*. But in the eagerness of giving, I had overlook'd a *pauvre honteux*, who had no one to ask a sous for him, and who, I believed, would have perish'd, ere he could have ask'd one for himself: he stood by the chaise a little without the circle, and wiped a tear from a face which I thought had seen better days—Good God! said I—and I have not one single sous left to give him—But you have a thousand! cried all the powers of nature, stirring within me—so I gave him—no matter what—I am ashamed to say *how much*, now —and was ashamed to think, how little, then: so if the reader can form any conjecture of my disposition, as these two fixed points are given him, he may judge within a livre or two what was the precise sum.

I could afford nothing for the rest, but, *Dieu vous benisse— Et le bon Dieu vous benisse encore*—said the old soldier, the dwarf, &c. The *pauvre honteux* could say nothing—he pull'd out a little handkerchief, and wiped his face as he turned away—and I thought he thank'd me more than them all.

THE BIDET

HAVING settled all these little matters, I got into my post-chaise with more ease than ever I got into a post-chaise in my life; and La Fleur having got one large jack-boot on the far side of a little *bidet**, and another on this (for I count nothing

* Post horse.

of his legs)—he canter'd away before me as happy and as perpendicular as a prince.—

—But what is happiness! what is grandeur in this painted scene of life! A dead ass, before we had got a league, put a sudden stop to La Fleur's career—his bidet would not pass by it—a contention arose betwixt them, and the poor fellow was kick'd out of his jack-boots the very first kick.

La Fleur bore his fall like a French christian, saying neither more or less upon it, than, Diable! so presently got up and came to the charge again astride his bidet, beating him up to it as he would have beat his drum.

The bidet flew from one side of the road to the other, then back again—then this way—then that way, and in short every way but by the dead ass.—La Fleur insisted upon the thing—and the bidet threw him.

What's the matter, La Fleur, said I, with this bidet of thine? —*Monsieur*, said he, *c'est un cheval le plus opiniatré du monde*— Nay, if he is a conceited beast, he must go his own way, replied I—so La Fleur got off him, and giving him a good sound lash, the bidet took me at my word, and away he scamper'd back to Montriul.—*Peste!* said La Fleur.

It is not *mal a propos* to take notice here, that tho' La Fleur availed himself but of two different terms of exclamation in this encounter—namely, *Diable!* and *Peste!* that there are nevertheless three, in the French language; like the positive, comparative, and superlative, one or the other of which serve for every unexpected throw of the dice in life.

Le Diable! which is the first, and positive degree, is generally used upon ordinary emotions of the mind, where small things only fall out contrary to your expectations—such as —the throwing once doublets[1]—La Fleur's being kick'd off his horse, and so forth—cuckoldom, for the same reason, is always—*Le Diable!*

But in cases where the cast has something provoking in it,

as in that of the bidet's running away after, and leaving La Fleur aground in jack-boots—'tis the second degree.

'Tis then *Peste!*

And for the third—

—But here my heart is wrung with pity and fellow-feeling, when I reflect what miseries must have been their lot, and how bitterly so refined a people must have smarted, to have forced them upon the use of it.—

Grant me, O ye powers which touch the tongue with eloquence in distress!—whatever is my *cast*, Grant me but decent words to exclaim in, and I will give my nature way.

—But as these were not to be had in France, I resolved to take every evil just as it befell me without any exclamation at all.

La Fleur, who had made no such covenant with himself, followed the bidet with his eyes till it was got out of sight— and then, you may imagine, if you please, with what word he closed the whole affair.

As there was no hunting down a frighten'd horse in jack-boots, there remained no alternative but taking La Fleur either behind the chaise, or into it.—

I preferred the latter, and in half an hour we got to the post-house at Nampont.

NAMPONT
THE DEAD ASS

AND this, said he, putting the remains of a crust into his wallet—and this, should have been thy portion, said he, hadst thou been alive to have shared it with me. I thought by the accent, it had been an apostrophe to his child; but 'twas to his ass, and to the very ass we had seen dead in the road, which had occasioned La Fleur's misadventure. The man seemed to lament it much; and it instantly brought into my mind Sancho's lamentation[1] for his; but he did it with more true touches of nature.

The mourner was sitting upon a stone bench at the door, with the ass's pannel[2] and its bridle on one side, which he took up from time to time—then laid them down—look'd at them and shook his head. He then took his crust of bread out of his wallet again, as if to eat it; held it some time in his hand—then laid it upon the bit of his ass's bridle—looked wistfully at the little arrangement he had made—and then gave a sigh.

The simplicity of his grief drew numbers about him, and La Fleur amongst the rest, whilst the horses were getting ready; as I continued sitting in the post-chaise, I could see and hear over their heads.

—He said he had come last from Spain, where he had been from the furthest borders of Franconia; and had got so far on his return home, when his ass died. Every one seem'd desirous to know what business could have taken so old and poor a man so far a journey from his own home.

It had pleased heaven, he said, to bless him with three sons, the finest lads in all Germany; but having in one week lost two of the eldest of them by the small-pox, and the youngest falling ill of the same distemper, he was afraid of being bereft of them all; and made a vow, if Heaven would not take him from him also, he would go in gratitude to St. Iago in Spain.

When the mourner got thus far on his story, he stopp'd to pay nature her tribute—and wept bitterly.

He said, Heaven had accepted the conditions; and that he had set out from his cottage with this poor creature, who had been a patient partner of his journey—that it had eat the same bread with him all the way, and was unto him as a friend.

Every body who stood about, heard the poor fellow with concern—La Fleur offered him money.—The mourner said, he did not want it—it was not the value of the ass—but the loss of him.—The ass, he said, he was assured loved him—and upon this told them a long story of a mischance upon their passage over the Pyrenean mountains which had separated them from each other three days; during which time the ass had sought him as much as he had sought the ass, and that they had neither scarce eat or drank till they met.

Thou hast one comfort, friend, said I, at least in the loss of thy poor beast; I'm sure thou hast been a merciful master to him.—Alas! said the mourner, I thought so, when he was alive—but now that he is dead I think otherwise.—I fear the weight of myself and my afflictions together have been too much for him—they have shortened the poor creature's days, and I fear I have them to answer for.—Shame on the world! said I to myself—Did we love each other, as this poor soul but loved his ass—'twould be something.—

NAMPONT
THE POSTILLION

THE concern which the poor fellow's story threw me into, required some attention: the postillion paid not the least to it, but set off upon the *pavè* in a full gallop.

The thirstiest soul in the most sandy desert of Arabia could not have wished more for a cup of cold water, than mine did for grave and quiet movements; and I should have had an high opinion of the postillion had he but stolen off with me in something like a pensive pace.—On the contrary, as the mourner finished his lamentation, the fellow gave an unfeeling lash to each of his beasts, and set off clattering like a thousand devils.

I called to him as loud as I could, for heaven's sake to go slower—and the louder I called the more unmercifully he galloped.—The deuce take him and his galloping too—said I—he'll go on tearing my nerves to pieces till he has worked me into a foolish passion, and then he'll go slow, that I may enjoy the sweets of it.

The postillion managed the point to a miracle: by the time he had got to the foot of a steep hill about half a league from Nampont,—he had put me out of temper with him—and then with myself, for being so.

My case then required a different treatment; and a good rattling gallop would have been of real service to me.—

—Then, prithee get on—get on, my good lad, said I.

The postillion pointed to the hill—I then tried to return back to the story of the poor German and his ass—but I had broke the clue[1]—and could no more get into it again, than the postillion could into a trot.—

—The deuce go, said I, with it all! Here am I sitting as candidly disposed to make the best of the worst, as ever wight was, and all runs counter.

There is one sweet lenitive at least for evils, which nature holds out to us; so I took it kindly at her hands, and fell asleep; and the first word which roused me was *Amiens*.

—Bless me! said I, rubbing my eyes—this is the very town where my poor lady is to come.

AMIENS

THE words were scarce out of my mouth, when the Count de L***'s post-chaise, with his sister in it, drove hastily by: she had just time to make me a bow of recognition—and of that particular kind of it, which told me she had not yet done with me. She was as good as her look; for, before I had quite finished my supper, her brother's servant came into the room with a billet, in which she said, she had taken the liberty to charge me with a letter, which I was to present myself to Madame R*** the first morning I had nothing to do at Paris. There was only added, she was sorry, but from what *penchant* she had not considered[1], that she had been prevented telling me her story—that she still owed it me; and if my rout should ever lay through Brussels, and I had not by then forgot the name of Madame de L***—that Madame de L*** would be glad to discharge her obligation.

Then I will meet thee, said I, fair spirit! at Brussels—'tis only returning from Italy through Germany to Holland, by the rout of Flanders, home—'twill scarce be ten posts out of my way; but were it ten thousand! with what a moral delight will it crown my journey, in sharing in the sickening incidents of a tale of misery told to me by such a sufferer? to see her weep! and though I cannot dry up the fountain of her tears, what an exquisite sensation is there still left, in wiping them away from off the cheeks of the first and fairest of women, as I'm sitting with my handkerchief in my hand in silence the whole night besides her.

There was nothing wrong in the sentiment; and yet I instantly reproached my heart with it in the bitterest and most reprobate[2] of expressions.

It had ever, as I told the reader, been one of the singular blessings of my life, to be almost every hour of it miserably in love with some one; and my last flame happening to be blown out by a whiff of jealousy on the sudden turn of a corner, I had lighted it up afresh at the pure taper of Eliza but about three months before—swearing as I did it, that it should last me through the whole journey—Why should I dissemble the matter? I had sworn to her eternal fidelity—she had a right to my whole heart—to divide my affections was to lessen them—to expose them, was to risk them: where there is risk, there may be loss—and what wilt thou have, Yorick! to answer to a heart so full of trust and confidence—so good, so gentle and unreproaching?

—I will not go to Brussels, replied I, interrupting myself—but my imagination went on—I recall'd her looks at that crisis of our separation when neither of us had power to say Adieu! I look'd at the picture she had tied in a black ribband about my neck—and blush'd as I look'd at it—I would have given the world to have kiss'd it,—but was ashamed—And shall this tender flower, said I, pressing it between my hands—shall it be smitten to its very root—and smitten, Yorick! by thee, who hast promised to shelter it in thy breast?

Eternal fountain of happiness! said I, kneeling down upon the ground—be thou my witness—and every pure spirit which tastes it, be my witness also, That I would not travel to Brussels, unless Eliza went along with me, did the road lead me towards heaven.

In transports of this kind, the heart, in spite of the understanding, will always say too much.

THE LETTER
AMIENS

FORTUNE had not smiled upon La Fleur; for he had been unsuccessful in his feats of chivalry—and not one thing had offer'd to signalize his zeal for my service from the time he had enter'd into it, which was almost four and twenty hours. The poor soul burn'd with impatience; and the Count de L***'s servant's coming with the letter, being the first practicable occasion which offered, La Fleur had laid hold of it; and in order to do honour to his master, had taken him into a back parlour in the Auberge, and treated him with a cup or two of the best wine in Picardy; and the Count de L***'s servant in return, and not to be behind hand in politeness with La Fleur, had taken him back with him to the

Count's hôtel[1]. La Fleur's *prevenancy*[2] (for there was a pass-port in his very looks) soon set every servant in the kitchen at ease with him; and as a Frenchman, whatever be his talents, has no sort of prudery in shewing them, La Fleur, in less than five minutes, had pull'd out his fife, and leading off the dance himself with the first note, set the *fille de chambre*, the *maitre d'hotel*, the cook, the scullion, and all the houshold, dogs and cats, besides an old monkey, a-dancing: I suppose there never was a merrier kitchen since the flood.

Madame de L***, in passing from her brother's apart-ments to her own, hearing so much jollity below stairs, rung up her *fille de chambre* to ask about it; and hearing it was the English gentleman's servant who had set the whole house merry with his pipe, she order'd him up.

As the poor fellow could not present himself empty, he had loaden'd himself in going up stairs with a thousand compli-ments to Madame de L***, on the part of his master—added a long apocrypha of inquiries after Madame de L***'s health—told her, that Monsieur his master was *au desespoire* for her re-establishment from the fatigues of her journey—and, to close all, that Monsieur had received the letter which Madame had done him the honour —— And he has done me the honour, said Madame de L***, interrupting La Fleur, to send a billet in return.

Madame de L*** had said this with such a tone of reliance upon the fact, that La Fleur had not power to disappoint her expectations—he trembled for my honour—and possibly might not altogether be unconcerned for his own, as a man capable of being attach'd to a master who could be a wanting *en egards vis a vis d'une femme*; so that when Madame de L*** asked La Fleur if he had brought a letter—*O qu'oui*, said La Fleur: so laying down his hat upon the ground, and taking hold of the flap of his right side pocket with his left hand, he began to search for the letter with his right—then contrary-wise—*Diable!*—then sought every pocket—pocket by pocket, round, not forgetting his fob[1]—*Peste!*—then La Fleur emptied them upon the floor—pulled out a dirty cravat —a handkerchief—a comb—a whip lash—a night-cap—then gave a peep into his hat—*Quelle etourderie!* He had left the letter upon the table in the Auberge—he would run for it, and be back with it in three minutes.

I had just finished my supper when La Fleur came in to give me an account of his adventure: he told the whole story simply as it was; and only added, that if Monsieur had forgot (*par hazard*) to answer Madame's letter, the arrangement gave him an opportunity to recover the *faux pas*—and if not, that things were only as they were.

Now I was not altogether sure of my *etiquette*, whether I ought to have wrote or no; but if I had—a devil himself could not have been angry: 'twas but the officious zeal of a well-meaning creature for my honour; and however he might have mistook the road—or embarrassed me in so doing—his heart was in no fault—I was under no necessity to write—and what weighed more than all—he did not look as if he had done amiss.

—'Tis all very well, La Fleur, said I.—'Twas sufficient. La Fleur flew out of the room like lightening, and return'd with pen, ink, and paper, in his hand; and coming up to the table, laid them close before me, with such a delight in his countenance, that I could not help taking up the pen.

I begun and begun again; and though I had nothing to say, and that nothing might have been express'd in half a dozen lines, I made half a dozen different beginnings, and could no way please myself.

In short, I was in no mood to write.

La Fleur stepp'd out and brought a little water in a glass to dilute my ink—then fetch'd sand and seal-wax—It was all one: I wrote, and blotted, and tore off, and burnt, and wrote again—*Le Diable l'emporte!* said I half to myself—I cannot write this self-same letter; throwing the pen down despairingly as I said it.

As soon as I had cast down the pen, La Fleur advanced with the most respectful carriage up to the table, and making a thousand apologies for the liberty he was going to take, told me he had a letter in his pocket wrote by a drummer in his regiment to a corporal's wife, which, he durst say, would suit the occasion.

I had a mind to let the poor fellow have his humour—Then prithee, said I, let me see it.

La Fleur instantly pull'd out a little dirty pocket-book cramm'd full of small letters and billet-doux in a sad condition, and laying it upon the table, and then untying the string which held them all together, run them over one by one, till he came to the letter in question—*La voila!* said he, clapping his hands: so unfolding it first, he laid it before me, and retired three steps from the table whilst I read it.

THE LETTER

MADAME,

JE suis penetré de la douleur la plus vive, et reduit en même temps au desespoir par ce retour imprevû du Corporal qui rend notre entrevue de ce soir la chose du monde la plus impossible.

Mais vive la joie! et toute la mienne sera de penser a vous.

L'amour n'est *rien* sans sentiment.[1]

Et le sentiment est encore *moins* sans amour.

On dit qu'on ne doit jamais se desesperer.

On dit aussi que Monsieur le Corporal monte la garde Mecredi: alors ce sera mon tour.

Chacun a son tour.

En attendant—Vive l'amour! et vive la bagatelle!

Je suis, MADAME,
Avec toutes les sentiments les plus respecteux et les plus
    tendres tout a vous,

JAQUES ROQUE.

It was but changing the Corporal into the Count—and saying
nothing about mounting guard on Wednesday—and the
letter was neither right or wrong—so to gratify the poor
fellow, who stood trembling for my honour, his own, and the
honour of his letter,—I took the cream gently off it, and
whipping it up in my own way—I seal'd it up and sent him
with it to Madame de L***—and the next morning we
pursued our journey to Paris.

PARIS

WHEN a man can contest the point by dint of equipage, and
carry all on floundering before him with half a dozen lackies
and a couple of cooks—'tis very well in such a place as Paris—
he may drive in at which end of a street he will.

A poor prince who is weak in cavalry, and whose whole
infantry does not exceed a single man, had best quit the field;
and signalize himself in the cabinet, if he can get up into it—
I say *up into it*—for there is no descending perpendicular
amongst 'em with a '*Me voici! mes enfans*'—here I am—
whatever many may think.

I own my first sensations, as soon as I was left solitary and
alone in my own chamber in the hotel, were far from being so
flattering as I had prefigured them. I walked up gravely to the
window in my dusty black coat, and looking through the glass
saw all the world in yellow, blue, and green, running at the
ring of pleasure[1].—The old with broken lances, and in

helmets which had lost their vizards—the young in armour bright which shone like gold, beplumed with each gay feather of the east—all—all tilting at it like fascinated knights in tournaments of yore for fame and love.—

Alas, poor Yorick! cried I, what art thou doing here? On the very first onset of all this glittering clatter, thou art reduced to an atom—seek—seek some winding alley, with a tourniquet[1] at the end of it, where chariot never rolled or flambeau shot its rays—there thou mayest solace thy soul in converse sweet with some kind *grisset*[2] of a barber's wife, and get into such coteries!—

—May I perish! if I do, said I, pulling out the letter which I had to present to Madame de R***.—I'll wait upon this lady, the very first thing I do. So I called La Fleur to go seek me a barber directly—and come back and brush my coat.

THE WIG
PARIS

WHEN the barber came, he absolutely refused to have any thing to do with my wig: 'twas either above or below his art: I had nothing to do, but to take one ready made of his own recommendation.

—But I fear, friend! said I, this buckle won't stand.—You may immerge it, replied he, into the ocean, and it will stand—

What a great scale is every thing upon in this city! thought I—The utmost stretch of an English periwig-maker's ideas could have gone no further than to have 'dipped it into a pail of water'—What difference! 'tis like time to eternity.

I confess I do hate all cold conceptions, as I do the puny ideas which engender them; and am generally so struck with the great works of nature, that for my own part, if I could help it, I never would make a comparison less than a mountain at least. All that can be said against the French sublime in this instance of it, is this—that the grandeur is *more* in the *word*; and *less* in the *thing*. No doubt the ocean fills the mind with vast ideas; but Paris being so far inland, it was not likely I should run post a hundred miles out of it, to try the experiment—the Parisian barber meant nothing.—

The pail of water standing besides the great deep, makes certainly but a sorry figure in speech—but 'twill be said—it has one advantage—'tis in the next room, and the truth of the buckle may be tried in it without more ado, in a single moment.

In honest truth, and upon a more candid revision of the matter, *The French expression professes more than it performs*.

I think I can see the precise and distinguishing marks of national characters more in these nonsensical *minutiæ*, than in the most important matters of state; where great men of all nations talk and stalk so much alike, that I would not give ninepence to chuse amongst them.

I was so long in getting from under my barber's hands, that it was too late to think of going with my letter to Madame R*** that night: but when a man is once dressed at all points for going out, his reflections turn to little account, so taking down the name of the Hotel de Modene where I lodged, I walked forth without any determination where to go—I shall consider of that, said I, as I walk along.

THE PULSE
PARIS

HAIL ye small sweet courtesies of life, for smooth do ye make the road of it! like grace and beauty which beget inclinations to love at first sight; 'tis ye who open this door and let the stranger in.

—Pray, Madame, said I, have the goodness to tell me which way I must turn to go to the Opera comique:—Most willingly, Monsieur, said she, laying aside her work—

I had given a cast with my eye into half a dozen shops as I came along in search of a face not likely to be disordered by such an interruption; till at last, this hitting my fancy, I had walked in.

She was working a pair of ruffles as she sat in a low chair on the far side of the shop facing the door—

—*Tres volentieres*; most willingly, said she, laying her work down upon a chair next her, and rising up from the low chair she was sitting in, with so chearful a movement and so chearful a look, that had I been laying out fifty louis d'ors with her, I should have said—'This woman is grateful.'

You must turn, Monsieur, said she, going with me to the door of the shop, and pointing the way down the street I was to take—you must turn first to your left hand—*mais prenez guarde*—there are two turns; and be so good as to take the second—then go down a little way and you'll see a church, and when you are past it, give yourself the trouble to turn directly to the right, and that will lead you to the foot of the *pont neuf*, which you must cross—and there, any one will do himself the pleasure to shew you—

She repeated her instructions three times over to me with the same good natur'd patience the third time as the first;—and if *tones and manners* have a meaning, which certainly they have, unless to hearts which shut them out

—she seem'd really interested, that I should not lose myself.

I will not suppose it was the woman's beauty, notwithstanding she was the handsomest grisset, I think, I ever saw, which had much to do with the sense I had of her courtesy; only I remember, when I told her how much I was obliged to her, that I looked very full in her eyes,—and that I repeated my thanks as often as she had done her instructions.

I had not got ten paces from the door, before I found I had forgot every tittle of what she had said—so looking back, and seeing her still standing in the door of the shop as if to look whether I went right or not—I returned back, to ask her whether the first turn was to my right or left—for that I had absolutely forgot.—Is it possible! said she, half laughing.— 'Tis very possible, replied I, when a man is thinking more of a woman, than of her good advice.

As this was the real truth—she took it, as every woman takes a matter of right, with a slight courtesy.

—Attendez! said she, laying her hand upon my arm to detain me, whilst she called a lad out of the back-shop to get ready a parcel of gloves. I am just going to send him, said she, with a packet into that quarter, and if you will have the complaisance to step in, it will be ready in a moment, and he shall attend you to the place.—So I walk'd in with her to the far side of the shop, and taking up the ruffle in my hand which she laid upon the chair, as if I had a mind to sit, she sat down herself in her low chair, and I instantly sat myself down besides her.

—He will be ready, Monsieur, said she, in a moment— And in that moment, replied I, most willingly would I say something very civil to you for all these courtesies. Any one may do a casual act of good nature, but a continuation of them shews it is a part of the temperature[1]; and certainly, added I, if it is the same blood which comes from the heart, which descends to the extremes (touching her wrist) I am sure you

must have one of the best pulses of any woman in the world—
Feel it, said she, holding out her arm. So laying down my hat,
I took hold of her fingers in one hand, and applied the two
fore-fingers of my other to the artery—

—Would to heaven! my dear Eugenius[1], thou hadst passed
by, and beheld me sitting in my black coat, and in my lack-a-
day-sical manner, counting the throbs of it, one by one, with
as much true devotion as if I had been watching the critical
ebb or flow of her fever—How wouldst thou have laugh'd
and moralized upon my new profession?—and thou shouldst
have laugh'd and moralized on—Trust me, my dear Eugenius,
I should have said, 'there are worse occupations in this world
than feeling a woman's pulse.'—But a Grisset's! thou wouldst
have said—and in an open shop! Yorick—

—So much the better: for when my views are direct,
Eugenius, I care not if all the world saw me feel it.

THE HUSBAND
PARIS

I HAD counted twenty pulsations, and was going on fast
towards the fortieth, when her husband coming unexpected
from a back parlour into the shop, put me a little out in my
reckoning—'Twas no body but her husband, she said—so
I began a fresh score—Monsieur is so good, quoth she, as
he pass'd by us, as to give himself the trouble of feeling my
pulse—The husband took off his hat, and making me a bow,
said, I did him too much honour—and having said that, he
put on his hat and walk'd out.

Good God! said I to myself, as he went out—and can this
man be the husband of this woman?

Let it not torment the few who know what must have been

the grounds of this exclamation, if I explain it to those who do not.

In London a shopkeeper and a shopkeeper's wife seem to be one bone and one flesh: in the several endowments of mind and body, sometimes the one, sometimes the other has it, so as in general to be upon a par, and to tally with each other as nearly as man and wife need to do.

In Paris, there are scarce two orders of beings more different: for the legislative and executive powers of the shop not resting in the husband, he seldom comes there—in some dark and dismal room behind, he sits commerceless in his thrum[1] night-cap, the same rough son of Nature that Nature left him.

The genius of a people where nothing but the monarchy is *salique*[2], having ceded this department, with sundry others, totally to the women—by a continual higgling with customers of all ranks and sizes from morning to night, like so many rough pebbles shook long together in a bag, by amicable collisions, they have worn down their asperities and sharp angles, and not only become round and smooth, but will receive, some of them, a polish like a brilliant—Monsieur *le Mari* is little better than the stone under your foot—

—Surely—surely man! it is not good for thee to sit alone[3]—thou wast made for social intercourse and gentle greetings, and this improvement of our natures from it, I appeal to, as my evidence.

—And how does it beat, Monsieur? said she.—With all the benignity, said I, looking quietly in her eyes, that I expected—She was going to say something civil in return—but the lad came into the shop with the gloves—*A propos*, said I; I want a couple of pair myself.

THE GLOVES
PARIS

THE beautiful Grisset rose up when I said this, and going behind the counter, reach'd down a parcel and untied it: I advanced to the side over-against her: they were all too large. The beautiful Grisset measured them one by one across my hand—It would not alter the dimensions—She begg'd I would try a single pair, which seemed to be the least—She held it open—my hand slipp'd into it at once—It will not do, said I, shaking my head a little—No, said she, doing the same thing.

There are certain combined looks of simple subtlety—where whim, and sense, and seriousness, and nonsense, are so blended, that all the languages of Babel set loose together could not express them—they are communicated and caught so instantaneously, that you can scarce say which party is the infecter. I leave it to your men of words to swell pages about it—it is enough in the present to say again, the gloves would not do; so folding our hands within our arms, we both loll'd upon the counter—it was narrow, and there was just room for the parcel to lay between us.

The beautiful Grisset look'd sometimes at the gloves, then side-ways to the window, then at the gloves—and then at me. I was not disposed to break silence—I follow'd her example: so I look'd at the gloves, then to the window, then at the gloves, and then at her—and so on alternately.

I found I lost considerably in every attack—she had a quick black eye, and shot through two such long and silken eyelashes with such penetration, that she look'd into my very heart and reins[1]—It may seem strange, but I could actually feel she did—

—It is no matter, said I, taking up a couple of the pairs next me, and putting them into my pocket.

I was sensible the beautiful Grisset had not ask'd above a single livre above the price—I wish'd she had ask'd a livre more, and was puzzling my brains how to bring the matter about—Do you think, my dear Sir, said she, mistaking my embarrassment, that I could ask a *sous* too much of a stranger —and of a stranger whose politeness, more than his want of gloves, has done me the honour to lay himself at my mercy?— *M'en croyez capable?*—Faith! not I, said I; and if you were, you are welcome—So counting the money into her hand, and with a lower bow than one generally makes to a shopkeeper's wife, I went out, and her lad with his parcel followed me.

THE TRANSLATION[1]
PARIS

THERE was no body in the box I was let into but a kindly old French officer. I love the character, not only because I honour the man whose manners are softened by a profession which makes bad men worse; but that I once knew one—for he is no more—and why should I not rescue one page from violation by writing his name in it, and telling the world it was Captain Tobias Shandy, the dearest of my flock and friends, whose philanthropy I never think of at this long distance from his death— but my eyes gush out with tears. For his sake, I have a predilection for the whole corps of veterans; and so I strode over the two back rows of benches, and placed myself beside him.

The old officer was reading attentively a small pamphlet, it might be the book of the opera, with a large pair of spectacles. As soon as I sat down, he took his spectacles off, and putting them into a shagreen case, return'd them and the book into his pocket together. I half rose up, and made him a bow.

Translate this into any civilized language in the world—the sense is this:

'Here's a poor stranger come in to the box—he seems as if he knew no body; and is never likely, was he to be seven years in Paris, if every man he comes near keeps his spectacles upon his nose—'tis shutting the door of conversation absolutely in his face—and using him worse than a German.'

The French officer might as well have said it all aloud; and if he had, I should in course have put the bow I made him into French too, and told him, 'I was sensible of his attention, and return'd him a thousand thanks for it.'

There is not a secret so aiding to the progress of sociality, as to get master of this *short hand*, and be quick in rendering the several turns of looks and limbs, with all their inflections and delineations, into plain words. For my own part, by long habitude, I do it so mechanically, that when I walk the streets of London, I go translating all the way; and have more than once stood behind in the circle, where not three words have been said, and have brought off twenty different dialogues with me, which I could have fairly wrote down and sworn to.

I was going one evening to Martini's concert[1] at Milan, and was just entering the door of the hall, when the Marquesina di F***[2] was coming out in a sort of a hurry—she was almost upon me before I saw her; so I gave a spring to one side to let her pass—She had done the same, and on the same side too; so we ran our heads together: she instantly got to the other side to get out: I was just as unfortunate as she had been; for I had sprung to that side, and opposed her passage again—We both flew together to the other side, and then back—and so on—it was ridiculous; we both blush'd intolerably; so I did at last the thing I should have done at first—I stood stock still, and the Marquesina had no more difficulty. I had no power to go into the room, till I had made her so much reparation as to wait and follow her with my eye to the end of the passage—She look'd back twice, and walk'd along it rather side-ways, as if she would make room for any one coming up stairs to pass her—No, said I—that's a vile translation: the Marquesina has a right to the best apology I can make her; and that opening is left for me to do it in—so I ran and begg'd pardon for the embarrassment I had given her, saying it was my intention to have made her way. She answered, she was guided by the same intention towards me—so we reciprocally thank'd each other. She was at the top of the stairs; and seeing no *chichesbee*[1] near her, I begg'd to hand her to her coach—so we went down the stairs, stopping at every third step to talk of the concert and the adventure—Upon my word, Madame, said I when I had handed her in, I made six different efforts to let you go out—And I made six efforts, replied she, to let you enter—I wish to heaven you would make a seventh, said I—With all my heart, said she, making room—Life is too short to be long about the forms of it—so I instantly stepp'd in, and she carried me home with her—And what became of the concert, St. Cecilia, who, I suppose, was at it, knows more than I.

I will only add, that the connection which arose out of that translation, gave me more pleasure than any one I had the honour to make in Italy.

THE DWARF
PARIS

I HAD never heard the remark made by any one in my life, except by one; and who that was, will probably come out in this chapter; so that being pretty much unprepossessed, there must have been grounds for what struck me the moment I cast my eyes over the *parterre*[2]—and that was, the unaccountable sport of nature in forming such numbers of dwarfs—No doubt, she sports at certain times in almost every corner of the world; but in Paris, there is no end to her amusements—The goddess seems almost as merry as she is wise.

As I carried my idea out of the *opera comique* with me, I measured every body I saw walking in the streets by it— Melancholy application! especially where the size was extremely little—the face extremely dark—the eyes quick— the nose long—the teeth white—the jaw prominent—to see so many miserables, by force of accidents driven out of their own proper class into the very verge of another, which it gives me pain to write down—every third man a pigmy!—some by ricketty heads and hump backs—others by bandy legs—a third set arrested by the hand of Nature in the sixth and seventh years of their growth—a fourth, in their perfect and natural state, like dwarf apple-trees; from the first rudiments and stamina of their existence, never meant to grow higher.

A medical traveller might say, 'tis owing to undue bandages —a splenetic one, to want of air—and an inquisitive traveller, to fortify the system, may measure the height of their houses —the narrowness of their streets, and in how few feet square in the sixth and seventh stories such numbers of the *Bourgoisie* eat and sleep together; but I remember, Mr. Shandy the elder[1], who accounted for nothing like any body else, in speaking one evening of these matters, averred, that children, like other animals, might be increased almost to any size, provided they came right into the world; but the misery was, the citizens of Paris were so coop'd up, that they had not actually room enough to get them—I do not call it getting any thing, said he —'tis getting nothing—Nay, continued he, rising in his argu- ment, 'tis getting worse than nothing, when all you have got, after twenty or five and twenty years of the tenderest care and most nutritious aliment bestowed upon it, shall not at last be as high as my leg. Now, Mr. Shandy being very short, there could be nothing more said upon it.

As this is not a work of reasoning, I leave the solution as I found it, and content myself with the truth only of the remark, which is verified in every lane and by-lane of Paris. I was walking down that which leads from the Carousal to the Palais Royal, and observing a little boy in some distress at the side of the gutter, which ran down the middle of it, I took hold of his hand, and help'd him over. Upon turning up his face to look at him after, I perceived he was about forty—Never mind, said I; some good body will do as much for me when I am ninety.

I feel some little principles within me, which incline me to be merciful towards this poor blighted part of my species, who have neither size or strength to get on in the world—I cannot bear to see one of them trod upon; and had scarce got seated beside my old French officer, ere the disgust was exercised, by seeing the very thing happen under the box we sat in.

At the end of the orchestra, and betwixt that and the first side-box, there is a small esplanade left, where, when the house is full, numbers of all ranks take sanctuary. Though you stand, as in the parterre, you pay the same price as in the orchestra. A poor defenceless being of this order had got thrust some how or other into this luckless place—the night was hot, and he was surrounded by beings two feet and a half higher than himself. The dwarf suffered inexpressibly on all sides; but the thing which incommoded him most, was a tall corpulent German, near seven feet high, who stood directly betwixt him and all possibility of his seeing either the stage or the actors. The poor dwarf did all he could to get a peep at what was going forwards, by seeking for some little opening betwixt the German's arm and his body, trying first one side, then the other; but the German stood square in the most un-accommodating posture that can be imagined—the dwarf might as well have been placed at the bottom of the deepest draw-well in Paris; so he civilly reach'd up his hand to the German's sleeve, and told him his distress—The German turn'd his head back, look'd down upon him as Goliah did upon David—and unfeelingly resumed his posture.

I was just then taking a pinch of snuff out of my monk's little horn box—And how would thy meek and courteous spirit, my dear monk! so temper'd to *bear and forbear!*—how sweetly would it have lent an ear to this poor soul's complaint!

The old French officer seeing me lift up my eyes with an emotion, as I made the apostrophe, took the liberty to ask me what was the matter—I told him the story in three words; and added, how inhuman it was.

By this time the dwarf was driven to extremes, and in his first transports, which are generally unreasonable, had told the German he would cut off his long queue[1] with his knife— The German look'd back coolly, and told him he was welcome if he could reach it.

An injury sharpened by an insult, be it to who it will, makes every man of sentiment a party: I could have leaped out of the box to have redressed it.—The old French officer did it with much less confusion; for leaning a little over, and nodding to a centinel, and pointing at the same time with his finger to the distress—the centinel made his way up to it.—There was no occasion to tell the grievance—the thing told itself; so thrusting back the German instantly with his musket—he took the poor dwarf by the hand, and placed him before him. —This is noble! said I, clapping my hands together—And yet you would not permit this, said the old officer, in England.

—In England, dear Sir, said I, *we sit all at our ease.*

The old French officer would have set me at unity with myself, in case I had been at variance,—by saying it was a *bon mot*—and as a *bon mot* is always worth something at Paris, he offered me a pinch of snuff.

THE ROSE
PARIS

IT was now my turn to ask the old French officer 'What was the matter?' for a cry of '*Haussez les mains, Monsieur l'Abbe,*' re-echoed from a dozen different parts of the parterre, was as unintelligible to me, as my apostrophe to the monk had been to him.

He told me, it was some poor Abbe in one of the upper loges[1], who he supposed had got planted perdu behind a couple of grissets in order to see the opera, and that the parterre espying him, were insisting upon his holding up both his hands during the representation.—And can it be supposed, said I, that an ecclesiastick would pick the Grisset's pockets? The old French officer smiled, and whispering in my ear, open'd a door of knowledge which I had no idea of—

Good God! said I, turning pale with astonishment—is it possible, that a people so smit with sentiment should at the same time be so unclean, and so unlike themselves—*Quelle grossierte!* added I.

The French officer told me, it was an illiberal sarcasm at the church, which had begun in the theatre about the time the Tartuffe was given in it, by Moliere—but, like other remains of Gothic manners, was declining—Every nation, continued he, have their refinements and *grossiertes*, in which they take the lead, and lose it of one another by turns—that he had been in most countries, but never in one where he found not some delicacies, which other seemed to want. *Le* POUR, *et le* CONTRE *se trouvent en chaque nation*; there is a balance, said he, of good and bad every where; and nothing but the knowing it is so can emancipate one half of the world from the prepossessions which it holds against the other—that the advantage of travel, as it regarded the *sçavoir vivre*, was by seeing a great deal both of men and manners; it taught us mutual toleration; and mutual toleration, concluded he, making me a bow, taught us mutual love.

The old French officer delivered this with an air of such candour and good sense, as coincided with my first favourable impressions of his character—I thought I loved the man; but I fear I mistook the object—'twas my own way of thinking—the difference was, I could not have expressed it half so well.

It is alike troublesome to both the rider and his beast—if the latter goes pricking up his ears, and starting all the way at every object which he never saw before—I have as little torment of this kind as any creature alive; and yet I honestly confess, that many a thing gave me pain, and that I blush'd at many a word the first month—which I found inconsequent and perfectly innocent the second.

Madame de Rambouliet[1], after an acquaintance of about six weeks with her, had done me the honour to take me in her coach about two leagues out of town—Of all women, Madame de Rambouliet is the most correct; and I never wish to see one of more virtues and purity of heart—In our return back, Madame de Rambouliet desired me to pull the cord—I ask'd her if she wanted any thing—*Rien que pisser*, said Madame de Rambouliet—

Grieve not, gentle traveller, to let Madame de Rambouliet p—ss on—And, ye fair mystic nymphs! go each one *pluck your rose*, and scatter them in your path—for Madame de Rambouliet did no more—I handed Madame de Rambouliet out of the coach; and had I been the priest of the chaste CASTALIA[2], I could not have served at her fountain with a more respectful decorum.

END OF VOL. I.

VOLUME II

THE FILLE DE CHAMBRE
PARIS

WHAT the old French officer had deliver'd upon travelling, bringing Polonius's advice to his son upon the same subject into my head—and that bringing in Hamlet; and Hamlet, the rest of Shakespear's works, I stopp'd at the Quai de Conti in my return home, to purchase the whole set.

The bookseller said he had not a set in the world—*Comment!* said I; taking one up out of a set which lay upon the counter betwixt us.——He said, they were sent him only to be got bound, and were to be sent back to Versailles in the morning to the Count de B****.

—And does the Count de B**** said I, read Shakespear? *C'est un Esprit fort*; replied the bookseller.—He loves English books; and what is more to his honour, Monsieur, he loves the English too. You speak this so civilly, said I, that 'tis enough to oblige an Englishman to lay out a Louis d'or or two at your shop—the bookseller made a bow, and was going to say something, when a young decent girl of about twenty, who by her air and dress, seemed to be *fille de chambre* to some devout woman of fashion, came into the shop and asked for *Les Egarments du Cœur & de l'Esprit*[1] : the bookseller gave her the book directly; she pulled out a little green sattin purse run round with a ribband of the same colour, and putting her finger and thumb into it, she took out the money, and paid for it. As I had nothing more to stay me in the shop, we both walked out at the door together.

——And what have you to do, my dear, said I, with *The Wanderings of the Heart*, who scarce know yet you have one? nor till love has first told you it, or some faithless shepherd has made it ache, can'st thou ever be sure it is so.—*Le Dieu m'en guard!* said the girl.—With reason, said I—for if it is a good one, 'tis pity it should be stolen: 'tis a little treasure to thee, and gives a better air to your face, than if it was dress'd out with pearls.

The young girl listened with a submissive attention, holding her sattin purse by its ribband in her hand all the time—'Tis a very small one, said I, taking hold of the bottom of it—she held it towards me—and there is very little in it, my dear, said I; but be but as good as thou art handsome, and heaven will fill it: I had a parcel of crowns in my hand to pay for Shakespear; and as she had let go the purse intirely, I put a single one in; and tying up the ribband in a bow-knot, returned it to her.

The young girl made me more a humble courtesy than a low one—'twas one of those quiet, thankful sinkings where the spirit bows itself down—the body does no more than tell it. I never gave a girl a crown in my life which gave me half the pleasure.

My advice, my dear, would not have been worth a pin to you, said I, if I had not given this along with it: but now, when you see the crown, you'll remember it—so don't, my dear, lay it out in ribbands.

Upon my word, Sir, said the girl, earnestly, I am incapable —in saying which, as is usual in little bargains of honour, she gave me her hand—*En verite, Monsieur, je mettrai cet argent apart*, said she.

When a virtuous convention is made betwixt man and woman, it sanctifies their most private walks: so notwithstanding it was dusky, yet as both our roads lay the same way, we made no scruple of walking along the Quai de Conti together.

She made me a second courtesy in setting off, and before we got twenty yards from the door, as if she had not done enough before, she made a sort of a little stop to tell me again,—she thank'd me.

It was a small tribute, I told her, which I could not avoid paying to virtue, and would not be mistaken in the person I had been rendering it to for the world—but I see innocence, my dear, in your face—and foul befal the man who ever lays a snare in its way!

The girl seem'd affected some way or other with what I said—she gave a low sigh—I found I was not impowered to enquire at all after it—so said nothing more till I got to the corner of the Rue de Nevers, where we were to part.

—But is this the way, my dear, said I, to the hotel de Modene? she told me it was—or, that I might go by the Rue de Guineygaude, which was the next turn.—Then I'll go, my dear, by the Rue de Guineygaude, said I, for two reasons; first I shall please myself, and next I shall give you the protection of my company as far on your way as I can. The girl was sensible I was civil—and said, she wish'd the hotel de Modene was in the Rue de St. Pierre——You live there? said I.—She told me she was *fille de chambre* to Madame R****—Good God! said I, 'tis the very lady for whom I have brought a letter from Amiens—The girl told me that Madame R****, she believed expected a stranger with a letter, and was impatient to see him—so I desired the girl to present my compliments to Madame R****, and say I would certainly wait upon her in the morning.

We stood still at the corner of the Rue de Nevers whilst this pass'd—We then stopp'd a moment whilst she disposed of her *Egarments de Cœur*, &c. more commodiously than carrying them in her hand—they were two volumes; so I held the second for her whilst she put the first into her pocket; and then she held her pocket, and I put in the other after it.

'Tis sweet to feel by what fine-spun threads our affections are drawn together.

We set off a-fresh, and as she took her third step, the girl put her hand within my arm—I was just bidding her—but she did it of herself with that undeliberating simplicity, which shew'd it was out of her head that she had never seen me before. For my own part, I felt the conviction of consanguinity so strongly, that I could not help turning half round to look in her face, and see if I could trace out any thing in it of a family likeness—Tut! said I, are we not all relations?

When we arrived at the turning up of the Rue de Guiney-gaude, I stopp'd to bid her adieu for good an all: the girl would thank me again for my company and kindness—She bid me adieu twice—I repeated it as often; and so cordial was the parting between us, that had it happen'd any where else, I'm not sure but I should have signed it with a kiss of charity, as warm and holy as an apostle.

But in Paris, as none kiss each other but the men—I did, what amounted to the same thing——

——I bid God bless her.

THE PASSPORT
PARIS

WHEN I got home to my hotel, La Fleur told me I had been enquired after by the Lieutenant de Police—The duce take it! said I——I know the reason. It is time the reader should know it, for in the order of things in which it happened, it was omitted; not that it was out of my head; but that had I told it then, it might have been forgot now—and now is the time I want it.

I had left London with so much precipitation, that it never

enter'd my mind that we were at war with France[1]; and had reach'd Dover, and look'd through my glass at the hills beyond Boulogne, before the idea presented itself; and with this in its train, that there was no getting there without a passport. Go but to the end of a street, I have a mortal aversion for returning back no wiser than I set out; and as this was one of the greatest efforts I had ever made for knowledge, I could less bear the thoughts of it: so hearing the Count de **** had hired the packet[2], I begg'd he would take me in his *suite*. The Count had some little knowledge of me, so made little or no difficulty—only said, his inclination to serve me could reach no further than Calais; as he was to return by way of Brussels to Paris: however, when I had once pass'd there, I might get to Paris without interruption; but that in Paris I must make friends and shift for myself.—Let me get to Paris, Monsieur le Count, said I—and I shall do very well. So I embark'd, and never thought more of the matter.

When La Fleur told me the Lieutenant de Police had been enquiring after me—the thing instantly recurred—and by the time La Fleur had well told me, the master of the hotel came into my room to tell me the same thing, with this addition to it, that my passport had been particularly ask'd after: the master of the hotel concluded with saying, He hoped I had one.—Not I, faith! said I.

The master of the hotel retired three steps from me, as from an infected person, as I declared this—and poor La Fleur advanced three steps towards me, and with that sort of movement which a good soul makes to succour a distress'd one—the fellow won my heart by it; and from that single *trait*, I knew his character as perfectly, and could rely upon it as firmly, as if he had served me with fidelity for seven years.

Mon seignior! cried the master of the hotel—but recollecting himself as he made the exclamation, he instantly changed the tone of it—If Monsieur, said he, has not a passport (*apparament*) in all likelihood he has friends in Paris who can procure him one.—Not that I know of, quoth I, with an air of indifference.—Then *certes*, replied he, you'll be sent to the Bastile or the Chatelet, *au moins*. Poo! said I, the king of France is a good natured soul—he'll hurt no body.—*Cela n'empeche pas*, said he—you will certainly be sent to the Bastile to-morrow morning.—But I've taken your lodgings for a month, answer'd I, and I'll not quit them a day before the time for all the kings of France in the world. La Fleur whisper'd in my ear, That no body could oppose the king of France.

Pardi! said my host, *ces Messieurs Anglois sont des gens tres extraordinaires*—and having both said and sworn it—he went out.

THE PASSPORT

The Hotel at Paris

I COULD not find in my heart to torture La Fleur's with a serious look upon the subject of my embarrassment, which was the reason I had treated it so cavalierly: and to shew him how light it lay upon my mind, I dropt the subject entirely; and whilst he waited upon me at supper, talk'd to him with more than usual gaiety about Paris, and of the opera comique. —La Fleur had been there himself, and had followed me through the streets as far as the bookseller's shop; but seeing me come out with the young *fille de chambre*, and that we walk'd down the Quai de Conti together, La Fleur deem'd it unnecessary to follow me a step further—so making his own reflections upon it, he took a shorter cut——and got to the hotel in time to be inform'd of the affair of the Police against my arrival.

As soon as the honest creature had taken away, and gone down to sup himself, I then began to think a little seriously about my situation.—

—And here, I know, Eugenius, thou wilt smile at the remembrance of a short dialogue which pass'd betwixt us the moment I was going to set out——I must tell it here.

Eugenius, knowing that I was as little subject to be over-burthen'd with money as thought, had drawn me aside to interrogate me how much I had taken care for; upon telling him the exact sum, Eugenius shook his head, and said it would not do; so pull'd out his purse in order to empty it into mine. —I've enough in conscience, Eugenius, said I.——Indeed, Yorick, you have not, replied Eugenius—I know France and Italy better than you.——But you don't consider, Eugenius, said I, refusing his offer, that before I have been three days in Paris, I shall take care to say or do something or other for which I shall get clapp'd up into the Bastile, and that I shall live there a couple of months entirely at the king of France's expence.—I beg pardon, said Eugenius, drily: really, I had forgot that resource.

Now the event I treated gaily came seriously to my door.

Is it folly, or nonchalance, or philosophy, or pertinacity—or what is it in me, that, after all, when La Fleur had gone down stairs, and I was quite alone, I could not bring down my mind to think of it otherwise than I had then spoken of it to Eugenius?

—And as for the Bastile! the terror is in the word—Make the most of it you can, said I to myself, the Bastile is but another word for a tower—and a tower is but another word for a house you can't get out of—Mercy on the gouty! for they are in it twice a year—but with nine livres a day, and pen and ink and paper and patience, albeit a man can't get out, he may do very well within—at least for a month or six weeks; at the end of which, if he is a harmless fellow his innocence appears, and he comes out a better and wiser man than he went in.

I had some occasion (I forget what) to step into the court-yard, as I settled this account; and remember I walk'd down stairs in no small triumph with the conceit of my reasoning—

Beshrew the *sombre* pencil![1] said I vauntingly—for I envy not its powers, which paints the evils of life with so hard and deadly a colouring. The mind sits terrified at the objects she has magnified herself, and blackened: reduce them to their proper size and hue she overlooks them—'Tis true, said I, correcting the proposition—the Bastile is not an evil to be despised—but strip it of its towers—fill up the fossè— unbarricade the doors—call it simply a confinement, and suppose 'tis some tyrant of a distemper—and not of a man which holds you in it—the evil vanishes, and you bear the other half without complaint.

I was interrupted in the hey-day of this soliloquy, with a voice which I took to be of a child, which complained 'it could not get out.'—I look'd up and down the passage, and seeing neither man, woman, or child, I went out without further attention.

In my return back through the passage, I heard the same words repeated twice over; and looking up, I saw it was a starling hung in a little cage.—'I can't get out—I can't get out,' said the starling[2].

I stood looking at the bird: and to every person who came through the passage it ran fluttering to the side towards which they approach'd it, with the same lamentation of its captivity— 'I can't get out', said the starling—God help thee! said I, but I'll let thee out, cost what it will; so I turn'd about the cage to get to the door; it was twisted and double twisted so fast with wire, there was no getting it open without pulling the cage to pieces—I took both hands to it.

The bird flew to the place where I was attempting his deliverance, and thrusting his head through the trellis, press'd his breast against it, as if impatient—I fear, poor creature! said I, I cannot set thee at liberty—'No,' said the starling— 'I can't get out—I can't get out,' said the starling.

I vow, I never had my affections more tenderly awakened; nor do I remember an incident in my life, where the dissipated spirits, to which my reason had been a bubble, were so suddenly call'd home. Mechanical as the notes were, yet so true in tune to nature were they chanted, that in one moment they overthrew all my systematic reasonings upon the Bastile; and I heavily walk'd up stairs, unsaying every word I had said in going down them.

Disguise thyself as thou wilt, still slavery! said I—still thou art a bitter draught; and though thousands in all ages have been made to drink of thee, thou art no less bitter on that account.—'tis thou, thrice sweet and gracious goddess, addressing myself to LIBERTY, whom all in public or in private worship, whose taste is grateful, and ever wilt be so, till NATURE herself shall change—no *tint* of words can spot thy snowy mantle, or chymic power turn thy sceptre into iron—with thee to smile upon him as he eats his crust, the swain is happier than his monarch, from whose court thou art exiled—Gracious heaven! cried I, kneeling down upon the last step but one in my ascent—grant me but health, thou great Bestower of it, and give me but this fair goddess as my companion—and shower down thy mitres, if it seems good unto thy divine providence, upon those heads which are aching for them.

THE CAPTIVE
PARIS

THE bird in his cage pursued me into my room; I sat down close to my table, and leaning my head upon my hand, I begun to figure to myself the miseries of confinement. I was in a right frame for it, and so I gave full scope to my imagination.

I was going to begin with the millions of my fellow creatures born to no inheritance but slavery; but finding, however affecting the picture was, that I could not bring it near me, and that the multitude of sad groups in it did but distract me.—

—I took a single captive, and having first shut him up in his dungeon, I then look'd through the twilight of his grated door to take his picture.

I beheld his body half wasted away with long expectation and confinement, and felt what kind of sickness of the heart it was which arises from hope deferr'd[1]. Upon looking nearer I saw him pale and feverish: in thirty years the western breeze had not once fann'd his blood—he had seen no sun, no moon in all that time—nor had the voice of friend or kinsman breathed through his lattice—his children—

—But here my heart began to bleed—and I was forced to go on with another part of the portrait.

He was sitting upon the ground upon a little straw, in the furthest corner of his dungeon, which was alternately his chair and bed: a little calender of small sticks were laid at the head notch'd all over with the dismal days and nights he had pass'd there—he had one of these little sticks in his hand, and with a rusty nail he was etching another day of misery to add to the heap. As I darkened the little light he had, he lifted up a hopeless eye towards the door, then cast it down—shook his head, and went on with his work of affliction. I heard his chains upon his legs, as he turn'd his body to lay his little stick upon the bundle—He gave a deep sigh—I saw the iron enter into his soul[2]—I burst into tears—I could not sustain the picture of confinement which my fancy had drawn—I startled up from my chair, and calling La Fleur, I bid him bespeak me a *remise*[3], and have it ready at the door of the hotel by nine in the morning.

—I'll go directly, said I, myself to Monsieur Le Duke de Choiseul.

La Fleur would have put me to bed; but not willing he should see any thing upon my cheek, which would cost the honest fellow a heart ache—I told him I would go to bed by myself—and bid him go do the same.

THE STARLING
ROAD TO VERSAILLES

I GOT into my *remise* the hour I proposed: La Fleur got up behind, and I bid the coachman make the best of his way to Versailles.

As there was nothing in this road, or rather nothing which I look for in travelling, I cannot fill up the blank better than with a short history of this self-same bird, which became the subject of the last chapter.

Whilst the Honourable Mr. **** was waiting for a wind at Dover it had been caught upon the cliffs before it could well fly, by an English lad who was his groom; who not caring to destroy it, had taken it in his breast into the packet—and by course of feeding it, and taking it once under his protection, in a day or two grew fond of it, and got it safe along with him to Paris.

At Paris the lad had laid out a livre in a little cage for the starling, and as he had little to do better the five months his master stay'd there, he taught it in his mother's tongue the four simple words—(and no more)—to which I own'd myself so much it's debtor.

Upon his master's going on for Italy—the lad had given it to the master of the hotel—But his little song for liberty, being in an *unknown* language at Paris—the bird had little or no store set by him—so La Fleur bough' both him and his cage for me for a bottle of Burgundy.

In my return from Italy I brought him with me to the country in whose language he had learn'd his notes—and telling the story of him to Lord A—Lord A begg'd the bird of me—in a week Lord A gave him to Lord B—Lord B made a present of him to Lord C—and Lord C's gentleman sold him to Lord D's for a shilling—Lord D gave him to Lord E— and so on—half round the alphabet—From that rank he pass'd into the lower house, and pass'd the hands of as many commoners——But as all these wanted to *get in*[1]—and my bird wanted to get out—he had almost as little store set by him in London as in Paris.

It is impossible but many of my readers must have heard of him; and if any by mere chance have ever seen him—I beg leave to inform them, that that bird was my bird—or some vile copy set up to represent him.

I have nothing further to add upon him, but that from that time to this, I have borne this poor starling as the crest to my arms.—Thus:

——And let the heralds officers twist his neck about if they dare.

I SHOULD not like to have my enemy take a view of my mind, when I am going to ask protection of any man: for which reason I generally endeavour to protect myself; but this going to Monsieur Le Duc de C***** was an act of compulsion—had it been an act of choice, I should have done it, I suppose, like other people.

How many mean plans of dirty address, as I went along, did my servile heart form! I deserved the Bastile for every one of them.

Then nothing would serve me, when I got within sight of Versailles, but putting words and sentences together, and conceiving attitudes and tones to wreath myself into Monsieur Le Duc de C*****'s good graces—This will do——said I—Just as well, retorted I again, as a coat carried up to him by an adventurous taylor, without taking his measure—Fool! continued I—see Monsieur Le Duc's face first—observe what character is written in it; take notice in what posture he stands to hear you—mark the turns and expressions of his body and limbs—And for the tone—the first sound which comes from his lips will give it you; and from all these together you'll compound an address at once upon the spot, which cannot disgust the Duke—the ingredients are his own, and most likely to go down.

Well! said I, I wish it well over—Coward again! as if man to man was not equal, throughout the whole surface of the globe; and if in the field—why not face to face in the cabinet[1] too? And trust me, Yorick, whenever it is not so, man is false to himself; and betrays his own succours[2] ten times, where nature does it once. Go to the Duc de C**** with the Bastile in thy looks—My life for it, thou wilt be sent back to Paris in half an hour, with an escort.

I believe so, said I—Then I'll go to the Duke, by heaven! with all the gaity and debonairness in the world.—

—And there you are wrong again, replied I—A heart at ease, Yorick, flies into no extremes—'tis ever on its center.— Well! well! cried I, as the coachman turn'd in at the gates— I find I shall do very well: and by the time he had wheel'd round the court, and brought me up to the door, I found myself so much the better for my own lecture, that I neither ascended the steps like a victim to justice, who was to part with life upon the topmost,—nor did I mount them with a skip and a couple of strides, as I do when I fly up, Eliza! to thee, to meet it[1].

As I enter'd the door of the saloon, I was met by a person who possibly might be the maitre d'hotel, but had more the air of one of the under secretaries, who told me the Duc de C**** was busy—I am utterly ignorant, said I, of the forms of obtaining an audience, being an absolute stranger, and what is worse in the present conjuncture of affairs, being an Englishman too.——He replied, that did not increase the difficulty.—I made him a slight bow, and told him, I had something of importance to say to Monsieur Le Duc. The secretary look'd towards the stairs, as if he was about to leave me to carry up this account to some one—But I must not mislead you, said I—for what I have to say is of no manner of importance to Monsieur Le Duc de C****—but of great importance to myself.—*C'est une autre affaire*, replied he——Not at all, said I, to a man of gallantry.—But pray, good sir, continued I, when can a stranger hope to have *accesse?* In not less than two hours, said he, looking at his watch. The number of equipages in the court-yard seem'd to justify the calculation, that I could have no nearer a prospect—and as walking backwards and forwards in the saloon, without a soul to commune with, was for the time as bad as being in the Bastile itself, I instantly went back to my *remise*, and bid the coachman drive me to the *cordon bleu*, which was the nearest hotel.

I think there is a fatality in it—I seldom go to the place I set out for.

LE PATISSER
VERSAILLES

BEFORE I had got half-way down the street, I changed my mind: as I am at Versailles, thought I, I might as well take a view of the town; so I pull'd the cord, and ordered the coachman to drive round some of the principal streets—I suppose the town is not very large, said I.—The coachman begg'd pardon for setting me right, and told me it was very superb, and that numbers of the first dukes and marquises and counts had hotels¹—The Count de B****, of whom the bookseller at the Quai de Conti had spoke so handsomely the night before, came instantly into my mind.—And why should I not go, thought I, to the Count de B****, who has so high an idea of English books, and Englishmen—and tell him my story? so I changed my mind a second time—In truth it was the third; for I had intended that day for Madame de R**** in the Rue St. Pierre, and had devoutly sent her word by her *fille de chambre* that I would assuredly wait upon her—but I am govern'd by circumstances—I cannot govern them: so seeing a man standing with a basket on the other side of the street, as if he had something to sell, I bid La Fleur go up to him and enquire for the Count's hotel.

La Fleur return'd a little pale; and told me it was a Chevalier de St. Louis selling *patès*—It is impossible, La Fleur! said I. —La Fleur could no more account for the phenomenon than myself; but persisted in his story: he had seen the croix set in

gold, with its red ribband, he said, tied to his button-hole—
and had look'd into the basket and seen the *patès* which the
Chevalier was selling; so could not be mistaken in that.

Such a reverse in man's life awakens a better principle than
curiosity: I could not help looking for some time at him as I
sat in the *remise*—the more I look'd at him—his croix and his
basket, the stronger they wove themselves into my brain—I
got out of the *remise* and went towards him.

He was begirt with a clean linen apron which fell below his
knees, and with a sort of a bib went half way up his breast;
upon the top of this, but a little below the hem, hung his croix.
His basket of little *patès* was cover'd over with a white damask
napkin; another of the same kind was spread at the bottom;
and there was a look of *propreté* and neatness throughout;
that one might have bought his *patès* of him, as much from
appetite as sentiment.

He made an offer of them to neither; but stood still with
them at the corner of a hotel, for those to buy who chose it,
without solicitation.

He was about forty-eight—of a sedate look, something
approaching to gravity. I did not wonder.—I went up rather
to the basket than him, and having lifted up the napkin and
taken one of his *patès* into my hand—I begg'd he would
explain the appearance which affected me.

He told me in a few words, that the best part of his life had
pass'd in the service, in which, after spending a small patri-
mony, he had obtain'd a company and the croix with it; but
that at the conclusion of the last peace, his regiment being
reformed, and the whole corps, with those of some other
regiments, left without any provision—he found himself in a
wide world without friends, without a livre—and indeed, said
he, without any thing but this—(pointing, as he said it, to his
croix)—The poor chevalier won my pity, and he finish'd the
scene, with winning my esteem too.

The king, he said, was the most generous of princes, but his generosity could neither relieve or reward every one, and it was only his misfortune to be amongst the number. He had a little wife, he said, whom he loved, who did the *patisserie*; and added, he felt no dishonour in defending her and himself from want in this way—unless Providence had offer'd him a better.

It would be wicked to with-hold a pleasure from the good, in passing over what happen'd to this poor Chevalier of St. Louis about nine months after.

It seems he usually took his stand near the iron gates which lead up to the palace, and as his croix had caught the eye of numbers, numbers had made the same enquiry which I had done—He had told them the same story, and always with so much modesty and good sense, that it had reach'd at last the king's ears—who hearing the Chevalier had been a gallant officer, and respected by the whole regiment as a man of honour and integrity—he broke up his little trade by a pension of fifteen hundred livres a year.

As I have told this to please the reader, I beg he will allow me to relate another out of its order, to please myself—the two stories reflect light upon each other,—and 'tis a pity they should be parted.

THE SWORD

RENNES

WHEN states and empires have their periods of declension, and feel in their turns what distress and poverty is—I stop not to tell the causes which gradually brought the house d'E**** in Britany into decay. The Marquis d'E**** had fought up against his condition with great firmness; wishing to preserve, and still shew to the world some little fragments of what his ancestors had been—their indiscretions had put it out of his power. There was enough left for the little exigencies of *obscurity*—But he had two boys who look'd up to him for *light*—he thought they deserved it. He had tried his sword—it could not open the way—the *mounting*[1] was too expensive—and simple œconomy was not a match for it— there was no resource but commerce.

In any other province in France, save Britany, this was smiting the root for ever of the little tree his pride and affection wish'd to see re-blossom—But in Britany, there being a provision for this, he avail'd himself of it; and taking an occasion when the states were assembled at Rennes, the Marquis, attended with his two boys, enter'd the court; and having pleaded the right of an ancient law of the duchy, which, though seldom claim'd, he said, was no less in force; he took his sword from his side—Here—said he—take it; and be trusty guardians of it, till better times put me in condition to reclaim it.

The president accepted the Marquis's sword—he stay'd a few minutes to see it deposited in the archives of his house —and departed.

The Marquis and his whole family embarked the next day for Martinico, and in about nineteen or twenty years of successful application to business, with some unlook'd for bequests from distant branches of his house—return'd home to reclaim his nobility and to support it.

It was an incident of good fortune which will never happen to any traveller, but a sentimental one, that I should be at Rennes at the very time of this solemn requisition: I call it solemn—it was so to me.

The Marquis enter'd the court with his whole family: he supported his lady—his eldest son supported his sister, and his youngest was at the other extreme of the line next his mother.—he put his handkerchief to his face twice—

—There was a dead silence. When the Marquis had

approach'd within six paces of the tribunal, he gave the Marchioness to his youngest son, and advancing three steps before his family—he reclaim'd his sword. His sword was given him, and the moment he got it into his hand he drew it almost out of the scabbard—'twas the shining face of a friend he had once given up—he look'd attentively along it, beginning at the hilt, as if to see whether it was the same—when observing a little rust which it had contracted near the point, he brought it near his eye, and bending his head down over it—I think I saw a tear fall upon the place: I could not be deceived by what followed.

'I shall find, said he, some *other way*, to get it off.'

When the Marquis had said this, he return'd his sword into its scabbard, made a bow to the guardians of it—and, with his wife and daughter and his two sons following him, walk'd out.

O how I envied him his feelings!

THE PASSPORT
VERSAILLES

I FOUND no difficulty in getting admittance to Monsieur Le Count de B****. The set of Shakespears was laid upon the table, and he was tumbling them over. I walk'd up close to the table, and giving first such a look at the books as to make him conceive I knew what they were—I told him I had come without any one to present me, knowing I should meet with a friend in his apartment who, I trusted, would do it for me—it is my countryman the great Shakespear, said I, pointing to his works—*et ayez la bontè, mon cher ami*, apostrophizing his spirit, added I, *de me faire cet honneur la*.——

The Count smil'd at the singularity of the introduction;

and seeing I look'd a little pale and sickly, insisted upon my taking an arm-chair: so I sat down; and to save him conjectures upon a visit so out of all rule, I told him simply of the incident in the bookseller's shop, and how that had impell'd me rather to go to him with the story of a little embarrassment I was under, than to any other man in France—And what is your embarrassment? let me hear it, said the Count. So I told him the story just as I have told it the reader—

—And the master of my hotel, said I, as I concluded it, will needs have it, Monsieur le Count, that I shall be sent to the Bastile—but I have no apprehensions, continued I—for in falling into the hands of the most polish'd people in the world, and being conscious I was a true man, and not come to spy the nakedness of the land, I scarce thought I laid at their mercy. —It does not suit the gallantry of the French, Monsieur le Count, said I, to shew it against invalids.

An animated blush came into the Count de B****'s cheeks, as I spoke this—*Ne craignez rien*—Don't fear, said he— Indeed I don't, replied I again—besides, continued I a little sportingly—I have come laughing all the way from London to Paris, and I do not think Monsieur le Duc de Choiseul is such an enemy to mirth, as to send me back crying for my pains.

——My application to you, Monsieur le Compte de B**** (making him a low bow) is to desire he will not.

The Count heard me with great good nature, or I had not said half as much—and once or twice said—*C'est bien dit*. So I rested my cause there—and determined to say no more about it.

The Count led the discourse: we talk'd of indifferent things; —of books and politicks, and men—and then of women— God bless them all! said I, after much discourse about them— there is not a man upon earth who loves them so much as I do: after all the foibles I have seen, and all the satires I have read against them, still I love them; being firmly persuaded that a man who has not a sort of an affection for the whole sex, is incapable of ever loving a single one as he ought.

Hèh bien! Monsieur l'Anglois, said the Count, gaily—You are not come to spy the nakedness of the land—I believe you —*ni encore*, I dare say, *that* of our women—But permit me to conjecture—if, *par hazard*, they fell in your way—that the prospect would not affect you.

I have something within me which cannot bear the shock of the least indecent insinuation: in the sportability of chit-chat I have often endeavoured to conquer it, and with infinite pain have hazarded a thousand things to a dozen of the sex together—the least of which I could not venture to a single one, to gain heaven.

Excuse me, Monsieur Le Count, said I—as for the naked-ness of your land, if I saw it, I should cast my eyes over it with tears in them—and for that of your women (blushing at the idea he had excited in me) I am so evangelical in this, and have such a fellow-feeling for what ever is *weak* about them, that I would cover it with a garment, if I knew how to throw it on—But I could wish, continued I, to spy the *nakedness* of their hearts, and through the different disguises of customs, climates, and religion, find out what is good in them, to fashion my own by—and therefore am I come.

It is for this reason, Monsieur le Compte, continued I, that I have not seen the Palais royal—nor the Luxembourg—nor the Façade of the Louvre—nor have attempted to swell the catalogues we have of pictures, statues, and churches—I con-ceive every fair being as a temple, and would rather enter in, and see the original drawings and loose sketches hung up in it, than the transfiguration of Raphael itself.

The thirst of this, continued I, as impatient as that which inflames the breast of the connoisseur, has led me from my own home into France—and from France will lead me through Italy—'tis a quiet journey of the heart in pur-suit of NATURE, and those affections which rise out of her, which make us love each other—and the world, better than we do.

The Count said a great many civil things to me upon the occasion; and added very politely how much he stood obliged to Shakespear for making me known to him—but, *a-propos*, said he—Shakespear is full of great things—He forgot a small punctillio of announcing your name—it puts you under a necessity of doing it yourself.

THE PASSPORT
VERSAILLES

THERE is not a more perplexing affair in life to me, than to set about telling any one who I am—for there is scarce any body I cannot give a better account of than of myself; and I have often wish'd I could do it in a single word—and have an end of it. It was the only time and occasion in my life, I could accomplish this to any purpose—for Shakespear lying upon the table, and recollecting I was in his books, I took up Hamlet, and turning immediately to the grave-diggers scene in the fifth act, I lay'd my finger upon YORICK, and advancing the book to the Count, with my finger all the way over the name—*Me Voici!* said I.

Now whether the idea of poor Yorick's skull was put out of the Count's mind, by the reality of my own, or by what magic he could drop a period of seven or eight hundred years, makes nothing in this account—'tis certain the French conceive better than they combine—I wonder at nothing in this world, and the less at this; inasmuch as one of the first of our own church, for whose candour and paternal sentiments I have the highest veneration, fell into the same mistake in the very same case.—'He could not bear, he said, to look into sermons wrote by the king of Denmark's jester.'[1]—Good, my lord! said I—but there are two Yorick's. The Yorick your lordship thinks of, has been dead and buried eight hundred years ago; he flourish'd in Horwendillus's[2] court—the other Yorick is myself, who have flourish'd my lord in no court—He shook his head—Good God! said I, you might as well confound Alexander the Great[3], with Alexander the Copper-smith, my lord——'Twas all one, he replied—

—If Alexander king of Macedon could have translated[4] your lordship, said I—I'm sure your Lordship would not have said so.

The poor Count de B**** fell but into the same *error*—

——*Et, Monsieur, est il Yorick?* cried the Count.—*Je le suis*, said I.—*Vous?—Moi—moi qui ai l'honneur de vous parler, Monsieur le Compte—Mon Dieu!* said he, embracing me—— *Vous etes Yorick.*

The Count instantly put the Shakespear into his pocket—and left me alone in his room.

THE PASSPORT
VERSAILLES

I COULD not conceive why the Count de B**** had gone so abruptly out of the room, any more than I could conceive why he had put the Shakespear into his pocket—*Mysteries which must explain themselves, are not worth the loss of time, which a conjecture about them takes up:* 'twas better to read Shakespear; so taking up, 'Much Ado about Nothing,' I transported myself instantly from the chair I sat in to Messina in Sicily, and got so busy with Don Pedro and Benedick and Beatrice, that I thought not of Versailles, the Count, or the Passport.

Sweet pliability of man's spirit, that can at once surrender itself to illusions, which cheat expectation and sorrow of their weary moments!—long—long since had ye number'd out my days, had I not trod so great a part of them upon this enchanted ground: when my way is too rough for my feet, or too steep for my strength, I get off it, to some smooth velvet path which fancy has scattered over with rose-buds of delights; and having taken a few turns in it, come back strengthen'd and refresh'd—When evils press sore upon me, and there is no retreat from them in this world, then I take a new course—I leave it—and as I have a clearer idea of the elysian fields[1] than I have of heaven, I force myself, like Eneas, into them—I see him meet the pensive shade of his forsaken Dido—and wish to recognize it—I see the injured spirit wave her head, and turn off silent from the author of her miseries and dishonours—I lose the feelings for myself in hers—and in those affections which were wont to make me mourn for her when I was at school.

Surely this is not walking in a vain shadow[2]—*nor does man disquiet himself* in vain, *by it*—he oftener does so in trusting the issue of his commotions to reason only.—I can safely say for myself, I was never able to conquer any one single bad sensation in my heart so decisively, as by beating up as fast as I could for some kindly and gentle sensation[3], to fight it upon its own ground.

When I had got to the end of the third act, the Count de B**** entered with my Passport in his hand. Mons. le Duc de C****, said the Count, is as good a prophet, I dare say, as he is a statesman—*Un homme qui rit*, said the duke, *ne sera jamais dangereuz.*—Had it been for any one but the king's jester, added the Count, I could not have got it these two hours.—*Pardonnez moi*, Mons. Le Compte, said I—I am not the king's jester.—But you are Yorick?—Yes.—*Et vous plaisantez?*—I answered, Indeed I did jest—but was not paid for it—'twas entirely at my own expence.

We have no jester at court, Mons. Le Compte, said I, the last we had was in the licentious reign of Charles the IId—since which time our manners have been so gradually refining, that our court at present is so full of patriots, who wish for *nothing* but the honours and wealth of their country—and our ladies are all so chaste, so spotless, so good, so devout—there is nothing for a jester to make a jest of—

Voila un persiflage! cried the Count.

THE PASSPORT
VERSAILLES

As the Passport was directed to all lieutenant governors, governors, and commandants of cities, generals of armies, justiciaries, and all officers of justice, to let Mr. Yorick, the king's jester, and his baggage, travel quietly along—I own the triumph of obtaining the Passport was not a little tarnish'd by the figure I cut in it—But there is nothing unmixt in this world; and some of the gravest of our divines have carried it so far as to affirm, that enjoyment itself was attended even with a sigh—and that the greatest *they knew of*, terminated *in a general way*, in little better than a convulsion.

I remember the grave and learned Bevoriskius[1], in his commentary upon the generations from Adam, very naturally breaks off in the middle of a note to give an account to the world of a couple of sparrows upon the out-edge of his window, which had incommoded him all the time he wrote, and at last had entirely taken him off from his genealogy.

—'Tis strange! writes Bevoriskius; but the facts are certain, for I have had the curiosity to mark them down one by one with my pen—but the cock-sparrow during the little time that I could have finished the other half this note, has actually interrupted me with the reiteration of his caresses three and twenty times and a half.

How merciful, adds Bevoriskius, is heaven to his creatures!

Ill fated Yorick! that the gravest of thy brethren should be able to write that to the world, which stains thy face with crimson, to copy in even thy study.

But this is nothing to my travels—So I twice—twice beg pardon for it.

CHARACTER
VERSAILLES

AND how do you find the French? said the Count de B****, after he had given me the Passport.

The reader may suppose that after so obliging a proof of courtesy, I could not be at a loss to say something handsome to the enquiry.

—*Mais passe, pour cela*—Speak frankly, said he; do you find all the urbanity in the French which the world give us the honour of?—I had found every thing, I said, which confirmed it—*Vraiment*, said the count.—*Les Francois sont polis.* —To an excess, replied I.

The count took notice of the word *excesse*; and would have it I meant more than I said. I defended myself a long time as well as I could against it—he insisted I had a reserve, and that I would speak my opinion frankly.

I believe, Mons. Le Compte, said I, that man has a certain compass, as well as an instrument; and that the social and other calls have occasion by turns for every key in him; so that if you begin a note too high or too low, there must be a want either in the upper or under part, to fill up the system of harmony.— The Count de B**** did not understand music, so desired me to explain it some other way. A polish'd nation, my dear Count, said I, makes every one its debtor; and besides urbanity itself, like the fair sex, has so many charms; it goes against the heart to say it can do ill; and yet, I believe, there is but a certain line of perfection, that man, take him altogether, is empower'd to arrive at—if he gets beyond, he rather exchanges qualities, than gets them. I must not presume to say, how far this has affected the French in the subject we are speaking of—but should it ever be the case of the English, in the progress of their refinements, to arrive at the same polish which distinguishes the French, if we did not lose the *politesse de cœur*, which inclines men more to human actions, than courteous ones—we should at least lose that distinct variety and originality of character, which distinguishes them, not only from each other, but from all the world besides.

I had a few king William's shillings as smooth as glass in my pocket; and foreseeing they would be of use in the illustration of my hypothesis, I had got them into my hand, when I had proceeded so far—

See, Mons. Le Compte, said I, rising up, and laying them before him upon the table—by jingling and rubbing one against another for seventy years together in one body's pocket or another's, they are become so much alike, you can scarce distinguish one shilling from another.

The English, like antient medals, kept more apart, and passing but few peoples hands, preserve the first sharpnesses which the fine hand of nature has given them—they are not so pleasant to feel—but in return, the legend is so visible, that at the first look you see whose image and superscription they bear.—But the French, Mons. Le Compte, added I, wishing to soften what I had said, have so many excellencies, they can the better spare this—they are a loyal, a gallant, a generous, an ingenious, and good temper'd people as is under heaven—if they have a fault—they are too *serious*.

Mon Dieu! cried the Count, rising out of his chair.

Mais vous plaisantez, said he, correcting his exclamation.— I laid my hand upon my breast, and with earnest gravity assured him, it was my most settled opinion.

The Count said he was mortified, he could not stay to hear my reasons, being engaged to go that moment to dine with the Duc de C****.

But if it is not too far to come to Versailles to eat your soup with me, I beg, before you leave France, I may have the pleasure of knowing you retract your opinion—or, in what manner you support it.—But if you do support it, Mons. Anglois, said he, you must do it with all your powers, because you have the whole world against you.—I promised the Count I would do myself the honour of dining with him before I set out for Italy—so took my leave.

THE TEMPTATION
PARIS

WHEN I alighted at the hotel, the porter told me a young woman with a band-box had been that moment enquiring for me.—I do not know, said the porter, whether she is gone away or no. I took the key of my chamber of him, and went up stairs; and when I had got within ten steps of the top of the landing before my door, I met her coming easily down.

It was the fair *fille de chambre* I had walked along the Quai de Conti with: Madame de R**** had sent her upon some commissions to a *merchande de modes* within a step or two of the hotel de Modene; and as I had fail'd in waiting upon her, had bid her enquire if I had left Paris; and if so, whether I had not left a letter address'd to her.

As the fair *fille de chambre* was so near my door she turned back, and went into the room with me for a moment or two whilst I wrote a card.

It was a fine still evening in the latter end of the month of May—the crimson window curtains (which were of the same colour as those of the bed) were drawn close—the sun was setting and reflected through them so warm a tint into the fair *fille de chambre*'s face—I thought she blush'd—the idea of it made me blush myself—we were quite alone; and that super-induced a second blush before the first could get off.

There is a sort of a pleasing half guilty blush, where the blood is more in fault than the man—'tis sent impetuous from the heart, and virtue flies after it—not to call it back, but to make the sensation of it more delicious to the nerves—'tis associated.—

But I'll not describe it.—I felt something at first within me which was not in strict unison with the lesson of virtue I had given her the night before—I sought five minutes for a card— I knew I had not one.—I took up a pen—I laid it down again —my hand trembled—the devil was in me.

I know as well as any one, he is an adversary, whom if we resist, he will fly from us—but I seldom resist him at all; from a terror, that though I may conquer, I may still get a hurt in the combat—so I give up the triumph, for security; and instead of thinking to make him fly, I generally fly myself.

The fair *fille de chambre* came close up to the bureau where I was looking for a card—took up first the pen I cast down, then offered to hold me the ink: she offer'd it so sweetly, I was going to accept it—but I durst not—I have nothing, my dear, said I, to write upon.—Write it, said she, simply, upon any thing.—

I was just going to cry out, Then I will write it, fair girl! upon thy lips.—

If I do, said I, I shall perish—so I took her by the hand, and led her to the door, and begg'd she would not forget the lesson I had given her—She said, Indeed she would not—and as she utter'd it with some earnestness, she turned about, and gave me both her hands, closed together, into mine—it was impossible not to compress them in that situation—I wish'd to let them go; and all the time I held them, I kept arguing within myself against it—and still I held them on.—In two minutes I found I had all the battle to fight over again—and I felt my legs and every limb about me tremble at the idea.

The foot of the bed was within a yard and a half of the place where we were standing—I had still hold of her hands—and how it happened I can give no account, but I neither ask'd her—nor drew her—nor did I think of the bed—but so it did happen, we both sat down.

I'll just shew you, said the fair *fille de chambre*, the little purse I have been making to-day to hold your crown. So she put her hand into her right pocket, which was next me, and felt for it for some time—then into the left—'She had lost it.'—I never bore expectation more quietly—it was in her right pocket at last —she pulled it out; it was of green taffeta, lined with a little bit of white quilted sattin, and just big enough to hold the crown —she put it into my hand—it was pretty; and I held it ten minutes with the back of my hand resting upon her lap— looking sometimes at the purse, sometimes on one side of it.

A stitch or two had broke out in the gathers of my stock—the fair *fille de chambre*, without saying a word, took out her little hussive[1], threaded a small needle, and sew'd it up—I foresaw it would hazard the glory of the day; and as she passed her hand in silence across and across my neck in the manœuvre, I felt the laurels shake which fancy had wreath'd about my head.

A strap had given way in her walk, and the buckle of her shoe was just falling off—See, said the *fille de chambre*, holding up her foot—I could not for my soul but fasten the buckle in return, and putting in the strap—and lifting up the other foot with it, when I had done, to see both were right—in doing it too suddenly—it unavoidably threw the fair *fille de chambre* off her center—and then—

THE CONQUEST

YES——and then—Ye whose clay-cold heads and luke-warm
hearts can argue down or mask your passions—tell me, what
trespass is it that man should have them? or how his spirit
stands answerable, to the father of spirits, but for his conduct
under them?

If nature has so wove her web of kindness, that some threads
of love and desire are entangled with the piece—must the
whole web be rent in drawing them out?—Whip me such
stoics, great governor of nature! said I to myself—Wherever
thy providence shall place me for the trials of my virtue—
whatever is my danger—whatever is my situation—let me feel
the movements which rise out of it, and which belong to me
as a man—and if I govern them as a good one—I will trust the
issues to thy justice, for thou hast made us—and not we ourselves.

As I finish'd my address, I raised the fair *fille de chambre* up
by the hand, and led her out of the room—she stood by me till
I lock'd the door and put the key in my pocket—*and then*—
the victory being quite decisive—and not till then, I press'd
my lips to her cheek, and, taking her by the hand again, led
her safe to the gate of the hotel.

THE MYSTERY
PARIS

IF a man knows the heart, he will know it was impossible to go
back instantly to my chamber—it was touching a cold key with
a flat third to it, upon the close of a piece of musick, which had
call'd forth my affections—therefore, when I let go the hand

of the *fille de chambre*, I remain'd at the gate of the hotel for some time, looking at every one who pass'd by, and forming conjectures upon them, till my attention got fix'd upon a single object which confounded all kind of reasoning upon him.

It was a tall figure of a philosophic serious, adust look, which pass'd and repass'd sedately along the street, making a turn of about sixty paces on each side of the gate of the hotel—the man was about fifty-two—had a small cane under his arm—was dress'd in a dark drab-colour'd coat, waistcoat, and breeches, which seem'd to have seen some years service—they were still clean, and there was a little air of frugal *propretè* throughout him. By his pulling off his hat, and his attitude of accosting a good many in his way, I saw he was asking charity; so I got a sous or two out of my pocket ready to give him, as he took me in his turn—he pass'd by me without asking any thing—and yet did not go five steps further before he ask'd charity of a little woman—I was much more likely to have given of the two—He had scarce done with the woman, when he pull'd off his hat to another who was coming the same way. —An ancient gentleman came slowly—and, after him, a young smart one—He let them both pass, and ask'd nothing: I stood observing him half an hour, in which time he had made a dozen turns backwards and forwards, and found that he invariably pursued the same plan.

There were two things very singular in this, which set my brain to work, and to no purpose—the first was, why the man should *only* tell his story to the sex—and secondly—what kind of story it was, and what species of eloquence it could be, which soften'd the hearts of the women, which he knew 'twas to no purpose to practise upon the men.

There were two other circumstances which entangled this mystery—the one was, he told every woman what he had to say in her ear, and in a way which had much more the air of a secret than a petition—the other was, it was always successful—he never stopp'd a woman, but she pull'd out her purse, and immediately gave him something.

I could form no system to explain the phenomenon.

I had got a riddle to amuse me for the rest of the evening, so I walk'd up stairs to my chamber.

THE CASE OF CONSCIENCE

PARIS

I WAS immediately followed up by the master of the hotel, who came into my room to tell me I must provide lodgings else where.—How so, friend? said I.—He answer'd, I had had a young woman lock'd up with me two hours that evening in my bed-chamber, and 'twas against the rules of his house. —Very well, said I, we'll all part friends then—for the girl is no worse—and I am no worse—and you will be just as I found you.——It was enough, he said, to overthrow the credit of his hotel.—*Voyez vous, Monsieur*, said he, pointing to the foot of the bed we had been sitting upon.—I own it had something of the appearance of an evidence; but my pride not suffering me to enter into any detail of the case, I exhorted him to let his soul sleep in peace, as I resolved to let mine do that night, and that I would discharge what I owed him at breakfast.

I should not have minded, *Monsieur*, said he, if you had had twenty girls—'Tis a score more, replied I, interrupting him, than I ever reckon'd upon—Provided, added he, it had been but in a morning.—And does the difference of the time of the day at Paris make a difference in the sin?—It made a difference, he said, in the scandal.—I like a good distinction in my heart; and cannot say I was intolerably out of temper with the man.—I own it is necessary, re-assumed the master of the hotel, that a stranger at Paris should have the opportunities presented to him of buying lace and silk stockings and ruffles, *et tout cela*—and 'tis nothing if a woman comes with a band box.——O' my conscience, said I, she had one; but I never look'd into it.—Then, *Monsieur*, said he, has bought nothing. —Not one earthly thing, replied I.—Because, said he, I could recommend one to you who would use you *en conscience*.— But I must see her this night, said I.—He made me a low bow and walk'd down.

Now shall I triumph over this *maitre d'hotel*, cried I—and what then?—Then I shall let him see I know he is a dirty fellow.—And what then?—What then!—I was too near myself to say it was for the sake of others.—I had no good answer left—there was more of spleen than principle in my project, and I was sick of it before the execution.

In a few minutes the Grisset came in with her box of lace— I'll buy nothing however, said I, within myself.

The Grisset would shew me every thing—I was hard to please: she would not seem to see it; she open'd her little magazine, laid all her laces one after another before me— unfolded and folded them up again one by one with the most patient sweetness—I might buy—or not—she would let me have every thing at my own price—the poor creature seem'd anxious to get a penny; and laid herself out to win me, and not so much in a manner which seem'd artful, as in one I felt simple and caressing.

If there is not a fund of honest cullibility[1] in man, so much the worse—my heart relented, and I gave up my second resolution as quietly as the first—Why should I chastise one for the trespass of another? if thou art tributary to this tyrant of an host, thought I, looking up in her face, so much harder is thy bread.

If I had not had more than four *Louis d'ors* in my purse, there was no such thing as rising up and shewing her the door, till I had first laid three of them out in a pair of ruffles[2].

—The master of the hotel will share the profit with her—
no matter—then I have only paid as many a poor soul has
paid before me for an act he *could* not do, or think of.

THE RIDDLE

PARIS

WHEN La Fleur came up to wait upon me at supper, he
told me how sorry the master of the hotel was for his affront
to me in bidding me change my lodgings.

A man who values a good night's rest will not lay down with
enmity in his heart if he can help it—So I bid La Fleur tell
the master of the hotel, that I was sorry on my side for the
occasion I had given him—and you may tell him, if you will,
La Fleur, added I, that if the young woman should call again,
I shall not see her.

This was a sacrifice not to him, but myself, having resolved,
after so narrow an escape, to run no more risks, but to leave
Paris, if it was possible, with all the virtue I enter'd in.

C'est deroger à noblesse, *Monsieur*, said La Fleur, making
me a bow down to the ground as he said it—*Et encore Monsieur*,
said he, may change his sentiments—and if (*par hazard*)
he should like to amuse himself—I find no amusement in it,
said I, interrupting him—

Mon Dieu! said La Fleur—and took away[1].

In an hour's time he came to put me to bed, and was more
than commonly officious—something hung upon his lips to
say to me, or ask me, which he could not get off: I could not
conceive what it was; and indeed gave myself little trouble to
find it out, as I had another riddle so much more interesting
upon my mind, which was that of the man's asking charity
before the door of the hotel—I would have given any thing to

have got to the bottom of it; and that, not out of curiosity—
'tis so low a principle of enquiry, in general, I would not purchase the gratification of it with a two-sous piece—but a secret,
I thought, which so soon and so certainly soften'd the heart
of every woman you came near, was a secret at least equal to
the philosopher's stone: had I had both the Indies, I would
have given up one to have been master of it.

I toss'd and turn'd it almost all night long in my brains to
no manner of purpose; and when I awoke in the morning, I
found my spirit as much troubled with my *dreams*, as ever
the king of Babylon[1] had been with his; and I will not hesitate
to affirm, it would have puzzled all the wise men of Paris, as
much as those of Chaldea, to have given its interpretation.

LE DIMANCHE
PARIS

IT was Sunday; and when La Fleur came in, in the morning, with my coffee and role and butter, he had got himself so
gallantly array'd, I scarce knew him.

I had covenanted at Montriul to give him a new hat with
a silver button and loop, and four Louis d'ors *pour s'adoniser*,
when we got to Paris; and the poor fellow, to do him justice,
had done wonders with it.

He had bought a bright, clean, good scarlet coat and a pair
of breeches of the same—They were not a crown worse, he
said, for the wearing—I wish'd him hang'd for telling me—
they look'd so fresh, that tho' I knew the thing could not be
done, yet I would rather have imposed upon my fancy with
thinking I had bought them new for the fellow, than that they
had come out of the *Rue de friperie*.

This is a nicety which makes not the heart sore at Paris.

He had purchased moreover a handsome blue sattin waist-coat, fancifully enough embroidered—this was indeed something the worse for the services it had done, but 'twas clean scour'd—the gold had been touch'd up, and upon the whole was rather showy than otherwise—and as the blue was not violent, it suited with the coat and breeches very well: he had squeez'd out of the money, moreover, a new bag and a solitaire[1]; and had insisted with the *fripier*, upon a gold pair of garters to his breeches knees—He had purchased muslin ruffles, *bien brodées*, with four livres of his own money—and a pair of white silk stockings for five more—and, to top all, nature had given him a handsome figure, without costing him a sous.

He enter'd the room thus set off, with his hair dress'd in the first stile, and with a handsome *bouquet* in his breast—in a word, there was that look of festivity in every thing about him, which at once put me in mind it was Sunday—and by combining both together, it instantly struck me, that the favour he wish'd to ask of me the night before, was to spend the day, as every body in Paris spent it, besides. I had scarce made the conjecture, when La Fleur, with infinite humility, but with a look of trust, as if I should not refuse him, begg'd I would grant him the day, *pour faire le galant vis à vis de sa maitresse*.

Now it was the very thing I intended to do myself *vis à vis* Madame de R****—I had retain'd the *remise* on purpose for it, and it would not have mortified my vanity to have had a servant so well dress'd as La Fleur was to have got up behind it: I never could have worse spared him.

But we must *feel*, not argue in these embarrassments—the sons and daughters of service part with liberty, but not with Nature in their contracts; they are flesh and blood, and have their little vanities and wishes in the midst of the house of bondage, as well as their task-masters—no doubt, they have set their self-denials at a price—and their expectations are so unreasonable, that I would often disappoint them, but that their condition puts it so much in my power to do it.

Behold!—Behold, I am thy servant[1]—disarms me at once of the powers of a master—

—Thou shalt go, La Fleur! said I.

—And what mistress, La Fleur, said I, canst thou have pick'd up in so little a time at Paris? La Fleur laid his hand upon his breast, and said 'twas a *petite demoiselle* at Monsieur Le Compte de B****'s.—La Fleur had a heart made for society; and, to speak the truth of him let as few occasions slip him as his master—so that some how or other; but how—heaven knows—he had connected himself with the *demoiselle* upon the landing of the stair-case, during the time I was taken up with my Passport; and as there was time enough for me to win the Count to my interest, La Fleur had contrived to make it do to win the maid to his—the family, it seems, was to be at Paris that day, and he had made a party with her, and two or three more of the Count's houshold, upon the *boulevards*.

Happy people! that once a week at least are sure to lay down all your cares together; and dance and sing and sport away the weights of grievance, which bow down the spirit of other nations to the earth.

THE FRAGMENT
PARIS

LA FLEUR had left me something to amuse myself with for the day more than I had bargain'd for, or could have enter'd either into his head or mine.

He had brought the little print of butter[2] upon a currant leaf; and as the morning was warm, and he had a good step to bring it, he had begg'd a sheet of waste paper to put betwixt the currant leaf and his hand—As that was plate sufficient, I bad him lay it upon the table as it was, and as I resolved to stay within all day I ordered him to call upon the *traiteur* to bespeak my dinner, and leave me to breakfast by myself.

When I had finish'd the butter, I threw the currant leaf out of the window, and was going to do the same by the waste paper—but stopping to read a line first, and that drawing me on to a second and third—I thought it better worth; so I shut the window, and drawing a chair up to it, I sat down to read it.

It was in the old French of Rabelais's time, and for ought I know might have been wrote by him—it was moreover in a Gothic letter, and that so faded and gone off by damps and length of time, it cost me infinite trouble to make any thing of it—I threw it down; and then wrote a letter to Eugenius— then I took it up again, and embroiled my patience with it afresh—and then to cure that, I wrote a letter to Eliza.—Still it kept hold of me; and the difficulty of understanding it increased but the desire.

I got my dinner; and after I had enlightened my mind with a bottle of Burgundy, I at it again[1]—and after two or three hours poring upon it, with almost as deep attention as ever Gruter or Jacob Spon[2] did upon a nonsensical inscription, I thought I made sense of it; but to make sure of it, the best way, I imagined, was to turn it into English, and see how it would look then—so I went on leisurely, as a trifling man does, some- times writing a sentence—then taking a turn or two—and then looking how the world went, out of the window; so that it was nine o'clock at night before I had done it—I then begun and read it as follows.

THE FRAGMENT
PARIS

——Now as the notary's wife disputed the point with the
notary with too much heat—I wish, said the notary, throwing
down the parchment, that there was another notary here only
to set down and attest all this——

—And what would you do then, Monsieur? said she, rising
hastily up—the notary's wife was a little fume of a woman[1],
and the notary thought it well to avoid a hurricane by a mild
reply—I would go, answer'd he, to bed.——You may go to
the devil, answer'd the notary's wife.

Now there happening to be but one bed in the house, the
other two rooms being unfurnish'd, as is the custom at Paris,
and the notary not caring to lie in the same bed with a woman
who had but that moment sent him pell-mell to the devil,
went forth with his hat and cane and short cloak, the night
being very windy, and walk'd out ill at ease towards the
pont neuf.

Of all the bridges which ever were built, the whole world
who have pass'd over the *pont neuf*, must own, that it is the
noblest—the finest—the grandest—the lightest—the longest
—the broadest that ever conjoin'd land and land together upon
the face of the terraqueous globe——

*By this, it seems, as if the author of the fragment had not been
a Frenchman.*

The worst fault which divines and the doctors of the
Sorbonne can allege against it, is, that if there is but a cap-full
of wind in or about Paris, 'tis more blasphemously *sacre
Dieu*'d there than in any other aperture of the whole city—
and with reason, good and cogent Messieurs; for it comes
against you without crying *garde d'eau*[2], and with such un-
premeditable puffs, that of the few who cross it with their

hats on, not one in fifty but hazards two livres and a half, which is its full worth.

The poor notary, just as he was passing by the sentry, instinctively clapp'd his cane to the side of it, but in raising it up the point of his cane catching hold of the loop of the sentinel's hat hoisted it over the spikes of the ballustrade clear into the Seine—

—'*Tis an ill wind*, said a boatsman, who catch'd it, *which blows no body any good.*

The sentry being a gascon[1] incontinently twirl'd up his whiskers, and levell'd his harquebuss.

Harquebusses in those days went off with matches; and an old woman's paper lanthorn at the end of the bridge happening to be blown out, she had borrow'd the sentry's match to light it—it gave a moment's time for the gascon's blood to run cool, and turn the accident better to his advantage—'*Tis an ill wind*, said he, catching off the notary's castor[2], and legitimating the capture with the boatman's adage.

The poor notary cross'd the bridge, and passing along the rue de Dauphine into the fauxbourgs of St. Germain, lamented himself as he walk'd along in this manner:

Luckless man! that I am, said the notary, to be the sport of hurricanes all my days——to be born to have the storm of ill language levell'd against me and my profession wherever I go —to be forced into marriage by the thunder of the church to a tempest of a woman—to be driven forth out of my house by domestic winds, and despoil'd of my castor by pontific[3] ones —to be here, bare-headed, in a windy night at the mercy of the ebbs and flows of accidents—where am I to lay my head?— miserable man! what wind in the two-and-thirty points of the whole compass can blow unto thee, as it does to the rest of thy fellow creatures, good!

As the notary was passing on by a dark passage, complaining in this sort, a voice call'd out to a girl, to bid her run for the next notary—now the notary being the next, and availing himself of his situation, walk'd up the passage to the door, and passing through an old sort of a saloon, was usher'd into a large chamber dismantled of every thing but a long military pike— a breast plate—a rusty old sword, and bandoleer[1], hung up equi-distant in four different places against the wall.

An old personage, who had heretofore been a gentleman, and unless decay of fortune taints the blood along with it was a gentleman at that time, lay supporting his head upon his hand in his bed; a little table with a taper burning was set close beside it, and close by the table was placed a chair—the notary sat him down in it; and pulling out his ink-horn and a sheet or two of paper which he had in his pocket, he placed them before him, and dipping his pen in his ink, and leaning his breast over the table, he disposed every thing to make the gentleman's last will and testament.

Alas! Monsieur le Notaire, said the gentleman, raising himself up a little, I have nothing to bequeath which will pay the expence of bequeathing, except the history of myself, which, I could not die in peace unless I left it as a legacy to the world; the profits arising out of it, I bequeath to you for the pains of taking it from me—it is a story so uncommon, it must be read by all mankind—it will make the fortunes of your house— the notary dipp'd his pen into his ink-horn—Almighty director of every event in my life! said the old gentleman, looking up earnestly and raising his hands towards heaven— thou whose hand has led me on through such a labyrinth of strange passages down into this scene of desolation, assist the decaying memory of an old, infirm, and broken-hearted man —direct my tongue, by the spirit of thy eternal truth, that this stranger may set down naught but what is written in that BOOK, from whose records, said he, clasping his hands together, I am to be condemn'd or acquitted!——the notary held up the point of his pen betwixt the taper and his eye—

—It is a story, Monsieur le Notaire, said the gentleman, which will rouse up every affection in nature—it will kill the humane, and touch the heart of cruelty herself with pity—

—The notary was inflamed with a desire to begin, and put his pen a third time into his ink-horn—and the old gentleman turning a little more towards the notary, began to dictate his story in these words—

—And where is the rest of it, La Fleur? said I, as he just then enter'd the room.

THE FRAGMENT
AND THE *BOUQUET
PARIS

WHEN La Fleur came up close to the table, and was made to comprehend what I wanted, he told me there were only two other sheets of it which he had wrapt round the stalks of a *bouquet* to keep it together, which he had presented to the *demoiselle* upon the *boulevards*—Then, prithee, La Fleur, said I, step back to her to the Count de B****'s hotel, and *see if you canst get*—There is no doubt of it, said La Fleur—and away he flew.

In a very little time the poor fellow came back quite out of breath, with deeper marks of disappointment in his looks than could arise from the simple irreparability of the fragment—*Juste ciel!* in less than two minutes that the poor fellow had taken his last tender farewel of her—his faithless mistress had given his *gage d'amour* to one of the Count's footmen—the footman to a young sempstress—and the sempstress to a fiddler, with my fragment at the end of it—Our misfortunes were involved together—I gave a sigh—and La Fleur echo'd it back again to my ear—

* Nosegay.

—How perfidious! cried La Fleur—How unlucky! said I.—
—I should not have been mortified, Monsieur, quoth La Fleur, if she had lost it—Nor I, La Fleur, said I, had I found it.

Whether I did or no, will be seen hereafter.

THE ACT OF CHARITY
PARIS

THE man who either disdains or fears to walk up a dark entry may be an excellent good man, and fit for a hundred things; but he will not do to make a good sentimental traveller. I count little of the many things I see pass at broad noon day, in large and open streets.—Nature is shy, and hates to act before spectators; but in such an unobserved corner, you sometimes see a single short scene of her's worth all the sentiments of a dozen French plays compounded together—and yet they are *absolutely* fine;—and whenever I have a more brilliant affair upon my hands than common, as they suit a preacher just as well as a hero, I generally make my sermon out of 'em—and for the text—'Capadosia, Pontus and Asia, Phrygia and Pamphilia'[1]—is as good as any one in the Bible.

There is a long dark passage issuing out from the opera comique into a narrow street; 'tis trod by a few who humbly wait for a *fiacre**, or wish to get off quietly o'foot when the opera is done. At the end of it, towards the theatre, 'tis lighted by a small candle, the light of which is almost lost before you get half-way down, but near the door—'tis more for ornament than use: you see it as a fix'd star of the least magnitude; it burns—but does little good to the world, that we know of.

In returning along this passage, I discern'd, as I approach'd within five or six paces of the door, two ladies standing arm in

* Hackney-coach.

arm, with their backs against the wall, waiting, as I imagined, for a *fiacre*—as they were next the door, I thought they had a prior right; so edged myself up within a yard or little more of them, and quietly took my stand—I was in black, and scarce seen.

The lady next me was a tall lean figure of a woman of about thirty-six; the other of the same size and make, of about forty; there was no mark of wife or widow in any one part of either of them—they seem'd to be two upright vestal sisters, un-sapp'd by caresses, unbroke in upon by tender salutations: I could have wish'd to have made them happy—their happiness was destin'd, that night, to come from another quarter.

A low voice, with a good turn of expression, and sweet cadence at the end of it, begg'd for a twelve-sous piece betwixt them, for the love of heaven. I thought it singular, that a beggar should fix the quota of an alms—and that the sum should be twelve times as much as what is usually given in the dark. They both seemed astonish'd at it as much as myself.— Twelve sous! said one—a twelve-sous piece! said the other —and made no reply.

The poor man said, He knew not how to ask less of ladies of their rank; and bow'd down his head to the ground.

Poo! said they—we have no money.

The beggar remained silent for a moment or two, and renew'd his supplication.

Do not, my fair young ladies, said he, stop your good ears against me—Upon my word, honest man! said the younger, we have no change—Then God bless you, said the poor man, and multiply those joys which you can give to others without change!—I observed the elder sister put her hand into her pocket—I'll see, said she, if I have a sous.—A sous! give twelve, said the supplicant; Nature has been bountiful to you, be bountiful to a poor man.

I would, friend, with all my heart, said the younger, if I had it.

My fair charitable! said he, addressing himself to the elder —What is it but your goodness and humanity which makes your bright eyes so sweet, that they outshine the morning even in this dark passage? and what was it which made the Marquis de Santerre and his brother say so much of you both as they just pass'd by?

The two ladies seemed much affected; and impulsively at the same time they both put their hands into their pocket, and each took out a twelve-sous piece.

The contest betwixt them and the poor supplicant was no more—it was continued betwixt themselves, which of the two should give the twelve-sous piece in charity—and to end the dispute, they both gave it together, and the man went away.

THE RIDDLE EXPLAINED

PARIS

I stepp'd hastily after him: it was the very man whose success in asking charity of the women before the door of the hotel had so puzzled me—and I found at once his secret, or at least the basis of it—'twas flattery.

Delicious essence! how refreshing art thou to nature! how strongly are all its powers and all its weaknesses on thy side! how sweetly dost thou mix with the blood, and help it through the most difficult and tortuous passages to the heart!

The poor man, as he was not straighten'd for time, had given it here in a larger dose: 'tis certain he had a way of bringing it into less form, for the many sudden cases he had to do with in the streets; but how he contrived to correct, sweeten, concentre[1], and qualify it—I vex not my spirit with the inquiry—it is enough, the beggar gain'd two twelve-sous pieces—and they can best tell the rest, who have gain'd much greater matters by it.

PARIS

WE get forwards in the world not so much by doing services, as receiving them: you take a withering twig, and put it in the ground; and then you water it, because you have planted it.

Mons. Le Compte de B****, merely because he had done me one kindness in the affair of my passport, would go on and do me another, the few days he was at Paris, in making me known to a few people of rank; and they were to present me to others, and so on.

I had got master of my *secret*, just in time to turn these honours to some little account; otherwise, as is commonly the case, I should have din'd or supp'd a single time or two round, and then by *translating* French looks and attitudes into plain English, I should presently have seen, that I had got hold of the *couvert** of some more entertaining guest; and in course, should have resigned all my places one after another, merely upon the principle that I could not keep them.—As it was, things did not go much amiss.

I had the honour of being introduced to the old Marquis de B****: in days of yore he had signaliz'd himself by some small feats of chivalry in the *Cour d'amour*, and had dress'd himself out to the idea of tilts and tournaments ever since—the Marquis de B**** wish'd to have it thought the affair was somewhere else than in his brain. 'He could like to take a trip to England,' and ask'd much of the English ladies. Stay where you are, I beseech you, Mons. le Marquise, said I— Les Messrs. Angloise can scarce get a kind look from them as it is.—The Marquis invited me to supper.

Mons. P**** the farmer-general[1] was just as inquisitive about our taxes.—They were very considerable, he heard— If we knew but how to collect them, said I, making him a low bow.

* Plate, napkin, knife, fork, and spoon.

I could never have been invited to Mons. P*****'s concerts upon any other terms.

I had been misrepresented to Madame de Q*** as an *esprit*—Madam de Q*** was an *esprit* herself; she burnt with impatience to see me, and hear me talk. I had not taken my seat, before I saw she did not care a sous whether I had any wit or no—I was let in, to be convinced she had.—I call heaven to witness I never once open'd the door of my lips[1].

Madame de Q*** vow'd to every creature she met, 'She had never had a more improving conversation with a man in her life.'

There are three epochas in the empire of a French-woman —She is coquette—then deist—then *devôte:* the empire during these is never lost—she only changes her subjects: when thirty-five years and more have unpeopled her dominions of the slaves of love, she re-peoples it with slaves of infidelity—and then with the slaves of the Church.

Madame de V*** was vibrating betwixt the first of these epochas: the colour of the rose was shading fast away—she ought to have been a deist five years before the time I had the honour to pay my first visit.

She placed me upon the same sopha with her, for the sake of disputing the point of religion more closely.—In short, Madame de V*** told me she believed nothing.

I told Madame de V*** it might be her principle; but I was sure it could not be her interest to level the outworks, without which I could not conceive how such a citadel as hers could be defended—that there was not a more dangerous thing in the world, than for a beauty to be a deist—that it was a debt I owed my creed, not to conceal it from her—that I had not been five minutes sat upon the sopha besides her, but I had begun to form designs—and what is it, but the sentiments of religion, and the persuasion they had existed in her breast, which could have check'd them as they rose up.

We are not adamant, said I, taking hold of her hand—and

there is need of all restraints, till age in her own time steals in and lays them on us—but, my dear lady, said I, kissing her hand—'tis too—too soon—

I declare I had the credit all over Paris of unperverting Madame de V***.—She affirmed to Mons. D*** and the Abbe M***, that in one half hour I had said more for revealed religion, than all their Encyclopedia[1] had said against it—I was listed directly into Madame de V***'s *Coterie*—and she put off the epocha of deism for two years.

I remember it was in this *Coterie*, in the middle of a discourse, in which I was shewing the necessity of a *first cause*, that the young Count de Faineant[2] took me by the hand to the furthest corner of the room, to tell me my *solitaire*[3] was pinn'd too strait about my neck—It should be *plus badinant*, said the Count, looking down upon his own—but a word, Mons. Yorick, to *the wise*—

—And from the wise, Mons. Le Compte, replied I, making him a bow—*is enough*.

The Count de Faineant embraced me with more ardour than ever I was embraced by mortal man.

For three weeks together, I was of every man's opinion I met.—*Pardi! ce Mons. Yorick a autant d'esprit que nous autres.*——*Il raisonne bien*, said another.—*C'est un bon enfant*, said a third.—And at this price I could have eaten and drank and been merry all the days of my life at Paris; but 'twas a dishonest *reckoning*—I grew ashamed of it—it was the gain of a slave—every sentiment of honour revolted against it—the higher I got, the more was I forced upon my *beggarly system*—the better the *Coterie*—the more children of Art—I languish'd for those of Nature: and one night, after a most vile prostitution of myself to half a dozen different people, I grew sick—went to bed—order'd La Fleur to get me horses in the morning to set out for Italy.

MARIA
MOULINES

I NEVER felt what the distress of plenty was in any one shape till now—to travel it through the Bourbonnois, the sweetest part of France—in the hey-day of the vintage, when Nature is pouring her abundance into every one's lap, and every eye is lifted up—a journey through each step of which music beats time to *Labour*, and all her children are rejoicing as they carry in their clusters—to pass through this with my affections flying out, and kindling at every group before me—and every one of 'em was pregnant with adventures.

Just heaven!—it would fill up twenty volumes—and alas! I have but a few small pages left of this to croud it into—and half of these must be taken up with the poor Maria[1] my friend, Mr. Shandy, met with near Moulines.

The story he had told of that disorder'd maid affect'd me not a little in the reading; but when I got within the neighbourhood where she lived, it returned so strong into my mind, that I could not resist an impulse which prompted me to go half a league out of the road to the village where her parents dwelt to enquire after her.

'Tis going, I own, like the Knight of the Woeful Countenance[2], in quest of melancholy adventures—but I know not how it is, but I am never so perfectly conscious of the existence of a soul within me, as when I am entangled in them.

The old mother came to the door, her looks told me the story before she open'd her mouth—She had lost her husband; he had died, she said, of anguish, for the loss of Maria's senses about a month before.—She had feared at first, she added, that it would have plunder'd her poor girl of what little understanding was left—but, on the contrary, it had brought her more to herself—still she could not rest—her poor daughter, she said, crying, was wandering somewhere about the road—

—Why does my pulse beat languid as I write this? and what made La Fleur, whose heart seem'd only to be tuned to joy, to pass the back of his hand twice across his eyes, as the woman stood and told it? I beckon'd to the postilion to turn back into the road.

When we had got within half a league of Moulines, at a little opening in the road leading to a thicket, I discovered poor Maria sitting under a poplar—she was sitting with her elbow in her lap, and her head leaning on one side within her hand—a small brook ran at the foot of the tree.

I bid the postilion go on with the chaise to Moulines—and La Fleur to bespeak my supper—and that I would walk after him.

She was dress'd in white, and much as my friend described her, except that her hair hung loose, which before was twisted within a silk net.—She had, superadded likewise to her jacket, a pale green ribband which fell across her shoulder to the waist; at the end of which hung her pipe.—Her goat had been as faithless as her lover; and she had got a little dog in lieu of him, which she had kept tied by a string to'her girdle; as I look'd at her dog, she drew him towards her with the string.—'Thou shalt not leave me, Sylvio,' said she. I look'd in Maria's eyes, and saw she was thinking more of her father than of her lover or her little goat; for as she utter'd them the tears trickled down her cheeks.

I sat down close by her; and Maria let me wipe them away as they fell with my handkerchief.—I then steep'd it in my own—and then in hers—and then in mine—and then I wip'd hers again—and as I did it, I felt such undescribable emotions within me, as I am sure could not be accounted for from any combinations of matter and motion.

I am positive I have a soul; nor can all the books with which materialists have pester'd the world ever convince me of the contrary.

MARIA

WHEN Maria had come a little to herself, I ask'd her if she remember'd a pale thin person of a man who had sat down betwixt her and her goat about two years before? She said, she was unsettled much at that time, but remember'd it upon two accounts—that ill as she was she saw the person pitied her; and next, that her goat had stolen his handkerchief, and she had beat him for the theft—she had wash'd it, she said, in the brook, and kept it ever since in her pocket to restore it to him in case she should ever see him again, which, she added, he had half promised her. As she told me this, she took the handkerchief out of her pocket to let me see it; she had folded it up neatly in a couple of vine leaves, tied round with a tendril —on opening it, I saw an S mark'd in one of the corners.

She had since that, she told me, stray'd as far as Rome, and walk'd round St Peter's once—and return'd back—that she found her way alone across the Apennines—had travell'd over all Lombardy without money—and through the flinty roads of Savoy without shoes—how she had borne it, and how she had got supported, she could not tell—but *God tempers the wind*, said Maria, to the shorn lamb[1].

Shorn indeed! and to the quick, said I; and wast thou in my own land, where I have a cottage, I would take thee to it and shelter thee: thou shouldst eat of my own bread, and drink of my own cup—I would be kind to thy Sylvio—in all thy weaknesses and wanderings I would seek after thee and bring thee back—when the sun went down I would say my prayers, and when I had done thou shouldst play thy evening song upon thy pipe, nor would the incense of my sacrifice be worse accepted for entering heaven along with that of a broken heart.

Nature melted within me, as I utter'd this; and Maria observing, as I took out my handkerchief, that it was steep'd too much already to be of use, would needs go wash it in the stream.—And where will you dry it, Maria? said I—I'll dry it in my bosom, said she—'twill do me good.

And is your heart still so warm, Maria? said I.

I touch'd upon the string on which hung all her sorrows— she look'd with wistful disorder for some time in my face; and then, without saying any thing, took her pipe, and play'd her service to the Virgin—The string I had touch'd ceased to vibrate—in a moment or two Maria returned to herself— let her pipe fall—and rose up.

And where art you going, Maria? said I.—She said to Moulines.—Let us go, said I, together.—Maria put her arm within mine, and lengthening the string, to let the dog follow —in that order we entered Moulines.

MARIA
MOULINES

Tho' I hate salutations and greetings in the market-place, yet when we got into the middle of this, I stopp'd to take my last look and last farewel of Maria.

Maria, tho' not tall, was nevertheless of the first order of fine forms—affliction had touch'd her looks with something that was scarce earthly—still she was feminine—and so much was there about her of all that the heart wishes, or the eye looks for in woman, that could the traces be ever worn out of her brain, and those of Eliza's out of mine, she should *not only eat of my bread and drink of my own cup*[1], but Maria should lay in my bosom, and be unto me as a daughter.

Adieu, poor luckless maiden!—imbibe the oil and wine which the compassion of a stranger, as he journieth on his way, now pours into thy wounds—the being who has twice bruised thee can only bind them up for ever.

THE BOURBONNOIS

THERE was nothing from which I had painted out for myself so joyous a riot of the affections, as in this journey in the vintage, through this part of France; but pressing through this gate of sorrow to it, my sufferings had totally unfitted me: in every scene of festivity I saw Maria in the back-ground of the piece, sitting pensive under her poplar; and I had got almost to Lyons before I was able to cast a shade across her——

——Dear sensibility! source inexhausted of all that's precious in our joys, or costly in our sorrows! thou chainest thy martyr down upon his bed of straw—and 'tis thou who lifts him up to HEAVEN—eternal fountain of our feelings!—'tis here I trace thee—and this is thy divinity which stirs within me——not, that in some sad and sickening moments, '*my soul shrinks back upon herself, and startles at destruction*'[1]—mere pomp of words!—but that I feel some generous joys and generous cares beyond myself—all comes from thee, great—great SENSORIUM of the world! which vibrates, if a hair of our heads but falls upon the ground, in the remotest desert of thy creation.—Touch'd with thee, Eugenius draws my curtain when I languish—hears my tale of symptoms, and blames the weather for the disorder of his nerves. Thou giv'st a portion of it sometimes to the roughest peasant who traverses the bleakest mountains—he finds the lacerated lamb of another's flock— This moment I beheld him leaning with his head against his crook, with piteous inclination looking down upon it—Oh! had I come one moment sooner!—it bleeds to death—his gentle heart bleeds with it——

Peace to thee, generous swain!—I see thou walkest off with anguish—but thy joys shall balance it—for happy is thy cottage—and happy is the sharer of it—and happy are the lambs which sport about you.

THE SUPPER

A SHOE coming loose from the fore-foot of the thill-horse[1], at the beginning of the ascent of mount Taurira, the postilion dismounted, twisted the shoe off, and put it in his pocket; as the ascent was of five or six miles, and that horse our main dependence, I made a point of having the shoe fasten'd on again, as well as we could; but the postilion had thrown away the nails, and the hammer in the chaise-box, being of no great use without them, I submitted to go on.

He had not mounted half a mile higher, when coming to a flinty piece of road, the poor devil lost a second shoe, and from off his other fore-foot; I then got out of the chaise in good earnest; and seeing a house about a quarter of a mile to the left-hand, with a great deal to do, I prevailed upon the postilion to turn up to it. The look of the house, and of every thing about it, as we drew nearer, soon reconciled me to the disaster.—It was a little farm-house surrounded with about twenty acres of vineyard, about as much corn—and close to the house, on one side, was a *potagerie* of an acre and a half, full of every thing which could make plenty in a French peasant's house—and on the other side was a little wood which furnished wherewithal to dress it. It was about eight in the evening when I got to the house—so I left the postilion to manage his point as he could—and for mine, I walk'd directly into the house.

The family consisted of an old grey-headed man and his wife, with five or six sons and sons-in-law and their several wives, and a joyous genealogy out of 'em.

They were all sitting down together to their lentil-soup; a large wheaten loaf was in the middle of the table; and a flaggon of wine at each end of it promised joy thro' the stages of the repast—'twas a feast of love.

The old man rose up to meet me, and with a respectful

cordiality would have me sit down at the table; my heart was sat down the moment I enter'd the room; so I sat down at once like a son of the family; and to invest myself in the character as speedily as I could, I instantly borrowed the old man's knife, and taking up the loaf cut myself a hearty luncheon; and as I did it I saw a testimony in every eye, not only of an honest welcome, but of a welcome mix'd with thanks that I had not seem'd to doubt it.

Was it this; or tell me, Nature, what else it was which made this morsel so sweet—and to what magick I owe it, that the draught I took of their flaggon was so delicious with it, that they remain upon my palate to this hour?

If the supper was to my taste—the grace which follow'd it was much more so.

THE GRACE

WHEN supper was over, the old man gave a knock upon the table with the haft of his knife—to bid them prepare for the dance: the moment the signal was given, the women and girls ran all together into a back apartment to tye up their hair —and the young men to the door to wash their faces, and change their sabots; and in three minutes every soul was ready upon a little esplanade before the house to begin—The old man and his wife came out last, and, placing me betwixt them, sat down upon a sopha of turf by the door.

The old man had some fifty years ago been no mean per-former upon the vielle[1]—and at the age he was then of, touch'd it well enough for the purpose. His wife sung now-and-then a little to the tune—then intermitted—and joined her old man again as their children and grand-children danced before them.

It was not till the middle of the second dance, when, from

some pauses in the movement wherein they all seemed to look up, I fancied I could distinguish an elevation of spirit different from that which is the cause or the effect of simple jollity.—In a word, I thought I beheld *Religion* mixing in the dance—but as I had never seen her so engaged, I should have look'd upon it now, as one of the illusions of an imagination which is eternally misleading me, had not the old man, as soon as the dance ended, said, that this was their constant way; and that all his life long he had made it a rule, after supper was over, to call out his family to dance and rejoice; believing, he said, that a chearful and contented mind was the best sort of thanks to heaven that an illiterate peasant could pay—

——Or a learned prelate either, said I.

THE CASE OF DELICACY

WHEN you have gained the top of mount Taurira, you run presently down to Lyons—adieu then to all rapid movements! 'Tis a journey of caution; and it fares better with sentiments, not to be in a hurry with them; so I contracted with a Voiturin to take his time with a couple of mules, and convey me in my own chaise safe to Turin through Savoy.

Poor, patient, quiet, honest people! fear not; your poverty, the treasury of your simple virtues, will not be envied you by the world nor will your vallies be invaded by it.—Nature! in the midst o thy disorders, thou art still friendly to the scantiness thou hast created—with all thy great works about thee, little hast thou left to give, either to the scithe or to the sickle—but to that little, thou grantest safety and protection; and sweet are the dwellings which stand so shelter'd.

Let the way-worn traveller vent his complaints upon the sudden turns and dangers of your roads—your rocks—your precipices—the difficulties of getting up—the horrors of getting down—mountains impracticable—and cataracts, which roll down great stones from their summits, and block his road up.—The peasants had been all day at work in removing a fragment of this kind between St. Michael and Madane; and by the time my Voiturin got to the place, it wanted full two hours of compleating before a passage could any how be gain'd: there was nothing but to wait with patience—'twas a wet and tempestuous night; so that by the delay, and that together, the Voiturin found himself obliged to take up five miles short of his stage at a little decent kind of an inn by the road side.

I forthwith took possession of my bed-chamber—got a good fire—order'd supper; and was thanking heaven it was no worse—when a voiture arrived with a lady in it and her servant-maid.

As there was no other bed-chamber in the house, the hostess, without much nicety, led them into mine, telling them, as she usher'd them in, that there was no body in it but an English gentleman—that there were two good beds in it, and a closet within the room which held another—the accent in which she spoke of this third bed did not say much for it—however, she said, there were three beds, and but three people —and she durst say, the gentleman would do any thing to accommodate matters.—I left not the lady a moment to make a conjecture about it—so instantly made a declaration I would do any thing in my power.

As this did not amount to an absolute surrender of my bed-chamber, I still felt myself so much the proprietor, as to have a right to do the honours of it—so I desired the lady to sit down—pressed her into the warmest seat—call'd for more wood—desired the hostess to enlarge the plan of the supper, and to favour us with the very best wine.

The lady had scarce warm'd herself five minutes at the fire, before she began to turn her head back, and give a look at the beds; and the oftener she cast her eyes that way, the more they return'd perplex'd—I felt for her—and for myself; for in a few minutes, what by her looks, and the case itself, I found myself as much embarrassed as it was possible the lady could be herself.

That the beds we were to lay in were in one and the same room, was enough simply by itself to have excited all this—but the position of them, for they stood parallel, and so very close to each other as only to allow space for a small wicker chair betwixt them, render'd the affair still more oppressive to us—they were fixed up moreover near the fire, and the projection of the chimney on one side, and a large beam which cross'd the room on the other, form'd a kind of recess for them that was no way favourable to the nicety of our sensations—if any thing could have added to it, it was, that the two beds were both of 'em so very small, as to cut us off from every idea of the lady and the maid lying together; which in either of them, could it have been feasible, my lying besides them, tho' a thing not to be wish'd, yet there was nothing in it so terrible which the imagination might not have pass'd over without torment.

As for the little room within, it offer'd little or no consolation to us; 'twas a damp cold closet, with a half dismantled window shutter, and with a window which had neither glass or oil paper in it to keep out the tempest of the night. I did not endeavour to stifle my cough when the lady gave a peep into it; so it reduced the case in course to this alternative—that the lady should sacrifice her health to her feelings, and take up with the closet herself, and abandon the bed next mine to her maid—or that the girl should take the closet, &c. &c.

The lady was a Piedmontese of about thirty, with a glow of health in her cheeks.—The maid was a Lyonoise of twenty, and as brisk and lively a French girl as ever moved.—There were difficulties every way—and the obstacle of the stone in the road, which brought us into the distress, great as it appeared whilst the peasants were removing it, was but a pebble to what lay in our ways now—I have only to add, that it did not lessen the weight which hung upon our spirits, that we were both too delicate to communicate what we felt to each other upon the occasion.

We sat down to supper; and had we not had more generous wine to it than a little inn in Savoy could have furnish'd, our tongues had been tied up, till necessity herself had set them at liberty—but the lady having a few bottles of Burgundy in her voiture sent down her Fille de Chambre for a couple of them; so that by the time supper was over, and we were left alone, we felt ourselves inspired with a strength of mind sufficient to talk, at least, without reserve upon our situation. We turn'd it every way, and debated and considered it in all kind of lights in the course of a two hours negociation; at the end of which the articles were settled finally betwixt us, and stipulated for in form and manner of a treaty of peace—and I believe with as much religion and good faith on both sides, as in any treaty which as yet had the honour of being handed down to posterity.

They were as follows:

First. As the right of the bed-chamber is in Monsieur— and he thinking the bed next to the fire to be the warmest, he insists upon the concession on the lady's side of taking up with it.

Granted, on the part of Madame; with a proviso, That as the curtains of that bed are of a flimsy transparent cotton, and appear likewise too scanty to draw close, that the Fille de Chambre, shall fasten up the opening, either by corking pins, or needle and thread, in such manner as shall be deemed a sufficient barrier on the side of Monsieur.

2dly. It is required on the part of Madame, that Monsieur shall lay the whole night through in his robe de chambre.

Rejected: inasmuch as Monsieur is not worth a robe de chambre; he having nothing in his portmanteau but six shirts and a black silk pair of breeches.

The mentioning the silk pair of breeches made an entire change of the article—for the breeches were accepted as an equivalent for the robe de chambre, and so it was stipulated and agreed upon that I should lay in my black silk breeches all night.

3dly. It was insisted upon, and stipulated for by the lady, that after Monsieur was got to bed, and the candle and fire extinguished, that Monsieur should not speak one single word the whole night.

Granted; provided Monsieur's saying his prayers might not be deem'd an infraction of the treaty.

There was but one point forgot in this treaty, and that was the manner in which the lady and myself should be obliged to undress and get to bed—there was but one way of doing it, and that I leave to the reader to devise; protesting as I do it, that if it is not the most delicate in nature, 'tis the fault of his own imagination—against which this is not my first complaint.

Now when we were got to bed, whether it was the novelty of the situation, or what it was, I know not; but so it was, I could not shut my eyes; I tried this side and that, and turn'd and turn'd again, till a full hour after midnight; when Nature and patience both wearing out—O my God! said I——

—You have broke the treaty, Monsieur, said the lady, who had no more slept than myself.—I begg'd a thousand pardons—but insisted it was no more than an ejaculation—she maintain'd 'twas an entire infraction of the treaty—I maintain'd it was provided for in the clause of the third article.

The lady would by no means give up her point, tho' she weakened her barrier by it; for in the warmth of the dispute, I could hear two or three corking pins fall out of the curtain to the ground.

Upon my word and honour, Madame, said I—stretching my arm out of bed, by way of asseveration—

—(I was going to have added, that I would not have

trespass'd against the remotest idea of decorum for the world)—

—But the Fille de Chambre hearing there were words between us, and fearing that hostilities would ensue in course, had crept silently out of her closet, and it being totally dark, had stolen so close to our beds, that she had got herself into the narrow passage which separated them, and had advanc'd so far up as to be in a line betwixt her mistress and me—

So that when I stretch'd out my hand, I caught hold of the Fille de Chambre's

END OF VOL. II.

THE JOURNAL TO
ELIZA

INTRODUCTION

'I HAVE brought your name *Eliza!* and Picture into my work —where they will remain—when You and I are at rest for ever', Sterne wrote in the *Journal* one day in June 1767. 'Some Annotator or explainer of my works in this place will take occasion, to speak of the Friendship which Subsisted so long and faithfully betwixt Yorick and the Lady he speaks of—Her Name he will tell the world was Draper—a Native of India— married there to a gentleman in the India Service of that Name—, who brought her over to England for the recovery of her health in the Year 65—where She continued to April the Year 1767. It was about three months before her Return to India, That our Author's acquaintance and hers began. Mrs Draper had a great thirst for Knowledge—was handsome —genteel—engaging—and of such gentle dispositions and so enlightend an understanding,—That Yorick, (whether he made much Opposition is not known) from an acquaintance— soon became her Admirer—they caught fire at each other at the same time—and they would often say, without reserve to the world, and without any Idea of saying wrong in it, That their Affections for each other were *unbounded*—'.

There is not much more that the 'Annotator or explainer' need say about Eliza Draper. Left an orphan at the age of four, she was only fourteen when she married Daniel Draper, a man eighteen years older than herself. Soon after Sterne met her, which was probably in January 1767, we find him signing himself hers 'faithfully if not affectionately', and it is clear that she was no less ready for a sentimental flirtation than the master of Sentiment himself. She called him her Bramin, by which she no doubt meant her wise man or spiritual teacher. Sterne characteristically gallicized the word and made it feminine, so that she became his Bramine.* Neither made any attempt to conceal the attachment, but soon the time came for Eliza to return to Bombay. Sterne saw her for the last time when he handed her into her post-chaise for Deal, and she sailed on 3 April. According to the statement at the beginning of the *Journal* they promised to write 'mutual testimonies to deliver hereafter to each other'. Eliza's 'Counterpart', if in fact it existed, has disappeared, as has the earlier part of the Bramin's *Journal*. What is printed here is all that remains.

The true significance of *The Journal to Eliza* is extremely hard to determine. The scholar who first published it, Wilbur Cross, welcomed its appearance on the ground that it 'completely reveals the pathological state of the emotions—long suspected but never quite known to a certainty—whence sprang the *Sentimental Journey*, during the composition of which Sterne was fast dying of consumption'. In the opinion of a distinguished French scholar, Henri Fluchère, 'c'est une confession totale, le cœur et le corps, mis à nu'. Against these judgements may be set the opinion of a more sceptical student of Sterne, Rufus Putney, who has argued forcibly that the *Journal* 'does not merit the confidence it has been accorded'. Putney maintains that the work is 'semi-fictitious rather than real autobiography', and believes that 'whatever place Eliza held in Sterne's life, she no more than ill health created the tone of the *Sentimental Journey*'. Putney's view is that Sterne 'mocked in the *Sentimental Journey* the foolish figure he had cut with Eliza Draper'.† The problem remains one of the most perplexing of the many which confront the would-be

---

* Sterne often inconsistently used this spelling in referring to himself.

† *The Life and Times of Laurence Sterne*, by Wilbur L. Cross (3rd ed., 1929), p. 460; *Laurence Sterne: de l'homme à l'œuvre*, by Henri Fluchère (1961), p. 174; 'The Evolution of *A Sentimental Journey*', by Rufus Putney, in *Philological Quarterly*, xix (1940), 349-69.

biographer of Laurence Sterne. All that can be offered here is a tentative suggestion or two for the consideration of the reader who is tempted to speculate on the relation between the two works.

As we have seen, the original idea of *A Sentimental Journey* seems to have been to exploit Sterne's 'excellence . . . in the PATHETIC', already demonstrated by such episodes in *Tristram Shandy* as the story of Le Fever and the description of Maria. He was planning his new book, but had not begun writing it, when he met Eliza. That he fell in love with her, after his own fashion, need not be doubted; but he was a man who fell in love easily and (in a sense) controlledly, and the view of Wilbur Cross that this was to prove 'the one great passion of his life, shining through a decade of flirtations' must be taken with a grain of salt. Perhaps he was attracted in part by the inevitable transitoriness of the affair. Although news of her association with the notorious Yorick could not yet have reached Daniel Draper in Bombay, he could not be expected to wait indefinitely for the arrival of his young wife.

The appeal of the *Journal* for Sterne may from the first have been literary as well as emotional; but while the heading and introductory sentences make it clear that at some point he thought of the possibility of publication, its initial importance to him as a writer was probably quite different:

Were your husband in England [we find him writing to Eliza shortly before her departure], I would freely give him five hundred pounds . . . to let you only sit by me two hours in a day, while I wrote my Sentimental Journey. I am sure the work would sell so much the better for it, that I should be re-imbursed the sum more than seven times told.

Nothing could be more characteristic of Sterne than this untroubled association of sentiment and calculation. As he wrote his clever new book, it appealed to him to look at his picture of Eliza (which was probably the work of the gifted Richard Cosway) and imagine her presiding over his labours. What could be more natural, or more becoming (as he no doubt noted himself), than his complaint on 3 June that he cannot write his 'Travels, or give one half hours close attention to them, upon Thy Account my dearest friend'? What source of inspiration could be more appropriate than this piquant young woman, whose unconcealed affection for a man more than twice her age had been a matter of notoriety for weeks before her husband summoned her away? What Muse could more fitly be invoked by the author of a Sentimental book that was also (as he came to see more and more clearly, as his *Journey* began to get under way) to have a mischievously erotic content?

Putney's view that *A Sentimental Journey* is 'a hoax by which Sterne persuaded his contemporaries that the humor he wanted to write was the pathos they wished to read' is an over-simplification of a very subtle book. Sterne's sensibility is self-conscious, ambivalent, sophisticated; but it is not wholly bogus. The suggestion that he was in a reasonably good state of health during the composition of the book can hardly be taken seriously. It is true that there are one or two optimistic remarks about his health in letters written at this time, but we also know that he had been desperately ill in the spring of 1767, and we have his own account of his spitting blood after his visit to the York Races in August. His health had been precarious for some time, and he was to die within three weeks of the publication of his book. In his more reasonable moments he knew that he was a dying man. In his more buoyant moments, on the other hand, with the optimism that so often accompanies his disease, we find him constructing an idyllic future for himself with a charming young widow as the helpmate and nurse of his declining days. At the end of the passage quoted above, in the first paragraph of this Introduction, he added the words 'except by a [*illegible*] of honour and Virtue', scored them out heavily, and continued:

Mr Draper dying in the Year *****—This Lady return'd to England, and Yorick the year after becoming a Widower—They were married—and retiring to one of his Livings in Yorkshire, where was a most romantic Situation—they lived and died happily.—and are spoke of with honour in the parish to this day—

Sterne's letters to Eliza contain numerous descriptions of the eminently practical preparations for her comfort which he delighted to make in Shandy Hall. Yet there is a certain unreality about the whole thing.

The Journal to Eliza is not (after all) the only lovers' journal to have begun as magic and continued as fantasy, and as we turn its pages it becomes evident that it was life itself that Sterne was in love with, rather than the particular woman called Eliza Draper. There is a self-consciousness about every entry that is very Sternean—and very understandable. He constantly repeats the comments of his friends and his servant on his forlorn condition, not only (one senses) as a reassurance to Eliza, but also as a reassurance to himself. *Amo ergo sum.*

It is more surprising that Sterne continued to make entries in the *Journal* for four months than that he went on with it no longer. The problem of conveying the *Journal* to Bombay was a formidable one, and when he found himself writing a passage like the last quoted above he realized that it was becoming impossible for him 'ever to send . . . this Journal to India'. The alternative—that he would one day be able to hand the *Journal* over to Eliza in person, after her return to England—must soon have become hard to believe in. And perhaps Sterne was less often in the mood to add to the *Journal*. The mischievous eroticism of *A Sentimental Journey* is (after all) very different from the predominant mood of the *Journal* itself. What Sterne longed for and required was feminine sympathy, and there were admirers more accessible than the fair Eliza: Mrs. James, 'Sheba', the mysterious Hannah, an unknown Countess, and particularly that 'dear part of me', his daughter Lydia. As the *Journal* could not really keep him in touch with Eliza, and as he could not see it becoming a publishable book, it is clear that he became bored with it. He wanted to devote himself to other matters, prominent among them the publication of *A Sentimental Journey*. And so we find him fibbing to Eliza and antedating his wife's return by a month, as an excuse for giving up his *Journal*.

The subsequent history of the manuscript is a curious one. Whether or not Sterne left it as a legacy to Eliza—as he had promised—the next we hear of it is an account of its discovery by a schoolboy during the first half of the nineteenth century. Fortunately the boy, whose name was Thomas Washbourne Gibbs and whose age was eleven, had already heard of Sterne, so he was careful to preserve the papers. In 1851 he lent them to Thackeray, who was preparing his lectures on *The English Humourists of the Eighteenth Century*. Today no one is likely to share Thackeray's view that Swift and Sterne are 'a couple of traitors and renegades' who are to be regarded 'with a scornful pity in spite of all their genius and greatness'. The papers which Master Gibbs rescued from oblivion do not (it is true) contain a major work of literature, nor do they support the view that Sterne was a flawless man or a devoted husband. But they throw a little more light on an enigmatic person whose oddity is the oddity of the human heart itself.

THE JOURNAL TO ELIZA

THIS Journal wrote under the fictitious Names of Yorick and Draper—and sometimes of the Bramin and Bramine—but tis a Diary of the miserable feelings of a person separated from a Lady for whose Society he languish'd—

The real Names—are foreigne—and the Account a Copy from a french Manuscript in M^r S——s hands—but wrote as it is, to cast a Viel over them—There is a Counterpart—which is the Lady's Account what transactions dayly happend—and what Sentiments occupied her mind, during this Separation from her Admirer—these are worth reading—the translator cannot say so much in favour of Yoricks—which seem to have little Merit beyond their honesty and truth—

Continuation of the Bramines Journal.

Sunday April 13[1].

wrote the last farewel to Eliza by Mr Wats* who sails this day for Bombay—inclosed her likewise the Journal kept from the day we parted, to this—so from hence continue it till the time we meet again—Eliza does the same, so we shall have mutual testimonies to deliver hereafter to each other, That the Sun has not more constantly rose and set upon the earth, than We have thought of and remember'd, what is more chearing than Light itself—eternal Sun-shine! Eliza!—dark to me is all this world without thee! and most heavily will every hour pass over my head, till that is come which brings thee, dear Woman back to Albion. dined with Hall[2] &c—at the brawn's head—the whole Pandamonium assembled—supp'd

* (he saild 23)

together at Halls—worn out both in body and mind, and paid a severe reckoning all the night.

April 14. got up tottering and feeble—then is it, Eliza, that I feel the want of thy friendly hand and friendly Council—and yet, with thee beside Me, thy Bramin would lose the merit of his virtue—he could not err—I will take thee upon any terms, Eliza! I shall be happy here—and I will be so just, so kind to thee, I will deserve not to be miserable hereafter—a Day dedicated to Abstinence and reflection—and what Object will employ the greatest part of mine—full well does my Eliza know—

Munday. April 15.

worn out with fevers of all kinds but most, by that fever of the heart with which I'm eternally wasting, and shall waste till I see Eliza again—dreadful Suffering of 15 Months!—it may be more—great Controuler of Events! surely thou wilt proportion this, to my Strength, and to that of my Eliza. pass'd the whole afternoon in reading her Letters, and reducing them to the order in which they were wrote to me—staid the whole evening at home—no pleasure or Interest in either Society or Diversions—What a change, my dear Girl, hast thou made in me!—but the Truth is, thou hast only turn'd the tide of my passions a new way—they flow, Eliza to thee—and ebb from every other Object in this world—and Reason tells me they do right—for my heart has rated thee at a Price, that all the world is not rich enough to purchase thee from me, at.   In a high fever all the night.

April 16. and got up so ill, I could not go to Mrs James[1] as I had promised her—took James's Powder[2] however—and leand the whole day with my head upon My hand; sitting most dejectedly at the Table with my Eliza's Picture before me—sympathizing and soothing me—O my Bramine! my Friend! my—Help-mate!—for that, (if I'm a prophet) is the Lot mark'd out for thee,—and such I consider thee now, and thence it is, Eliza, I Share so righteously with thee, in all the evil or good which befalls thee—But all our portion is Evil now, and all our hours grief—I look forwards towards the Elysium we have so often and rapturously talk'd of—Cordelia's Spirit will fly to tell thee in some sweet Slumber, the moment the door is opend for thee—and The Bramin of the Vally, shall follow the track wherever it leads him, to get to his Eliza, and invite her to his Cottage.—

5 in the afternoon—I have just been eating my Chicking, sitting over my repast upon it, with Tears—a bitter Sause— Eliza! but I could eat it with no other—when Molly spread the Table Cloath, my heart fainted with in me—one solitary plate —one knife—one fork—one Glass!—O Eliza! twas painfully distressing—I gave a thousand pensive penetrating Looks at the Arm chair thou so often graced on these quiet, sentimental Repasts—and Sighed and laid down my knife and fork,—and took out my handkerchiff, clap'd it across my face, and wept like a child—I shall read the same affecting Account of many a sad Dinner which Eliza has had no power to taste of, from the same feelings and recollections, how She and her Bramin have eat their bread in peace and Love together.

April 17. with my friend Mrs James in Gerard street, with a present of Colours and apparatus for painting:—Long Conversation about thee my Eliza—sunk my heart with an infamous Account of Draper and his detested Character at Bombay—for What a Wretch art thou thou hazarding thy life, my dear friend, and what thanks is his nature capable of returning?—thou wilt be repaid with Injuries and Insults! Still there is a blessing in store for the meek and gentle, and Eliza will not be disinherited of it: her Bramin is kept alive by this hope only—otherwise he is so sunk both in Spirits and looks, Eliza would scarse know him again. dined alone again to day; and begin to feel a pleasure in this kind of resigned Misery arising from this Situation, of heart unsupported by aught but its own tenderness—Thou owest me much Eliza!—and I will have patience; for thou wilt pay me all—But the Demand is equal;—much I owe thee, and with much shalt thou be requited.——Sent for a Chart of the Atlantic Ocean, to make conjectures upon what part of it my Treasure was floating—O! tis but a little way off—and I could venture after it in a Boat, methinks—I'm sure I could, was I to know Eliza was in distress—but fate has chalk'd out other roads. for us—We must go on with many a weary step, each in our separate heartless track, till Nature——

April 18.

This day, set up my Carriage,—new Subject of heartache, That Eliza is not here to share it with me.

Bought Orm's account of India[1]—why?—Let not my Bramine ask me—her heart will tell her Why I do this, and every Thing—

April 19. poor Sick-headed, sick hearted Yorick! Eliza has made a Shadow of thee—I am absolutely good for nothing, as every mortal is who can think and talk but upon one thing!—how I shall rally my powers, alarms me; for Eliza thou has melted them all into one—the power of loving thee[2]—and with such ardent affection as triumphs over all other feelings—was with our faithful friend all the morning; and dined with her and James—What is the Cause, that I can never talk about my Eliza to her, but I am rent in pieces—I burst into tears a dozen different times after dinner, and such affectionate gusts of passion, That She was ready to leave the room, —and sympathize in private for us—I weep for You both, said she (in a whisper,) for Elizas Anguish is as sharp as yours —her heart as tender—her constancy as great—heaven join Your hands I'm sure together!—James was occupied in reading a pamphlet upon the East India affairs—so I answerd her with a kind look, a heavy sigh, and a stream of tears—What was passing in Eliza's breast, at this affecting Crisis?—something kind, and pathetic! I will lay my Life.

8 o'clock—retired to my room, to tell my dear this—to run back the hours of Joy I have pass'd with her—and meditate

upon those which are still in reserve for Us.—By this time Mr James tells me, You will have got as far from me, as the Maderas—and that in two months more, you will have doubled the Cape of good hope—I shall trace thy track every day in the Map, and not allow one hour for contrary Winds, or Currents—every engine of nature shall work together for us—Tis the Language of Love—and I can speak no other. And so, good night, to thee, and may the gentlest delusions of love impose upon thy dreams, as I forbode they will, this night, on those of thy Bramine.

April 20. Easter Sunday.

was not disappointed—yet awoke in the most acute pain— Something Eliza is wrong with me—you should be ill out of Sympathy—and yet you are too ill already—my dear friend—. all day at home—in extream dejection.

April 21. The Loss of Eliza, and attention to that one Idea, brought on a fever—a consequence, I have for some time, for-seen—but had not a sufficient Stock of cold philosophy to remedy—to satisfy my friends, call'd in a Physician—Alas! alas! the only Physician, and who carries the Balm of my Life along with her,—is Eliza.—why did I suffer thee to go from me?—surely thou hast more than once call'd thyself, my Eliza, to the same Account.—twil cost us both dear! but it could not be otherwise—We have submitted—we shall be rewarded.

Twas a prophetic Spirit, which dictated the Account of Corporal Trim's uneasy night[1] when the fair Beguin ran in his head,—for every night and almost every Slumber of mine, since the day We parted, is a repe[ti]tion of the same description—dear Eliza! I am very ill—very ill for thee—but I could still give thee greater proofs of my Affection. parted with 12 Ounces of blood, in order to quiet what was left in me—tis a vain experiment,—physicians cannot understand this; tis enough for me that Eliza does.—I am worn down my dear Girl to a Shadow, and but that I'm certain thou wilt not read this, till I'm restored—thy Yorick would not let the Winds hear his Complaints—4 o'clock—sorrowful Meal! for twas upon our old dish.—We shall liv[e] to eat it, my Dear Bramine, with comfort.

8. at night, our dear friend Mrs James, from the forbodings of a good heart, thinking I was ill; sent her Maid to enquire after me—I had alarm'd her on Saturday; and not being with her on sunday,—her friendship supposed the Condition, I was in—She suffers most tenderly for Us, my Eliza!—and We owe her more than all the Sex—or indeed both Sexes if not, all the world put together—adieu! my sweet Eliza! for this night—thy Yorick is going to waste himself on a restless bed, where he will turn from side to Side a thousand times— and dream by Intervals of things terrible and impossible— That Eliza is false to Yorick, or Yorick is false to Eliza——

April 22^d—rose with utmost difficulty—my Physician order'd me back to bed as soon as I had got a dish of Tea— was bled again; my arm broke loose and I half bled to death in bed before I felt it. O Eliza! how did thy Bramine mourn the want of thee to tye up his wounds, and comfort his dejected heart—still something bids me hope—and hope, I will—and it shall be the last pleasurable Sensation I part with.

4 o'clock They are making my bed—how shall I be able to continue my Journal, in it?—If there remains a chasm here— think Eliza, how ill thy Yorick must have been.—this moment received a Card from our dear friend, beging me to take [care] of a Life so valuable to my friends—but most so—She adds, to my poor dear Eliza.—not a word from the Newnhams! but they had no such exhortation in their harts, to send thy Bramine—adieu to em!—

April 23.—a poor night. and am only able to quit my bed at 4 this afternoon—to say a word to my dear—and fulfill my engagement to her, 'of letting no day pass over my head without some kind communication with thee—faint resemblance, my dear girl, of x and how our days are to pass, when one kingdom holds us—visited in bed by 40 friends, in the Course of the Day—is not one warm affectionate call, of that friend, for whom I sustain Life, worth 'em all?—What thinkest thou my Eliza.—

April 24.

So ill, I could not write a word all this morning—not so much, as Eliza! farewel to thee;—I'm going———am a little better.—

So Shall not depart, as I apprehended—being this morning something better—and my Symptoms become milder, by a tolerable easy night.—and now, if I have strength and Spirits to trail my pen down to the bottom of the page, I have as whimsical a Story to tell you, and as comically disastrous as ever befell one of our family—Shandy's Nose—his *name*—his Sash-Window are fools to it. It will serve at *least* to amuse You. The Injury I did myself in catching cold upon James's pouder, fell, you must know, upon the worst part it could,—the most painful, and most dangerous of any in the human Body—It was on this Crisis, I call'd in an able Surgeon and with him an able physician (both my friends) to inspect my disaster—tis a venerial Case, cried my two Scientifick friends. —'tis impossible. at least to be that, replied I—for I have had no commerce whatever with the Sex—not even with my wife, added I, these 15 Years—You are ***** however my good friend, said the Surgeon, or there is no such Case in the world —what the Devil! said I without knowing Woman—we will not reason about it, said the Physician, but you must undergo a course of Mercury,—I'll lose my life first, said I,—and trust to Nature, to Time—or at the worst—to Death,—so I put an end with some Indignation to the Conference; and determined to bear all the torments I underwent, and ten times more rather than, submit to be treated as a *Sinner*, in a point where I had acted like a *Saint*. Now as the father of mischief would have it, who has no pleasure like that of dishonouring the righteous—it so fell out, That from The moment I dismiss'd my Doctors—my pains began to rage with a violence not to be express'd, or supported. every hour became more intollerable—I was got to bed—cried out and raved the whole night—and was got up so near dead, That my friends insisted upon my sending again for my Physician and Surgeon—I told them upon the word of a man of Strict honour, They were both mistaken as to my case—but tho' they had reason'd wrong—they might act right—but that sharp as my sufferings were, I felt them not so sharp as the Imputation, which a venerial treatment of my case, laid me under—They answerd that these taints of the blood laid dormant 20 Years—but that they would not reason with me in a matter wherein I was so delicate—but Would do all the Office for which they were call'd in—namely, to put an end to my torment, which otherwise would put an end to me. —and so have I been compell'd. to surrender myself—and thus Eliza is your Yorick, your Bramine—your friend with all his sensibilities, suffering the Chastisement of the grossest Sensualist—Is it not a most ridiculous Embarassment, as ever Yorick's Spirit could be involved in—

Tis needless to tell Eliza, that nothing but the purest consciousness of Virtue, could have tempted Eliza's friend to have told her this Story—Thou art too good my Eliza to love aught but Virtue—and too discerning not to distinguish the open Character which bears it, from the artful and double one which affects it—This, by the way, would make no bad anecdote in T. Shandy's Life—however I thought at least it would amuse you, in a Country where *less Matters* serve.— This has taken me three Sittings—it ought to be a good picture—I'm more proud, That it is a true one. In ten Days, I shall be able to get out—my room allways full of friendly Visiters—and my rapper eternally going with Cards and enquiries after me. I should be glad of the Testimonies—without the Tax.

Every thing convinces me, Eliza, We shall live to meet again —So—Take care of your health, to add to the comfort of it.

April 25. after a tolerable night, I am able, Eliza, to sit up and hold a discourse with the sweet Picture thou hast left behind thee of thyself, and tell it how much I had dreaded the catastrophe, of never seeing its dear Original more in this world—never did that Look of sweet resignation appear so eloquent as now; it has said more to my heart—and cheard it up more effectually above little fears and *may be's*—Than all the Lectures of philosophy I have strength to apply to it, in my presènt Debility of mind and body.—as for the latter—my men of Science, will set it properly a going again—tho' upon what principles—the Wise Men of Gotham[1] know as much as they—If they *act right*—What is it to me, how *wrong they think*; for finding my machine a much less tormenting one to me than before, I become reconciled to my Situation, and to their Ideas of it——but don't You pity me, after all, my dearest and my best of friends? I know to what an amount thou wilt Shed over Me, this tender Tax—and tis the Consolation springing out of that, of what a good heart it is which pours this friendly balm on mine, That has already, and will for ever heal every evil of my Life.   and What is becoming, of my Eliza, all this time!—where is she sailing?—What Sickness or other evils have befallen her? I weep often my dear Girl, for those my Imagination surrounds thee with—What would be the measure of my Sorrow, did I know thou wast distressd?—adieu—adieu. and trust my dear friend—my dear Bramine, that there still wants nothing to kill me in a few days, but the certainty, That thou wast suffering, what I am—and yet I know thou art ill—but when thou returnest back to England, all shall be set right.—so heaven waft thee to us upon the wings of Mercy—that is, as speedily as the winds and tides can do thee this friendly office. This is the 7th day That I have tasted nothing better than Water gruel—am going, at the solicitation of Hall, to eat of a boild fowl—so he dines with me on it—and a dish of Macaruls—

7 o'clock—I have drank to thy Name Eliza! everlasting

peace and happiness (for my Toast) in the first glass of Wine I have adventured to drink. my friend has left me—and I am alone,—like thee in thy solitary Cabbin after thy return from a tastless meal in the round house and like thee I fly to my Journal, to tell thee, I never prized thy friendship so high, or loved thee more—or wish'd so ardently to be a sharer of all the weights which Providence has laid upon thy tender frame —Than this moment—when upon taking up my pen, my poor pulse quickend—my pale face glowed—and tears stood ready in my Eyes to fall upon the paper, as I traced the word Eliza. O Eliza! Eliza! ever best and blessed of all thy Sex! blessed in thyself and in thy Virtues—and blessed and endearing to all who know thee—to Me, Eliza, most so; because I *know more* of thee than any other—This is the true philtre by which Thou hast charm'd me and wilt for ever charm and hold me thine, whilst Virtue and faith hold this world together; tis the simple Magick, by which I trust, I have won a place in that heart of thine on which I depend so satisfied, That Time and distance, or change of every thing which might allarm the little hearts of little men, create no uneasy suspence in mine—It scorns to doubt—and scorns to be doubted—tis the only exception—When Security is not the parent of Danger.

My Illness will keep me three weeks longer in town.—but a Journey in less time would be hazardous, unless a short one across the Desert which I should set out upon to morrow, could I carry a Medcine with me which I was sure would prolong one Month of Your Life—or should it happen————

but why make Suppositions?—when Situations happen— tis time enough to shew thee That thy Bramin is the truest and most friendly of mortal Spirits, and capable of doing more for his Eliza, than his pen will suffer him to promise.

April 26. Slept not till three this morning—was in too delicious Society to think of it; for I was all the time with thee besides me, talking over the projess of our friendship, and turning the world into a thousand Shapes to enjoy it. got up much better for the Conversation—found myself improved in body and mind and recruited beyond any thing I lookd for; My Doctors, stroked their beards, and look'd ten per Cent wiser upon feeling my pulse, and enquiring after my Symptoms —am still to run thro' a course of Van Sweetens corrosive Mercury, or rather Van Sweeten's Course of Mercury is to run thro' me—I shall be sublimated to an etherial Substance by the time my Eliza sees me—she must be sublimated and uncorporated too, to be able to see me—but I was always transparent and a Being easy to be seen thro', or Eliza had never loved me nor had Eliza been of any other *Cast* herself, could her Bramine have held *Communion* with her. hear every day from our worthy sentimental friend—who rejoyces to think that the Name of Eliza is still to vibrate upon Yoricks ear—this, my dear Girl, many who loved me dispair'd off— poor Molly who is all attention to me—and every day brings in the name of poor Mrs Draper, told me last night, that She and her Mistress had observed, I had never held up my head, since the Day you last dined with me—That I had seldome laughd or smiled—had gone to no Diversions—but twice or thrice at the most, dined out—That they thought I was broken hearted, for She never enterd the room or passd by the door, but she heard me sigh heavily—That I neither eat or slept or took pleasure in any Thing as before, except writing——

The Observation will draw a Sigh, Eliza, from thy feeling heart—and yet, so thy heart would wish to have it—tis fit in truth We suffer equally—nor can it be otherwise—when the Causes of Anguish in two hearts are so proportion'd, as in ours.—Surely—Surely—Thou art mine Eliza! for dear have have I bought thee!

April 27. Things go better with me, Eliza! and I shall be reestablish'd soon, except in bodily weakness; not yet being able to rise from my arm chair, and walk to the other corner

of my room, and back to it again, without fatigue—I shall
double my Journey to morrow, and if the day is warm the day
after be got into my Carriage and be transported into Hyde
park for the advantage of air and exercise—wast thou but
besides me, I could go to Salt hill, Im sure, and feel the
Journey short and pleasant.—another Time!—the present,
alas! is not ours. I pore so much on thy Picture—I have it *off
by heart*—dear Girl—oh tis sweet! tis kind! tis reflecting! tis
affectionate! tis—thine my Bramine—I say my matins and
Vespers to it—I quiet my Murmurs, by the Spirit which
speaks in it—'all will end Well my Yorick.'—I declare my
dear Bramine I am so secured and wrapt up in this Belief,
That I would not part with the Imagination, of how happy I
am to be with thee, for all the Offers of present Interest or
Happiness the whole world could tempt me with; in the
loneliest Cottage that Love and Humility ever dwelt in, with
thee along with me, I could possess more refined Content,
Than in the most glittering Court; and with thy Love and
fidelity, taste truer joys, my Eliza! and make thee also partake
of more, than all the senseless parade of this silly world could
compensate to either of us—with this, I bound all my desires
and worldly views—what are they worth without Eliza? Jesus!
grant me but this, I will deserve it—I will make My Bramine,
as Happy, as thy goodness wills her—I will be the Instrument
of her recompense for the sorrows and disappointments thou
has suffer'd her to undergo; and if ever I am false, unkind or
ungentle to her; so let me be dealt with by thy Justice.

9 o'clock, I am preparing to go to bed my dear Girl, and
first pray for thee, and then to Idolize thee for two wakeful
hours upon my pillow—I shall after that, I find dream all
night of thee, for all the day have I done nothing but think
of thee—something tells, that thou hast this day, been
employd exactly in the same Way. good night, fair Soul—
and may the sweet God of sleep close gently thy eyelids—and
govern and direct thy Slumbers—adieu—adieu, adieu!

April 28. I was not decieved Eliza! by my presentiment that I should find thee out in my dreams; for I have been with thee almost the whole night, alternately soothing thee, or telling thee my sorrows—I have rose up comforted and strengthend —and found myself so much better, that I orderd my Carriage, to carry me to our mutual friend—Tears ran down her cheeks when She saw how pale and wan I was—and never gentle Creature sympathiz'd more tenderly—I beseech you, cried the good Soul, not to regard either difficulties or expences but fly to Eliza directly—I see you will dye without her—save yourself for her—how shall I look her in the face? What can I say to her, when on her return, I have to tell her, That her Yorick is no more!—Tell her my dear friend, said I, That I will meet her in a better world—and that I have left this, because I could not live without her; tell Eliza, my dear friend added I—That I died broken hearted—and that you were a Witness to it—as I said this, She burst into the most pathetick flood of Tears—that ever kindly nature shed   you never beheld so affecting a Scene—! 'twas too much for Nature! Oh! she is good—I love her as my Sister!—and could Eliza have been a witness, hers would have melted down to Death and scarse have been brought back, from an Extacy so celestial, and savouring of another world.—I had like to have fainted, and to that Degree was my heart and Soul affected, it was with difficulty I could reach the Street door; I have got home, and shall lay all day upon my Sopha—and to morrow morning my dear Girl write again to thee; for I have not strength to drag my pen—

April 29.

I am so ill to day, my dear, I can only tell you so—I wish I was put into a Ship for Bombay—I wish I may otherwise hold out till the hour We might otherwise have met—I have too many evils upon me at once—and yet I will not faint under them—Come!—Come to me soon my Eliza and save me!

April 30. Better to day—but am too much visited and find

my Strength wasted by the attention I must give to all concern'd for me—I will go Eliza, be it but by ten mile Journeys,
home to my thatchd Cottage—and there I shall have no
respit—for I shall do nothing but think of thee—and burn
out this weak Taper of Life. by the flame thou hast superadded to it—fare well My dear **** to morrow begins a new
month—and I hope to give thee in it, a more sunshiny Side
of myself—Heaven! how is it with my Eliza—

May 1. got out into the park to day—Sheba¹ there on Horse-
back; pass'd twice by her without knowing her—She stop'd
the third time—to ask me how I did—I would not have askd
you, Solomon! said She, but your Looks affected me—for
you'r half dead I fear—I thank'd Sheba, very kindly, but without any emotion but what sprung from gratitude—Love
alas! was fled with thee Eliza!—I did not think Sheba could
have changed so much in grace and beauty—Thou hadst
shrunk poor Sheba away into Nothing,—but a good natured
girl, without powers or charms—I *fear* your Wife is dead,
quoth Sheba—no, you don't *fear* it Sheba said I—Upon my
Word Solomon! I would quarrel with You, was you not so ill
—If you knew the Cause of my Illness, Sheba, replied I, you
would quarrel but the more with me—You lie, Solomon!
answered Sheba, for I know the Cause already—and am so
little out of Charity with You upon it—That I give You leave
to come and drink Tea with me before You leave Town—
you're a good honest Creature Sheba—no! you Rascal, I am
not—but I'm in Love, as much as you can be for your Life—
I'm glad of it Sheba! said I—You Lie. said Sheba, and so
canter'd away.—O My Eliza, had I ever truely loved another
(which I never did) Thou hast long ago, cut the Root of all
Affection in me—and planted and waterd and nourish'd it, to
bear fruit only for thyself—Continue to give me proofs I have
had and shall preserve the same rights over thee my Eliza!
and if I ever murmur at the sufferings of Life, after that, Let
me be numberd with the ungrateful.—I look now forwards

with Impatience for the day thou art to get to Madras—and
from thence shall I want to hasten thee to Bombay—where
heaven will make all things Conspire to lay the Basis of thy
health and future happiness—be true my dear girl, to thy
self—and the rights of Self preservation which Nature has
given thee!—persevere—be firm—be pliant be placid—be
courteous—but still be true to thy self—and never give up
your Life,—or suffer the disquieting altercations, or small out-
rages you may undergo in this momentous point, to weigh a
Scruple in the Ballance—Firmness—and fortitude and per-
severance gain almost impossibilities—and *Skin* for *Skin*,
saith *Job, nay all that a Man has, will he give* for his Life'—[1]
oh My Eliza! That I could take the Wings of the Morning, and
fly to aid thee in *this* virtuous Struggle. went to Ranelagh
at 8 this night, and sat still till ten—came home ill.

May 2nd
I fear I have relapsed—sent afresh for my Doctor—who
has confined me to my Sopha—being able neither able to
walk, stand or sit upright, without aggravating my Symptoms
—I'm still to be treated as if I was a Sinner—and in truth have
some appearances so strongly implying it, That was I not
conscious I had had no Commerce with the Sex these 15
Years, I would decamp to morrow for Montpellier in the
South of France, where Maladies of this sort are better treated
and all taints more radically driven out of the Blood—than in
this Country; but If I continue long ill—I am still determined to repair there—not to undergo a Cure of a distemper
I cannot have, but for the bettering my Constitution by a
better Climate.—I write this as I lie upon my back—in which
posture I must continue, I fear some days—If I am able—
will take up my pen again before night—

4 o'clock.—an hour dedicated to Eliza! for I have dined
alone—and ever since the Cloath has been laid, have done
nothing but call upon thy dear Name—and ask why tis not
permitted thou shouldst sit down, and share my Macarel and

foul—there would be enough, said Molly as she place'd it upon the Table to have served both You and poor Mrs Draper—I never bring in the Knives and forks, added She, but I think of her—There was no more trouble with you both, than with one of You—I never heard a high or a hasty word from either of You—You were surely made, added Molly, for one another, You are both so kind so quiet and so friendly —Molly furnished me with Sause to my Meat—for I wept my plate full, Eliza! and now I have begun, could shed tears till Supper again—and then go to bed weeping for thy absence till morning. Thou hast bewitch'd me with powers, my dear Girl, from which no power shall unlose me—and if fate can put this Journal of my Love into thy hands, before we meet, I know with what warmth it will inflame the kindest of hearts, to receive me. peace be with thee, my Eliza, till that happy moment!—

9 at night I shall never get possession of myself, Eliza! at this rate—I want to Call off my Thoughts from thee, that I may now and then, apply them to some con[c]erns which require both my attention and genius; but to no purpose— I had a Letter to write to Lord Shelburn—and had got my apparatus in order to begin—when a Map of India coming in my Way—I begun to study the length and dangers of my Eliza's Voiage to it, and have been amusing and frightening myself by turns, as I traced the path-way of the Earl of Chatham, the whole Afternoon—good god! what a voiage for any one! —but for the poor relax'd frame of my tender Bramine to cross the Line twice! and be subject to the Intolerant heats, and the hazards which must be the consequence of em to such an unsupported Being!—O Eliza! 'tis too much—and if thou conquerest these, and all the other difficulties of so tremendous an alienation from thy Country, thy Children and thy friends, tis the hand of Providence which watches over thee for most merciful purposes—Let this persuasion, my dear Eliza! stick close to thee in all thy tryals—as it shall in those thy

faithful Bramin is put to—till the mark'd hour of deliverance comes. I'm going to sleep upon this religious Elixir—may the Infusion of it distil into the gentlest of hearts—for that Eliza! is thine—sweet, dear, faithful Girl, most kindly does thy Yorick greet thee with the wishes of a good night. and—of Millions yet to come—

May 3rd Sunday What can be the matter with me! Some thing is wrong, Eliza! in every part of me—I do not gain strength; nor have I the feelings of health returning back to me; even my best moments seem merely the efforts of my mind to get well again, because I cannot reconcile myself to the thoughts of never seeing thee Eliza more.—for something is out of tune in every Chord of me—still with thee to nurse and sooth me, I should soon do well—The Want of thee is half my distemper—but not the whole of it—I must see Mrs James tonight, tho' I know not how to get there—but I shall not sleep, if I don't talk of You to her—so shall finish this Days Journal on my return—/May 4th—

Directed by Mrs James how to write Over-Land to thee, my Eliza!—would gladly tear out thus much of my Journal to send to thee—but the Chances are too many against it's getting to Bombay—or of being deliverd into your own hands —shall write a long long Letter—and trust it to fate and thee. was not able to say three words at Mrs James, thro' utter weakness of body and mind; and when I got home—could not get up stairs with Molly's aid—have rose a little better, my dear girl—and will live for thee—do the same for thy Bramin, I beseech thee. a Line from thee now, in this state of my Dejection,—would be worth a Kingdome to me!—

May 4. Writing by way of Vienna and Bussorah to My Eliza.—this and Company took up the day.

5th writing to Eliza.—and trying l'*Extraite de* Saturne upon myself.—(a french Nostrum)—

6th Dined out for the first time—came home to enjoy a More harmonious evening with my Eliza, than I could expect at Soho Con[c]ert[1]—every Thing my dear Girl, has lost its former relish to me—and for thee eternally does it quicken! writing to thee over Land—all day.

7. continue poorly, my dear!—but my blood warms, every moment I think of our future Scenes.—so must grow strong, upon the Idea—what shall I do upon the Reality?—O God!—

8th employ'd in writing to my Dear all day—and in projecting happiness for her—tho in misery myself. O! I have undergone Eliza!—but the worst is over—(I hope)—so adieu to those Evils, and let me hail the happiness to come.

9th, 10th and 11th so unaccountably disorder'd—I cannot Say more—but that I would suffer ten times more with Smiles for my Eliza—adieu bless'd Woman!—

12th O Eliza! That my weary head was now laid upon thy Lap—(tis all that's left for it)—or that I had thine, reclining upon my bosome, and there resting all its disquietudes;— my Bramine—the world or Yorick must perish, before that foundation shall fail thee!—I continue poorly—but I turn my Eyes *Eastward* the oftener, and with more earnestness for it—

Great God of Mercy! shorten the Space betwixt us,— Shorten the space of our miseries!

13th Could not get the General post Office to take charg[e] of my Letters to You—so gave thirty shillings to a Merchant to further them to Aleppo and from thence to Bassorah—so you will receive 'em, (I hope in god) sa[fe] by Christmas— Surely 'tis not impossible, but [I] may be made happy as my Eliza, by so[me] transcript from her, by that time—If not I shall hope—and hope, every week, and every hour of it, for Tidings of Comfort—we taste not of it *now*, my dear Bramine —but we will make full meals upon it hereafter.—Cards from 7 or 8 of our Grandies to dine with them before I leave Town —shall go like a Lamb to the Slaughter—'*Man delights not me—nor Woman*'[2]

14. a little better to day—and would look pert, if my heart

would but let me—dined with Lord and Lady Bellasis.[1]—
so beset with Company—not a moment to write.

15—Undone with too much Society yesterday,—You
scarse can Conceive my dear Eliza what a poor Soul I am—
how I shall be got down to Coxwould—heaven knows—for
I am as weak as a Child—You would not like me the worse
for it, Eliza, if you was here—My friends like me, the more,—
and Swear I shew more true fortitude and eveness of temper
in my Suffering than Seneca, or Socrates—I am, My Bramin,
resigned.

16—Taken up all day with wor[l]dly matters, just as my
Eliza was, the week before her departure—breakfasted with
Lady Spencer[2]—[c]aught her with the Character of your
Portrait—caught her passions still more with that of yourself
—and my Attachment to the most amiable of Beings.—drove
at night to Ranalagh[3]—staid an hour—returnd to my Lodgings, dissatisfied.

17. At Court—every thing in this world seems in Masque-
rade, but thee dear Woman—and therefore I am sick of all the
world b[ut] thee—one Evening *so spent*, as the [S]*aturday's
which preceeded our Separation—would sicken all the Conversation of the world— I relish no Converse since*—when will
the like return?—tis hidden from us both, for the wisest ends
—and the hour will come my Eliza! when We shall be convinced, that every event has been order'd for the best for Us
—Our fruit is not ripend—the accidents of time and Seasons
will ripen every Thing *together* for Us—a little better to day—
or could not have wrote this. dear Bramine rest thy Sweet
Soul in peace!.

18. Laid sleepless all the night, with thinking of the many
dangers and sufferings, my dear Girl! that thou art exposed
to—from thy Voiage and thy sad state of health—but I find
I must think no more upon them—I have rose wan and
trembling with the Havock they have made upon my Nerves—
tis death to me to apprehend for you—I must flatter my

Imagination, That every Thing goes well with You—Surely no evil can have befallen You—for if it had—I had felt some monitory sympathetic Shock within me, which would have spoke like Revelation.—So farewell to all tormenting *May be's*, in regard to my Eliza—She is well—she thinks of her Yorick with as much Affection and true esteem as ever—and values him as much above the World, as he values his Bramine—

19—Packing up, or rather Molly for me, the whole day—tormenting! had not Molly all the time talk'd of poor Mrs Draper—and recounted every Visit She had made me, and every repast She had shared with me—how good a Lady!—How sweet a temper!—how beautiful!—how genteel!—how gentle a Carriage—and how soft and engaging a look!.—the poor girl is bewitch'd with us both—infinitely interested in our Story, tho' She knows nothing of it but from her penetration and Conjectures—She says however tis Impossible not to be in Love with her—

—In heart felt truth, Eliza! I'm of Molly's Opinion—

20—Taking Leave of all the Town, before my departure to morrow.

21. detaind by Lord and Lady Spence[r] who had made a party to dine and sup on my Account. Impatient to set out for my Solitude—there the Mind, Eliza! gains strength, and learns to lean upon herself,—and seeks refuge in its own Constancy and Virtue—in the world it seeks or accepts of a few treacherous supports—the feign'd Compassion of one—the flattery of a second—the Civilities of a third—the friendship of a fourth—they all decieve—and bring the Mind back to where mine is retreating—that is Eliza! to itself—to thee (who art my second self) to retirement, reflection & Books—When The Stream of Things, dear Bramine, Brings Us both together to this Haven—will not your heart take up its rest for ever? and will not your head Leave the world to those who can make a better thing of it—if there are any who know

how.—Heaven take thee Eliza! under it's Wing—adieu!
adieu.——

   22nd Left Bond Street and London with it, this Morning—
What a Creature I am! my heart has ached this week to get
away—and still was ready to bleed in quiting a Place where
my Connection with my dear dear Eliza began—Adieu to it!
till I am summon'd up to the Downs by a Message, to fly to
her—for I think I shall not be able to support Town without
you—and would chuse rather to sit solitary here, till the End
of the next Summer—to be made happy altogether,—then
seek for happiness,—or even suppose I can have it, but in
Eliza's Society.

   —23d bear my Journey badly—ill—and dispirited all
the Way [?28 May]—staid two days on the road at the
Archbishops of Yorks—shewd his Grace and his Lady and
Sister your portrait—with a short but interesting Story of
my friendship for the Original—kindly nursed and honourd
both—arrived at my Thatched Cottage the 28th of May

   29th and 30th confined to my bed—so emaciated, and unlike
what I was, I could scarse be angry with thee Eliza, if thou
Coulds not remember me, did heaven send me across thy
way—Alas! poor Yorick!—'remember thee! Pale Ghost—
remember thee—whilst Memory holds a seat in this distracted
World—Remember thee,—Yes, from the Table of her
Memory, shall just Eliz[a] wipe away all trivial men[1]—and
leave a thron[e] for Yorick—adieu dear constant Girl—adieu
—adieu.—and Remember my Truth and eternal fidelity
—Remember how I Love—remember What I suffer.—Thou
art mine Eliza by Purchace—had I not earn'd thee with a
better price.—

   31 Going this day upon a long course of Corrosive Mercury
—which in itself, is deadly poyson, but given in a certain
preparation, not very dangerous—I was forced to give it up
in Town, from the terrible Cholicks both in Stomach and
Bowels—but the Faculty thrust it down my Throat again—

These Gentry have got it into their Noddles, That mine is an Ecclesiastick Rhum as the french call it—god help em! I submit as my Uncle Toby did,[1] in drinking Water, upon the wound he received in his Groin—*Merely for quietness sake.*'

June 1 The Faculty, my dear Eliza! have mistaken my Case —why not Yours? I wish I could fly to you and attend You but one month as a physician—You'l Languish and dye where you are,—(if not by the climate)—most certainly by their *Ignorance of your Case*, and the unskilful Treatment you must be a martyr for in such a place as Bombay.—I'm Languishing here myself with every Aid and help—and tho' I shall conquer it—yet have had a cruel Struggle—Would my dear friend, I could ease yours, either by my advice—my attention—my Labour—my purse—They are all at Your Service, such as they are—and that You know Eliza—or my friendship for you is not worth a rush.

June 2d

This morning surpriz'd with a Letter from my Lydia— that She and her Mama, are coming to pay me a Visit—but on Condition I promise not to detain them in England beyond next April—when, they purpose, by my Consent, to retire into France, and establish themselves for Life—To all which I have freely given my parole of Honour—and so shall have them with me for the Summer—from October to April—they take Lodgings in York—When they Leave me for good and all I suppose. ☞ —Every thing for the best! Eliza.

This unexpected visit, is neither a visit of friendship or form—but tis a visit, such as I know you will never make me, —of pure Interest—to pillage What they can from me. In the first place to sell a small estate I have of sixty pounds a year— and lay out the purchase money in joint annuitys for them in the french Funds; by this they will obtain 200 pounds a year, to be continued to the longer Liver—and as it rids me of all future care—and moreover transfers their In[c]ome to the Kingdom where they purpose to live—I'm truely acquiescent

—tho' I lose the Contingency of surviving them—but 'tis no matter—I shall have enough—and a hundred or two hundred Pounds for Eliza whenever She will honour me with putting her hand into my Purse—In the main time, I am not sorry for this Visit, as every Thing will be finally settled between us by it—only as their Annuity will be too strait—I shall engage to remit them a 100 Guineas a year more, during my Wife's Life—and then, I will think, Eliza, of living for myself and the Being I love as much!—But I shall be pillaged in a hundred small Item's by them—which I have a Spirit above saying, *no*-to; as Provisions of all sorts of Linnens—for house use—Body Use—printed Linnens for Gowns—Maga-zeens of Teas—Plate, all I have (but 6 Silver Spoons)—In short I shall be pluck'd bare—all but of your Portrait and Snuff Box and your other dear Presents—and the neat furni-ture of my thatch'd Palace—and upon those I set up Stock again; Eliza What Say You, Eliza! shall we join our little *Capitals* together?—will Mr Draper give us leave?—he may safely—if your Virtue and Honour are only concernd,—'twould be safe in Yoricks hands, as in a Brothers—I would not wish Mr Draper to allow you above half I allow Mrs Sterne—Our Capital would be too great, and tempt us from the Society of poor Cordelia—who begins to wish for You.

By this time, I trust You have doubled the Cape of good hope—and sat down to your writing Drawer, and look'd in Yoricks face, as you took out your Journal; to tell him so—I hope he seems to smile as kindly upon You Eliza, as ever—Your Attachment and Love for me, will make him do so to eternity—if ever he should change his Air, Eliza!—I charge you catechize your own Heart.—Oh! twil never happen!—

June 3^d—Cannot write my Travels, or give one half hours close attention to them, upon Thy Account, my dearest friend —Yet write I must, and what to do with You, whilst I write— I declare I know not—I want to have you ever before my

Imagination—and cannot keep You out of my heart or head—
In short thou enterst my Library, Eliza! (as thou one day
shalt) without tapping—or sending for—by thy own Right of
ever being close to thy Bramine—now I must shut you out
out sometimes—or meet you Eliza! with an empty purse upon
the Beach—pity my entanglements from other passions—my
Wife with me every moment of the Summer—think what
restraint upon a Fancy that should Sport and be in all points
at its ease—O had I, my dear Bramine this Summer, to soften
—and modulate my feelings—to enrich my fancy, and fill my
heart brim full with bounty—my Book would be worth the
reading—

It will be by stealth if I am able to go on with my Journal at
all—It will have many Interruptions—and Hey ho's! most
sentimentally utter'd—Thou must take it as it pleases God.—
as thou must take the Writer—eternal Blessings be about You,
Eliza! I am a little better, and now find I shall be set right in
all points—my only anxiety is about You—I want to pre-
scribe for you. My Eliza—for I think I understand your *Case*
better than all the Faculty. adieu. adieu.

June 4. Hussy!—I have employ'd a full hour upon your
sweet sentimental Picture—and a couple of hours upon yourself—and with as much kind friendship, as the hour You left
me—I deny it—Time lessens no Affections which honour
and merit have planted—I would give more, and hazard more
now for your happiness than in any one period, since I first
learn'd to esteem you—is it so with thee my friend? has
absence weakend my Interest—has time worn out any Impression—or is Yoricks Name less Musical in Eliza's ears?
—my heart smites me, for asking the question—tis Treason
against thee Eliza and Truth—Ye are dear Sisters, and your
Brother Bramin Can never live to see a Separation amongst
us.—What a similitude in our Trials, Whilst asunder!—
Providence has order'd every Step better, than we could have
order'd them, for the particular good we wish each other—

This you will comment upon and find the Sense of without my explanation.

I wish this Summer and Winter with all I am to go through with in them, in business and Labour and Sorrow, well over—I have much to compose—and much to discompose me—have my Wife's projects—and my own Views arising out of them, to harmonize and turn to account—I have Millions of heart aches to suffer and reason with—and in all this Storm of Passions, I have but one small anchor, Eliza! to keep this weak Vessel of mine from perishing—I trust all I have to it—as I trust Heaven, which cannot leave me, without a fault, to perish.—may the same just Heaven my Eliza, be that eternal Canopy which shall shelter thy head from evil till we meet—Adieu—adieu. adieu.—

June 5.

I Sit down to write this day, in good earnest—so read Eliza! quietly besides me—I'll not give you a Look—except one of kindness.—dear Girl! if thou lookest so bewitching once more—I'll turn thee out of my Study—You may bid me defiance, Eliza.—You cannot conceive how much and how universally I'm pitied, upon the Score of this unexpected Visit from france—my friends think it will kill me—If I find myself in danger I'll fly to You to Bombay—will Mr Draper receive me?—he ought—but he will never know What reasons make it his *Interest* and *Duty*—We must leave all all to that Being—who is infinitely removed above all Straitness of heart . . . and is a friend to the friendly, as well as to the friendless.

June 6.—am quite alone in the depth of that sweet Recesse, I have so often described to You—tis sweet in itself—but You never come across me—but the perspective brightens up —and every Tree and Hill and Vale and Ruin about me— smiles as if you was amidst 'em—delusive moments!—how pensive a price do I pay for you—fancy sustains the Vision, whilst She has Strength—but Eliza! Eliza is not with me!—

I sit down upon the first Hillock Solitary as a sequester'd
Bramin—I wake from my delusion to a thousand Disquietudes, which many talk of—my Eliza!—but few feel—
then weary my Spirit with thinking, plotting, and projecting
—and when Ive brought my System to my mind—am only
Doubly miserable, That I cannot execute it—

Thus—Thus my dear Bramine are we tost at present in this
tempest—Some Haven of rest will open to us. assuredly—
God made us not for Misery and Ruin—he has orderd all our
Steps—and influenced our Attachments for what is worthy of
them—It must end well—Eliza!—

June 7.

I have this week finish'd a sweet little apartment which all
the time it was doing, I flatter'd the most delicious of Ideas, in
thinking I was making it for you—Tis a neat little simple
elegant room, overlook'd only by the Sun—just big enough to
hold a Sopha,—for us—a Table, four Chairs, a Bureau—and
a Book case.—They are to be all yours, Room and all—and
there Eliza! shall I enter ten times a day to give thee Testimonies of my Devotion—Was't thou this moment sat down,
it would be the sweetest of earthly Tabernacles—I shall
enrich it, from time to time, for thee—till Fate lets me lead
thee by the hand into it—and then it can want no Ornament.
—tis a little oblong room—with a large Sash at the end—a
little elegant fireplace—with as much room to dine around it,
as in Bond street.—But in sweetness and Simplicity, and
silence beyond any thing—Oh my Eliza!—I shall see thee
surely Goddesse of this Temple,—and the most sovereign
one, of all I have—and of all the powers heaven has trusted me
with—They were lent me, Eliza! only for thee—and for thee
my dear Girl shall be kept and employ'd.—You know *What
rights* You have over me—wish to heaven I could Convey the
Grant more amply than I have *done*—but 'tis the same—tis
register'd where it will longest last—and that is in the feeling
and most sincere of human hearts—You know I mean this

reciprocally—and whenever I mention the Word Fidelity and
Truth, in Speaking of your Reliance on mine—I always
Imply the same Reliance upon the same Virtues in my Eliza.
—I love thee Eliza! and will love thee for ever. Adieu.—
    June 8.
    Begin to recover, and sensibly to gain strength every day—
and have such an appetite as I have not had for some Years—
I prophecy I shall be the better, for the very Accident which
has occasiond my Illness, and that the Medcines and Regimen
I have submitted to, will make A thorough Regeneration of
me, and that I shall have more health and Strength, than I
have enjoy'd these ten Years—Send me such an Account of
thy self Eliza, by the first sweet Gale—but tis impossible You
should from Bombay—twil be as fatal to You, as it has been
to thousands of your Sex—England and Retirement in it, can
only save you—Come!—Come away—
    June 9th I keep a post Chaise and a couple of fine horses,
and take the Air every day in it—I go out—and return to my
Cottage Eliza! alone—'tis melancholly, what should be matter
of enjoyment; and the more so for that reason—I have a
thousand things to remark and say as I roll along—but I want
You to say them to—I could sometimes be wise—and often
Witty—but I feel it a reproach to be the latter whilst Eliza is
so far from hearing me—and What is Wisdome to a foolish
weak heart like mine!—Tis like the Song of Melody to a
broken Spirit—You must teach me fortitude my dear Bramine
—for with all the tender qualities which make you the most
precious of Women—and most wanting of all other Women
of a kind protector—yet you have a passive kind of sweet
Courage which bears You up—more than any one Virtue I
can summon up in my own Case—We were made with
Tempers for each other, Eliza! and You are blessd with such a
certain turn of Mind and reflection—that if Self love does not
blind me—I resemble no Being in the world so nearly as I do
You—do you wonder tha[t] I have such friendship for you?—

for my own part, I should not be astonish'd, Eliza, if you was to declare, 'You was up to the ears in Love with Me'.

June 10th—You are stretching over now in the Trade Winds from the Cape to Madrass—(I hope)—but I know it not. some friendly Ship You possibly have met with, and I never read an Account of an India Man arrived—but I expect that it is the Messenger of the news my heart is upon the rack for.—I calculate, That you will arrive at Bombay by the beginning of October—by February, I shall surely hear from you thence—but from Madrass sooner.—I expect you Eliza in person, by September—and shall scarse go to London till March—for what have I to do there, when (except printing my Book) I have no Interest or Passion to gratify—I shall return in June to Coxwould—and there wait for the glad Tidings of your arrival in the Downs—won't You write to me Eliza! by the first Boat?—would not you wish to be greeted by your Yorick upon the Beech?—or be met by him to hand you out of your postchaise, to pay him for the Anguish he underwent, in handing you in to it?—I know your answers— my Spirit is with You. farewel dear friend—

June 11. I am every day negociating to sell my little Estate besides me—to send the money into France, to purchace peace to myself—and a certainty of never having it inter- rupted by Mrs Sterne—who when She is sensible I have given her all I can part with—will be at rest herself—Indeed her plan to purchace annuities in france—is a pledge of Security to me—That She will live her days out there—otherwise She could have no end in transporting this two thousand pounds out of England——nor would I consent but upon that plan— but I may be at rest!—if my imagination will but let me—Hall says tis no matter where she lives; If we are but separate, tis as good as if the Ocean rolld between us—and so I should Argue to another Man—but, tis an Idea which won't do so well for me—and tho' nonsensical enough—Yet I shall be most at rest when there is that Bar between Us—was I never so sure,

I should never be interrupted by her, in England—but I may
be at rest I say, on that head—for they have left all their
Cloaths and plate and Linnen behind them in france—and
have joind in the most earnest Entreaty, That they may return
and fix in france—to which I have give[n] my word and
honour—You will be bound with me Eliza! I hope, for performance of my promise—I never yet broke it, in cases where
Interest or pleasure could have tempted me,—and shall hardly
do it, now, when tempted only by misery.—In Truth Eliza!
thou art the Object to which every act of mine is directed—
You interfere in every Project—I rise—I go to sleep with this
in my Brain—how will my dear Bramine approve of this?—
which way will it conduce to make her happy? and how will it
be a proof of my Affection to her? are all the Enquiries I make.
—Your Honour, your Conduct, your Truth and regard for
my esteem—I know will equally direct every Step—and movement of your Desires—and with that Assurance, is it, my dear
Girl, That I sustain Life,—But when will those Sweet eyes of
thine, run over these Declarations?—how—and with Whom
are they to be entrusted; to be conveyd to You?—unless M^{rs}
James's friendship to us, finds some expedient—I must wait—
till the first evening I'm with You—when I shall present You
with—them as a better Picture of me, than Cosway[1] Could do
for You. .—have been dismally ill all day—oweing to my
course of Medecines which are too strong and forcing for this
gawsy Constitution of mine—I mend with them however—
good God! how is it with You?—

June 12. I have return'd from a delicious Walk of Romance,
my Bramine, which I am to tread a thousand times over with
You swinging upon my arm—tis to my Convent—and I have
pluckd up a score Bryars by the roots which grew near the
edge of the foot way, that they might not scratch or incom-
mode you—had I been sure of your taking that walk with me
the very next day, I could not have been more serious in
my employment—dear Enthusiasm!—thou bringst things

forwards in a moment, which Time keeps for Ages back—I
have you ten times a day besides me—I talk to You Eliza, for
hours together—I take your Council—I hear your reasons—I
admire you for them!—to this magic of a warm Mind, I owe
all that's worth living for, during this State of our Trial—
Every Trincket you gave or exchanged with me, has its force
—Your Picture is Yourself—all Sentiment, Softness, and
Truth—It speaks—it listens—'tis convincd—it resignes—
Dearest Original! how like unto thee does it seem—and will
seem—till thou makest it vanish, by thy presence—I'm but
so, so—but advancing in health—to meet you.—to nurse you,
to nourish you against you come—for I fear, You will not
arrive, but in a State that calls out to Yorick for support—
Thou art Mistress, Eliza, of all the powers he has to sooth and
protect thee—for thou art Mistress of his heart; his affections;
and his reason—and beyond that, except a paltry purse, he
has nothing worth giving thee—.

June 13.

This has been a year of presents to me—my Bramine—
How many presents have I received from You, in the first
place?—Lord Spencer has loaded me with a grand Ecritoire
of 40 Guineas—I am to recieve this week a fourty Guinea-
present of a gold Snuff Box, as fine as Paris can fabricate one—
with an Inscription on it, more valuable, than the Box itself—
I have a present of a portrait, (which by the by, I have im-
mortalized in my Sentimental Journey) worth them both—
I say nothing of a gold Stock buccle and Buttons—tho' I rate
them above rubies, because they were Consecrated by the hand
of Friendship, as She fitted them to me.—I have a present of
the Sculptures upon poor Ovid's Tomb, who died in Exile,
tho' he wrote so well upon the Art of Love—These are in six
beautiful Pictures executed on Marble at Rome—and these
Eliza, I keep sacred as Ornaments for your Cabinet, on
Condition I hang them up.—and last of all, I have had a
present, Eliza! this Year, of a Heart so finely set—with such

rich materials—and Workmanship—That Nature must have
had the chief hand in it—If I am able to keep it—I shall be
a rich Man; If I lose it—I shall be poor indeed—so poor! I
shall stand begging at your gates.—But what can all these
presents portend—That it will turn out a fortunate earnest,
of what is to be given me hereafter—

June 14.

I want you to comfort me my dear Bramine—and reconcile
my mind to 3 Months misery—some days I think lightly of it
—on others—my heart sinks down to the earth—but tis the
last Trial of conjugal Misery—and I wish it was to begin this
moment, That it might run its period the faster—for sitting as
I do, expecting sorrow—is suffering it—I am going to Hall
to be philosophizd with for a Week or ten Days on this point—
but one hour with you would calm me more and furnish me
with stronger Supports, under this weight upon my Spirits,
than all the world—put together—Heaven! to what distressful
Encountres hast thou thought fit to expose me—and was it not,
that thou hast blessd me with a chearfulness of disposition—and
thrown an Object in my Way, That is to render that Sun Shine
perpetual—Thy dealings with me, would be a mystery.—

June 15—from morning to night every moment of this day
held in Bondage at my friend Lord ffauconberg's[1]—so have
but a moment. left to close the day, as I do every one—with
wishing thee a sweet nights rest—would I was at the feet of
your Bed—fanning breezes to You, in your Slumbers—
Mark!—you will dream of me this night—and if it is not
recorded in your Journal—Ill say, you could not recollect it
the day following—adieu.—

June 16.

My Chaise is so large—so high—so long—so wide—so
Crawford's like,[2]—That I am building a coach house on purpose for it—do you dislike it for this gigantick Size?—now I
remember, I heard You once say—You hated a small post
Chaise—which you must know determined my Choice to

this—because I hope to make you a present of it—and if you are squeamish I shall be as squeamish as You, and return you all your presents—but one—which I cannot part with—and what that is—I defy you to guess. I have bought a milch Asse this Afternoon—and purpose to live by Suction, to save the expences of houskeeping—and have a Score or two guineas in my purse, next September——

June 17

I have brought your name *Eliza!* and Picture into my work—where they will remain—when You and I are at rest for ever—Some Annotator or explainer of my works in this place will take occasion, to speak of the Friendship which Subsisted so long and faithfully betwixt Yorick and the Lady he speaks of—Her Name he will tell the world was Draper—a Native of India—married there to a gentleman in the India Service of that Name—, who brought her over to England for the recovery of her health in the Year 65—where She continued to April the Year 1767. It was about three months before her Return to India, That our Author's acquaintance and hers began. Mrs Draper had a great thirst for Knowledge—was handsome—genteel—engaging—and of such gentle dispositions and so enlightend an understanding,—That Yorick, (whether he made much Opposition is not known) from an acquaintance—soon became her Admirer—they caught fire at each other at the same time—and they would often say, without reserve to the world, and without any Idea of saying wrong in it, That their Affections for each other were *unbounded*—Mr Draper dying in the Year *****—This Lady return'd to England, and Yorick the year after becoming a Widower—They were married—and retiring to one of his Livings in Yorkshire, where was a most romantic Situation—they lived and died happily.—and are spoke of with honour in the parish to this day—

June 18

How do you like the History, of this couple, Eliza?—is it

to your mind?—or shall it be written better some sentimental Evening after your return—tis a rough Sketch—but I could make it a pretty picture, as the outlines are just—we'll put our heads together and try what we can do. This last Sheet[1] has put it out of my power, ever to send you this Journal to India—I had been more guarded—but that You have often told me, 'twas in vain to think of writing by Ships which sail in March,—as you hoped to be upon your return again by their Arrival at Bombay—If I can write a Letter, I will—but this Journal must be put into Eliza's hands by Yorick only—God grant you to read it soon.—

June. 19. I never was so well and alert, as I find myself this day—tho' with a face as pale and clear as a Lady after her Lying in, Yet you never saw me so Young by 5 Years If You do not leave Bombay soon—You'l find me as young as Yourself—at this rate of going on——Summon'd from home. adieu.

June 20

I think my dear Bramine—That nature is turn'd upside down—for Wives go to visit Husbands, at greater perils, and take longer journies to pay them this Civility now a days out of ill Will—than good—Mine is flying post a Journey of a thousand Miles—with as many Miles to go back—merely to see how I do, and whether I am fat or lean—and how far are you going to see your Helpmate—and at such hazards to your Life, as few Wives' best affections would be able to surmount—But Duty and Submission Eliza govern thee—by what impulses my Rib is bent towards me—I have told you—and yet I would to God, Draper but received and treated you with half the courtesy and good nature—I wish you was with him—for the same reason I wish my Wife at Coxwould—That She might the sooner depart in peace.—She is ill—of a Diarhea which she has from a weakness on her bowels ever since her paralitic Stroke.—Travelling post in hot weather, is not the best remedy for her—but my girl says—she is determined to venture—She wrote me word in Winter, She would not leave france, till her end approach'd—surely this journey is not prophetick! but twould invert the order of Things on the other side of this *Leaf*—and what is to be on the next Leaf— The Fates, Eliza only can tell us—rest satisfied.

June 21.

have left off all medcines—not caring to tear my frame to pieces with 'em—as I feel perfectly well.—set out for Crasy Castle to morrow morning—where I stay ten days—take my sentimental Voyage—and this Journal with me, as certain as the two first Wheels of my Chariot—I cannot go on without them—I long to see Yours—I shall read it a thousand times over If I get it before your Arrival—What would I now give for it—tho' I know there are *circumstances* in it, That will make my heart bleed and waste within me—*but if all blows over*— tis enough—we will not recount our Sorrows, but to shed tears of Joy over them—O Eliza! Eliza!—Heaven nor any Being it created, ever so possessd a Man's heart—as thou possessest mine—use it kindly—Hussy—that is, eternally be true to it.—

June 22. Ive been as far as York to day with no Soul with me in my Chase, but your Picture—for it has a *Soul*, I think— or something like one which has talk'd to me, and been the best Company I ever took a Jou[r]ney with (always excepting a Journey I once took with a friend of Yours to Salt hill, and Enfield Wash—The pleasure I had in those Journies, have left *Impressions* upon my Mind, which will last my Life—You may tell her as much when You see her—she will not take it ill—I set out early to morrow morning to see Mr Hall—but take my Journal along with me.

June 24th

as pleasant a Journey as I am capable of taking Eliza! without thee—Thou shalt take it with me, when time and tide serve hereafter, and every other Journey which ever gave me pleasure, shall be rolled over again with thee besides me.—

Arno's Vale shall look gay again upon Eliza's Visit.—and the Companion of her Journey, will grow young again as he sits upon her Banks with Eliza seated besides him—I have this and a thousand little parties of pleasure—and systems of living out of the common high road; of Life, hourly working in my fancy for you—there wants only the *Dramatis Pers*onee for the performance—the play is wrote—the Scenes are painted—and the Curtain ready to be drawn up.—the whole Piece waits for thee, my Eliza—

June 25.—In a course of continual visits and Invitations here[1]—*Bombay-Lascelles*[2] dined here to day—(his Wife yesterday brought to bed)—(he is a poor sorry soul! but has taken a house two miles from Crasy Castle—What a stupid, selfish, unsentimental set of Beings are the Bulk of our Sex! by Heaven! not one man out of 50, informd with feelings—or endow'd either with heads or hearts able to possess and fill the mind of such a Being as thee, with one Vibration like its own—I never See or converse with one of my Sex—but I give this point a reflection—how would such a creature please my Bramine? I assure thee Eliza I have not been able to find one, whom I thought could please You—the turn of Sentiment, with which I left your Character possess'd—must improve, hourly upon You—Truth, fidelity, honour and Love mix'd up with Delicacy, garrantee one another—and a taste so improved as Yours, by so delicious fare, can never degenerate—I shall find you, my Bramine, if possible, more valuable and lovely, than when You first caught my esteem and kindness for You—and tho' I see not this change—I give you so much Credit for it—that at this moment, my heart glowes more warmly as I think of you—and I find myself more your Husband than contracts can make us—I stay here till the 29th—had intended a longer Stay—but much company and Dissipation rob me of the only comfort my mind takes, which is in retirement, where I can think of You Eliza! and enjoy you quietly and without Interruption—tis the Way

We must expect all that is to be had of *real* enjoyment in this vile world—which being miserable itself—seems so confederated against the happiness of the Happy,—that they are forced to secure it in private—Variety must still be had;—and that, Eliza! and every thing with it which Yorick's sense, or generosity has to furnish to one he loves so much as thee—need I tell thee—Thou wilt be as much a Mistress of—as thou art eternally of thy Yorick—adieu adieu.—

June 26. el[e]ven at night—out all the day—dined with a large Party—shewd your Picture from the fullness of my heart—highly admired—alas! said I—did You but see the Original!—good night.—

June 27.

Ten in the morning, with my Snuff open at the Top of this sheet,—and your gentle sweet face opposite to mine, and saying 'what I write will be cordially read'—possibly you may be precisely engaged at this very hour, the same way—and telling me some interesting Story about your health, Your sufferings—your heartarches—and other Sensations which friendship—absence and Uncertainty create within You. for my own part, my dear Eliza, I am a prey to every thing in its turn—and was it not for that sweet clew of hope which is perpetual[ly] opening me a Way which is to lead me to thee thro' all this Labyrinth—was it not for this, my Eliza! how could I find rest for this bewilderd heart of mine?—I should wait for you till September came—and if you did not arrive with it—should sicken and die.—but I will live for thee—so count me Immortal—3 India Men arrived within ten days—will none of 'em bring me Tidings of You?—but I am foolish—but ever thine—my dear, dear Bramine.—

June 28.

O What a tormenting night have my dreams led me about You Eliza—Mrs Draper a Widow!—with a hand at Liberty to give!—and gave it to another!—She told me—I must acquiesce—it could not be otherwise—Acquies[c]e! cried I, waking in agonies—God be prais'd cried I—tis a dream—fell asleep after—dreamd You was married to the Captain of the Ship—I waked in a fever—but 'twas the Fever in my blood which brought on this painful chain of Ideas—for I am ill to day—and for want of more cheary Ideas, I torment my Eliza with these—whose Sensibility will suffer, if Yorick could dream but of her Infidelity! and I suffer Eliza in my turn, and think my self at present little better than an old Woman or a Dreamer of Dreams in the Scripture Language—I am going to ride myself into better health and better fancies, with Hall—whose Castle lying near the Sea—We have a Beach as even as a mirrour of 5 miles in Length, before it, where we dayly run races in our Chaises, with one wheel in the Sea, and the other on the Sand—O Eliza, with what fresh ardour and impatience when I'm viewing this element, do I sigh for thy return—But I need no *memento*'s of my Destitution and misery, for want of thee—I carry them about me,—and shall not lay them down—(for I worship and Idolize these tender sorrows) till I meet thee upon the Beech and present the handkerchiefs staind with blood which broke out, from my heart upon your departure—This token of What I felt at that Crisis, Eliza, shall never, never be wash'd out. Adieu my dear Wife—you are still mine—notwithstanding all the Dreams and Dreamers in the World.—Mr Lascells dined with us—Mem^d I have to tell you a Conversation—I will not write, it—.

June 29. am got home from Halls—to Coxwould—O 'tis a delicious retreat! both from its beauty, and air of Solitude; and so sweetly does every thing about it invite the mind to rest from its Labours and be at peace with itself and the world —That tis the only place, Eliza, I could live in at this juncture —I hope one day, you will like it as much as your Bramine—It shall be decorated and made more worthy of You—by the time, fate encourages me to look for you—I have made you, a sweet Sitting Room (as I told You) already—and am pro-jecting a good Bed-chamber adjoi[ni]ng it, with a pretty dressing room for You, which connects them together—and when they are finishd, will be as sweet a set of romantic Apartments, as You ever beheld—the Sleeping room will be very large—The dressing room, thro' which You pass into your Temple, will be little—but Big enough to hold a dressing Table—a couple of chairs, with room for your Nymph to stand at her ease both behind and on either side of you—with spare Room to hang a dozen petticoats—gowns, &c—and Shelves for as many Bandboxes—Your little Temple I have described—and what it will hold—but if it ever it holds You and I, my Eliza—the Room will not be too little for us—but We shall be *too big* for the Room.—

June 30—Tis now a quarter of a year (wanting 3 days) since You sail'd from the Downs—in one month more—You will be (I trust,) at Madras—and there you will stay I suppose 2 long long months, before you set out for Bombay—Tis there I shall want to hear from you,—most impatiently—because the most interesting Letters, must come from Eliza when she is there—at present, I can hear of your health, and tho' that of all Accounts affects me most—yet still I have hopes taking their Rise from that—and those are—What Impression you can make upon Mr Draper, towards setting You at Liberty—and leaving you to pursue the best measures for Your pre-servation—and these are points, I would go to Aleppo, to know certainly: I have been possess'd all day and night with an opinion, That Draper will change his behaviour totally towards you—That he will grow friendly and caressing—and as he know[s] your Nature is easily to be won with gentleness, he will practice it to turn you from your purpose of quitting him—In short when it comes to the point of your going from him to England—it will have so much the face, if not the reality, of an alienation on your side from India for-ever, as a place you cannot live at—that he will part with You by no means, he can prevent—You will be cajolled my dear Eliza thus out of your Life—but what serves it to write this, unless means can be found for You to read it—If you come not—I will take the Safest Cautions I can, to have it got to You—and risk every thing, rather than You should not know how much I think of You—and how much stronger hold You have got of me, than ever.—Dillon¹ has obtain'd his fair Indian—and has this post wrote a kind Letter of enquiry after Yorick and his Bramine—he is a good Soul—and interests himself much in our fate—I have wrote him a whole Sheet of paper about us— it ought to have been copied into this Journal—but the uncertainty of your ever reading it, makes me omit that, with a thousand other things, which when we meet, shall beguile us of many a long winters night.—*those precious Nights!*—my Eliza!—You rate them as high as I do.—and look back upon the manner the hours glided over our heads in them, with the same Interest and Delight as the man you *spent them with*— They are all that remains to us—except the *Expectation* of their return—the Space between is a dismal Void—full of doubts, and suspence——Heaven and its kindest Spirits, my dear, rest over your thoughts by day—and free them from all disturbance at night adieu. adieu Eliza!—I have got over this Month—so fare wel to it, and the Sorrows it has brought with it—the next month, I prophecy will be worse—

July 1.—But who can foretell what a a month may produce— Eliza—I have no less than seven different chances—not one of which is improbable—and any one of [which] would set me much at Liberty—and some of 'em render me compleatly happy—as they would facilitate and open the road to thee— What these chances are I leave thee to conjecture, my Eliza— some of them You cannot divine—tho' I once hinted them to You—but those are pecuniary chances arising out of my Prebend—and so not likely to stick in thy brain—nor could they occupy mine a moment, but on thy account . . .: I hope before I meet thee Eliza on the Beach, to have every thing plann'd; that depends on me properly—and for what depends upon him who orders every Event for us, to him I leave and trust it—We shall be happy at last. I know—tis the Corner Stone of all my Castles—and tis all I bargain for. I am perfectly recoverd—or more than recover'd—for never did I feel such Indications of health or Strength and promptness of mind—notwithstanding the Cloud hanging over me, of a Visit—and all its tormenting consequences—Hall has wrote an affecting little poem upon it—the next time I see him, I will get it, and trans[cr]ibe it in this Journal, for You. . He has persuaded me to trust her with no more than fifteen hundred pounds into—Franc—twil purchase 150 pounds a year—and to let the rest come annually from myself. the advice is wise enough, If I can get her Off with it—Ill summon up the Husband a little (if I can)—and keep the 500 pounds remaining for emergencies—Who knows, Eliza, what sort of Emergencies may cry out for it—I conceive some—and you Eliza are not backward in Conception—so may conceive others. *I wish I was in Arno's Vale!*—

July 2ᵈ—But I am in the Vale of Coxwould and wish You saw in how princely a manner I live in it—tis a Land of Plenty—I sit down alone to Venison, fish or Wild foul—or a couple of dishes of fouls—with Curds, and strawberrys and Cream, and all the simple clean plenty which a rich Vally can produce—with a Bottle of wine on my right hand (as in Bond street) to drink your health—I have a hundred hens and chickens about my yard—and not a parishoner catches a hare a rabbit or a Trout—but he brings it as an Offering—In short tis a golden Vally—and will be the golden Age when You govern the rural feast, my Bramine, and are the Mistress of my table and spread it with elegancy and that natural grace and bounty with which heaven has disti[n]guish'd You.

—Time goes on slowly—every thing stands still—hours seem days and days seem Years whilst you lengthen the Distance between us—from Madras to Bombay—I shall think it shortening—and then desire and expectation will be upon the rack again—come—come—

July 3ᵈ

Hail! Hail! my dear Eliza—I steal something every day
from my sentimental Journey—to obey a more sentimental
impulse in writing to you—and giving you the present Picture
of myself—my wishes—my Love, my sincerity—my hopes—
my fears—tell me, have I varied in any one Lineament, from
the first Sitting—to this last—have I been less warm—less
tender and affectionate than you expected or could have
wish'd me in any one of 'em—or, however varied in the
expressions of what I was and what I felt, have I not still presented the same air and face towards thee?—take it as a
Sample of what I ever shall be—My dear Bramine—and that
is—such as my honour, my Engagements and promises and
desires have fix'd me—I want You to be on the other side of
my little table, to hear how sweetly your Voice will be in
Unison to all this—I want to hear what You have to say to
Your Yorick upon this Text.—what heavenly Consolation
would drop from your Lips and how pathetically you would
enforce your Truth and Love upon my heart to free it from
every Aching doubt—Doubt! did I say—but I have none—
and as soon would I doubt the Scripture I have preach'd on—
as question thy promises, or Suppose one Thought in thy
heart during thy absence from me, unworthy of my Eliza.—
for if thou art false, my Bramine—the whole world—and
Nature itself are lyars—and—I will trust to nothing on this side
of heaven—but turn aside from all Commerce with expectation, and go quietly on my way alone towards a State where no
disappointments can follow me—you are grieved when I talk
thus; it implies what does not exist in either of us—so cross it
out, if thou wilt—or leave it as a part of the picture of a heart
that *again* Languishes for Possession—and is disturbed at
every Idea of its Uncertainty.—So heaven bless thee—and
ballance thy passions better than I have power to regulate mine
—farewel my dear Girl—I sit in dread of tomorrows post
which is to bring me an Account when *Madame* is to arrive.—

July 4th—Hear nothing of her—so am tortured from post to post, for I want to know certainly *the day and hour of this Judgment*—She is moreover ill, as my Lydia writes me word—and I'm impatient to know whether tis that—or what other Cause detains her, and keeps me in this vile state of Ignorance—I'm pitied by every Soul, in proportion as her Character is detested—and her Errand known—She is coming, every one says, to flea poor Yorick or slay him—and I am spirited up by every friend I have to sell my Life dear, and fight valiantly in defence both of my property and Life—Now my Maxim, Eliza, is quietly in three [words]—'Spare my Life, and take all I have—If She is not content to decamp with that—One kingdome shall not hold us—for If she will not betake herself to France—I will. but these, I verily believe my fears and nothing more—for she will be as impatient to quit England—as I could wish her—but of this—you will know more, before I have gone thro' this month's Journal.—I get 2000 pounds for my Estate—that is, I had the Offer this morning of it—and think tis enough.—when that is gone—I will begin saving for thee—but in Saving myself for thee, That and every other kind Act is implied.

—get on slowly with my Work—but my head is too full of other Matters—yet will I finish it before I see London—for I am of too scrupulous honour to break faith with the world—great Authors make no scruple of it—but if they are great Authors—I'm sure they are little Men.—and I'm sure also of another Point which concerns yourself—and that is Eliza, that You shall never find me one hair breadth a less Man than you [*illegible deletion*]—farewell—I love thee eternally—

July 5. Two Letters from the South of France by this post, by which by some fatality, I find not one of my Letters have got to them this month—This gives me concern—because it has the Aspect of an unseasonable unkindness in me—to take no notice of what has the appearance at least of a Civility in desiring to pay me a Visit—my daughter besides has not

deserved ill of me—and tho' her mother has, I would not un-
generously take that Opportunity, which would most over-
whelm her, to give any mark of my resentment—I have besides
long since forgiven her—and am the more inclined now as she
proposes a plan, by which I shall never more be disquieted—
in these 2 last, she renews her request to have leave to live
where she has transfer'd her fortune—and purposes, with my
leave she says, to end her days in the South of france—to all
which I have just been writing her a Letter of Consolation and
good will—and to crown my professions, entreat her to take
post with my girl to be here time enough to enjoy York races
—and so having done my duty to them—I continue writing,
to do it to thee Eliza who art the *Woman of my heart*, and for
whom I am ordering and planning this, and every thing else—
be assured by Bramine that ere every thing is ripe for our
Drama,—I shall work hard to fit out and decorate a little
Theatre for us to act on—but not before a crouded house—
no Eliza—it shall be as secluded as the elysian fields—retirement is the nurse of Love and kindness—and I will Woo and
caress thee in it in such sort, that every thicket and grotto we
pass by, *shall* sollicit the remembrance of the mutual pledges
We have exchanged of Affection with one another—Oh! these
expectations—make me sigh, as I recite them—and many a
heart-felt Interjection! do they cost me, as I saunter alone in
the tracks we are to tread together hereafter—still I think thy
heart is with me—and whilst I think so, I prefer it to all the
Society this world can offer—and tis in truth my dear oweing
to this—That tho I've received half a dozen Letters to press
me to join my friends at Scarborough—that I've found pretences not to quit You *here*—and sacrifice the many sweet
Occasions I have of giving my thoughts up to You—, for
Company I cannot rellish *since* I *have tasted* my dear Girl, the
sweets of thine.—

July 6

Three long Months and three long days are pass'd and gone,

since my Eliza sighed on taking her leave of Albions cliffs, and of all in Albion, which was dear to her—How oft have I smarted at the Idea, of that last longing Look by which thou badest adieu to all thy heart Sufferd at that dismal Crisis— twas the Separation of Soul and Body—and equal to nothing but what passes on that tremendous Moment.—and like it in one Consequence, that thou art in another World; where I would give a world, to follow thee, or hear even an Account of thee—for this I shall write in a few days to our dear friend Mrs James—she possibly may have heard a single Syllable or two about You—but it cannot be; the same must have been directed towards Yoricks ear, to whom you would have wrote the name of *Eliza*, had there been no time for more. I would almost now compound with Fate,—and was I sure Eliza only breathd—I would thank heaven and acquiesce. I kiss your Picture—your Shawl—and every trinket I exchanged with You—every day I live—alas! I shall soon be debarrd of that— in a fortnight I must lock them up and clap my seal and yours upon them in the most secret Cabinet of my Bureau—You may divine the reason, Eliza! adieu—adieu!

July 7.

—But not Yet—for I will find means to write to you every night whilst my people are here—if I sit up till midnight, till they are asleep.—I should not dare to face you, if I was worse than my word in the smallest Item—and this Journal I promissed You Eliza should be kept without a chasm of a day in it. and had I my time to myself and nothing to do, but gratify my propensity—I should write from sun rise to Sun set to thee—But a Book to write—a Wife to receive and make Treaties with—an estate to sell—a Parish to superintend— and a disquieted heart perpetually to reason with, are eternal calls upon me—and yet I have you more in my mind than ever —and in proportion as I am thus torn from your embraces— *I cling the closer to the Idea of you*—Your Figure is ever before my eyes—the sound of your voice vibrates with its sweetest tones the live long day in my ear—I can see and hear nothing but my Eliza. remember this, when You think my Journal too short, and compare it not with thine, which tho' it will exceed it in length, can do no more than equal it in Love and truth of esteem—for esteem thee I do beyond all the powers of eloquence to tell thee how much—and I love thee my dear Girl, and prefer thy Love to me, more than the whole world—

    night.—have not eat or drunk all day thro' vexation of heart at a couple of ungrateful unfeeling Letters from that Quarter, from whence, had it pleas'd God, I should have lookd for all my Comforts—but he has will'd they should come from the east—and he knows how I am satisfyed with all his Dispensations—but with none, my dear Bramine, so much as this—with which Cordial upon my Spirits—I go to bed, in hopes of seeing thee in my Dreams.

July 8th

    eating my fowl, and my trouts and my cream and my strawberries, as melancholly and sad as a Cat; for want of you—by the by, I have got one which sits quietly besides me, purring all day to my sorrows—and looking up gravely from time to time in my face, as if she knew my Situation.—how soothable my heart is Eliza, when such little things sooth it! for in some pathetic sinkings I feel even some support from this poor Cat—I attend to her purrings—and think, they harmonize me—they are *pianissimo* at least, and do not disturb me.—poor Yorick! to be driven, with all his sensibilities, to these ressources—all powerful Eliza, that has had this Magical authority over him; to bend him thus to the dust— But I'll have my revenge, Hussy!

    July 9. I have been all day making a sweet Pavillion in a retired Corner of my garden—but my Partner and Companion and friend for whom I make it, is fled from me, and when she return[s] to me again, Heaven who first brought us together, best knows—When that hour is foreknown What a Paradice will I plant for thee—till then I walk as Adam did whilst there was no help-meet found for it, and could almost wish a deep Sleep would come upon me till that Moment When I can say as he did—'*Behold the Woman Thou has given me for Wife*'[1] She shall be call'd La Bramine. Indeed Indeed Eliza! my Life will be little better than a dream, till we approach nearer to each other—I live scarse conscious of my existence—or as if I wanted a vital part; and could not live above a few hours. and yet I live, and live, and live on, for thy Sake, and the sake of thy truth to me; which I measure by my own,—and I fight against every evil and every danger, that I may be able to support and shelter thee from danger and evil also.—upon my word, dear Girl, thou owest me much—but tis cruel to dun thee when thou art not in a condition to pay—I think Eliza has not run off in her Yoricks debt—

July 10.

I cannot suffer you to be longer upon the Water—in 10 days time, You shall be at Madrass—the element roles in my head as much as yours, and I am sick at the sight and smell of it—for all this, my Eliza, I feel in Imagination and so strongly—I can bear it no longer—on the 20th therefore Instant I begin to write to you as a terrestrial Being—I must deceive myself—and think so I will notwithstanding all that Lascelles has told me—but there is no truth in him.—I have just kiss'd your picture—even that sooths many an anxiety—I have found out the Body is too little for the head—it shall not be rectified, till I sit by the Original, and direct the Painter's Pencil, and that done, will take a Scamper to *Enfield* and see your dear Children—if You tire by the Way, there are *one or two* places to rest at.—I never stand out. God bless thee. I am thine as *ever*

July 11.

Sooth me—calm me—pour thy healing Balm Eliza, into the sorest of hearts—I'm pierced with the Ingratitude and unquiet Spirit of a restless unreasonable Wife whom neither gentleness or generosity can conquer—She has now enterd

upon a new plan of waging War with me, a thousand miles off
—thrice a week this last month, has the quietest man under
heaven been outraged by her Letters—I have offer'd to give
her every Shilling I was worth, except my preferment, to be
let alone and left in peace by her—Bad Woman! nothing must
now purchace this, unless I borrow 400 pounds to give her
and carry into france more—I would perish first, my Eliza!
e're I would give her a shilling of another man's, which I must
do if I give her a Shilling more than I am worth.

—How I now feel the want of thee! my dear Bramine—my
generous unworldly honest Creature—I shall die for want
of thee for a thousand reasons—every emergency and every
Sorrow each day brings along with it—tells me what a Treasure I am bereft off,—whilst I want thy friendship and Love to
keep my head up from sinking—Gods will be done. but I
think she will send me to my grave.—She will now keep me in
torture till the end of September——and writing me word to
day—she will delay her Journey two Months beyond her first
Intention—it keeps me in eternal Suspence all the while—for
she will come unawars at last upon me—and then adieu to the
dear sweets of my retirement.

How cruelly are our Lots drawn, my dear—both made for
happiness—and neither of us made to taste it! In feeling so
acutely for my own disappointment I drop blood for thine, I
call thee in, to my Aid—and thou wantest mine as much—
Were we together we should recover—but never, never till
then *nor by any other Recipe.*—

July 12.

am ill all day with the Impressions of Yesterdays account.—
can neither eat or drink or sit still and write or read—I walk
like a disturbed Spirit about my Garden—calling upon heaven
and thee, to come to my Succour—couldst thou but write one
word to me, it would be worth the world to me—my friends
write me millions—and every one invites me to flee from my
Solitude and come to them—I obey the commands of my

friend Hall who has sent over on purpose to fetch me—
or he will come himself for me—so I set off to morrow
morning to take Sanctuary in Crasy Castle—The news
papers have sent me there already by putting in the following
paragraph.

'We hear from Yorkshire, That Skelton Castle is the
present Rendevouz, of the most brilliant Wits of the Age—
the admired Author of Tristram—Mr Garrick &c. been ing
there, and Mr Coleman and many other men of Wit and
Learning being every day expected'—when I get there, which
will be to morrow night, My Eliza will hear from her Yorick—
her Yorick—who loves her more than ever.

July 13. Skelton Castle. Your picture has gone round the
Table after supper—and your health after it, my invaluable
friend!—even the Ladies, who hate grace in another, seemd
struck with it in You—but Alas! you are as a dead Person—
and Justice, (as in all such Cases,) is paid you in course—when
thou returnest it will be render'd more Sparingly—but I'll
make up all deficiencies—by honouring You more than ever
Woman was honourd by man—every good Quality That ever
good heart possess'd—thou possessest my dear Girl, and so
sovereignly does thy temper and sweet sociability, which
harmonize all thy other properties make me thine, that whilst
thou art true to thyself and thy Bramin—he thinks thee worth
a world—and would give a World was he master of it, for the
undisturbed possession of thee—Time and Chance are busy
throwing this Die for me—a fortunate Cast, or two, at the
most, makes our fortune—it gives us each other—and then
for the World—I will not give a pinch of Snuff.—Do take care
of thyself—keep this prospect before thy eyes—have a view
to it in all your Transactions, Eliza,—In a word Remember
You are mine—and stand answerable for all you say and do to
me—I govern myself by the same Rule—and such a History
of myself can I lay before you, as shall create no blushes, but
those of pleasure—tis midnight—and so sweet Sleep to thee

the remai[ni]ng hours of it. I am more thine, my dear Eliza! than ever—but that cannot be—

July 14.

dining and feasting all day at Mʳ Turner's¹—his Lady a fine Woman herself, in love with your picture—O my dear Lady, cried I, did you but know the Original—but what is she to you, Tristram—nothing; but that I am in Love with her —et caetera——said She—no I have given over dashes— replied I——I verily think my Eliza I shall get this Picture set, so as to wear it, as I first purposed—about my neck—I do not like the place tis in—it shall be nearer my heart—Thou art ever in its centre—good night—

July 15. From home. (Skelton Castle) from 8 in the morning till late at Supper—I seldom have put thee so off, my dear Girl—and yet to morrow will be as bad—

July 16. for Mʳ Hall has this Day left his Crasy Castle to come and sojourn with me at Shandy Hall for a few days— for so they have long christend our retired Cottage—we are just arrived at it—and whilst he is admiring the premises— I have stole away to converse a few minutes with thee, and in thy own dressing room—for I make every thing thine and call it so, before hand, that thou art to be mistress of hereafter. This *Hereafter*, Eliza, is but a melancholly term—but the Certainty of its coming to us, brightens it up—pray do not forget my prophecy in the Dedication of the Almanack—I have the utmost faith in it myself—but by what impulse my mind was struck with 3 Years—heaven, whom I believe it's author, best knows—but I shall see your face before—but that I leave to You—and to the Influence such a Being must have over all inferior ones—We are going to dine with the Arch Bishop to morrow—and from thence to Harrogate for three days, whilst thou dear Soul art pent up in sultry Nastiness— without Variety or change of face or Conversation—Thou shalt have enough of both when I cater for thy happiness Eliza—and if an Affectionate husband and 400 pounds a year in a sweeter Vally than that of Jehosophat will do—less thou shalt never have—but I hope more—and were it millions, tis the same—twould be laid at thy feet—Hall is come in in raptures with every thing—and so I shut up my Journal for to day and tomorrow for I shall not be able to open it where I go —adieu my dear Girl—

18—was yesterday all the day with our Archbishop[1]—this good Prelate, who is one of our most refined Wits—and the most of a gentleman of our order—oppresses me with his kindness—he shews in his treatment of me, what he told me upon taking my Leave—that he loves me, and has a high Value for me—his Chaplains tell me, he is perpetually talking of me—and has such an Opinion of my head and heart that he begs to stand Godfather for my next Literary production— so has done me the honour of putting his name in a List which I am most proud of because my Eliza's name is in it—I have just a moment to scrawl this to thee, being at York—where I want to be employd in taking you a little house, where the prophet may be accomodated with a '*Chamber in the Wall apart, with a stool and a Candlestick*'[2]—where his Soul can be at rest from the distractions of the world, and lean only upon his kind hostesse, and repose all his Cares, and melt them *along with hers* in her sympathetic bosom.

July 19. Harrogate Spaws.—drinking the waters here till the 26th—to no effect, but a cold dislike of every one of your sex.—I did nothing, but make comparisons betwixt thee my Eliza, and every woman I saw and talk'd to—thou has made me so unfit for every one else—than I am thine as much from necessity, as Love—I am thine by a thousand sweet ties, the least of which shall never be relax'd—be assured my dear Bramine of this—and repay me in so doing, the Confidence I repose in thee—your Absence, your distresses, your sufferings; your conflicts; all make me rely but the more upon that fund in you, which is able to sustain so much weight—Providence I know will relieve you from one part of it—and it shall be the pleasure of my days to ease my dear friend of the other—I Love thee Eliza, more than the heart of Man ever loved Woman's—I even love thee more than I did, the day thou badest me farewel!—Farewell!—Farewell! to thee again —I'm going from hence to York. Races.—

July 27. arrived at York.—where I had not been 2 hours before My heart was overset with a pleasure, which beggard every other, that fate could give me—save thyself—It was thy dear Packets from Iago[1]—I cannot give vent to all the emotions I felt even before I opend them—for I knew thy hand—and my seal,—which was only in thy possession.—O tis from my Eliza, said I.—I instantly shut the door of my Bed-Chamber, and orderd myself to be denied—and spent the whole evening, and till dinner the next day, in reading over and over again the most interesting Account—and the most endearing one, that ever tried the tenderness of man—I read and wept—and wept and read till I was blind—then grew sick, and went to bed— and in an hour calld again for the Candle—to read it once more—as for my dear Girls pains and her dangers I cannot write about them—because I cannot write my feelings or express them any how to my mind—O Eliza! but I will talk them over with thee with a sympathy that shall woo thee, so much better than I have ever done—That we will both be gainers in the end—'*Ill love thee for the dangers thou hast past*[2] —and thy Affection shall go hand in hand with me, because I'll pity thee—as no man ever pitied Woman—but Love like mine is never satisfied—else your second Letter from Iago— is a Letter so warm, so simple, so tender! I defy the world to produce such another—by all thats kind and gracious! I will so entreat thee Eliza! so k[i]ndly—that thou shalt say, I merit much of it—nay all—for my merit to thee, is my truth.

I now want to have this week of nonsensical Festivity over— that I may get back, with thy picture which I ever carry about me—to my retreat and to Cordelia—when the days of our Afflictions are over, I oft amuse my fancy, with an Idea, that thou wilt come down to me by Stealth, and hearing where I have walk'd out to—surprize me some sweet moon Shiney Night at Cordelia's grave, and catch me in thy Arms over it— O My Bramin! my Bramin!—

July 31. am tired to death with the hurrying pleasures of these Races—I want still and *silent* ones—so return home to-morrow, in search of them—I shall find them as I sit contemplating over thy passive picture; sweet Shadow! of what is to come! for tis all I can now grasp—first and best of Woman kind! remember me, as I remember thee—tis asking a great deal, my Bramine!—but I cannot be satisfied with less— farwell—fare—happy till fate will let me cherish thee myself. —O my Eliza! thou writest to me with an Angels pen—and thou wouldst win me by thy Letters, had I never seen thy face, or known thy heart.

August 1. what a sad Story thou hast told me of thy Sufferings and Despondences, from St Iago, till thy meeting with the Dutch Ship—twas a sympathy above Tears—I trembled every Nerve as I went from line to line—and every moment the Account comes across me—I suffer all I felt, over and over again—will providence suffer all this anguish without end— and without pity?—'*it no can be*'—I am tried my dear Bramine in the furnace of Affliction as much as thou—by the time we meet, We shall be fit only for each other—and should cast away upon any other Harbour.

August 2. my wife—uses me most unmercifully—every Soul advises me to fly from her—but where can I fly If I fly not to thee? The Bishop of Cork and Ross[1] has made me great Offers in Ireland—but I will take no step without thee—and till heaven opens us some track—He is the best of feeling tender hearted men—knows our Story—sends You his Blessing—and says if the Ship you return in touches at Cork (which many India men do)—he will take you to his palace, till he can send for me to join You—he only hopes, he says, to join us together for ever—but more of this good Man, and his attachment to me—hereafter and of a couple of Ladies in the family &c. &c.

August 3rd

I have had an offer of exchanging two pieces of preferment I hold here (but sweet Cordelia's Parish is not one of 'em) for a living of 350 pounds a year in Surry about 30 miles from London —and retaining Coxwould and my Prebendaryship—which are half as much more—the Country also is sweet—but I will not[1] —I cannot take any step unless I had thee my Eliza for whose sake I live, to consult with—and till the road is open for me as my heart wishes to advance—with thy sweet light Burden in my Arms, I could get up fast the hill of preferment, if I chose it— but without thee I feel Lifeless—and if a Mitre was offer'd me, I would not have it, till I could have thee too, to make it sit easy upon my brow—I want kindly to smooth thine, and not only wipe away thy tears but dry up the Sourse of them for ever—

—August 4[2]—Hurried backwards and forwards about the arrival of Madame, this whole week—and then farewel I fear to this journal—till I get up to London—and can pursue it as I wish. at present all I can write would be but the History of my miserable feelings—She will be ever present—and if I take up my pen for thee—something will jarr within me as I do it—that I must lay it down again—I will give you one general Account of all my sufferings together—but not in Journals—I shall set my wounds a-bleeding every day afresh by it—and the Story cannot be too short.—so worthiest, best, kindest and [most] affectionate of Souls farewell—every Moment will I have thee present—and sooth my sufferings with the looks my fancy shall cloath thee in.—Thou shalt lye down and rise up with me—about my bed and about my paths, and shalt see out all my Ways.—adieu—adieu—and remember one eternal truth, My dear Bramine, which is not the worse, because I have told it thee a thousand times before—That I am thine—and thine only, and for ever.

L. Sterne

November 1st. All my dearest Eliza has turnd out more favourable than my hopes—Mrs S—— and my dear Girl have been 2 Months with me and they have this day left me to go to spend the Winter at York, after having settled every thing to their hearts content—Mrs Sterne retired into france, whence she purposes not to stir, till her death—and never, has she vow'd, will give me another sorrowful or discontented hour—I have conquerd her, as I would every one else, by humanity and Generosity—and she leaves me, more than half in Love with me—She goes into the South of france, her health being insupportable in England—and her age, as she now confesses ten Years more, than I thought—being on the edge of sixty—so God bless—and make the remainder of her Life happy—in order to which I am to remit her three hundred guineas a year—and give my dear Girl two thousand pounds—which with all Joy, I agree to,—but tis to be sunk into an annuity in the french Loans—

—And now Eliza! Let me talk to thee—But What can I say, What can I write—But the Yearnings of heart wasted with looking and wishing for thy Return—Return—Return! my dear Eliza! May heaven smooth the Way for thee to send thee safely to us, and soj[ourn] for Ever

A Political Romance,

Addressed

To ——— ———, *Esq ;*

OF *YORK*.

To which is subjoined a
KEY.

Ridiculum acri
Fortius et melius magnas plerumque secat Res.[1]

INTRODUCTION

THE writing of *A Political Romance* marks the opening of the major phase of Sterne's literary career. About the year 1758, according to the account he later gave one of his friends, 'a squabble breaking out at York ... he sided with the Dean and his friends, and tried to throw the laugh on the other party, by writing The History of an Old Watchcoat ... About 500 copies were printed off, and all committed to the flames but three or four.' In fact some half-dozen of the original edition are known to survive. In 1769, a year after Sterne's death, the first half of the work was reprinted in London: in this edition the text is tidied up in a manner that would have infuriated Sterne, and the satirical *Key* (an integral part of the satire) is omitted, as are the appended letters. Reprints of this later version can occasionally be found, but it is surprising that the original edition has seldom been reprinted. Admirers of Sterne who have been obliged to rely on secondary sources for their knowledge of this amusing *jeu d'esprit* can now read it for themselves.

The answer Sterne gave to a lady who asked him for news of 'an extraordinary book' that he was rumoured to be writing, in November 1759, reveals the impulse that had led him to begin *Tristram Shandy*:

Now for your desire of knowing the reason of my turning author? why truly I am tired of employing my brains for other people's advantage. — 'Tis a foolish sacrifice I have made for some years to an ungrateful person ...

Although its affinities are with *Tristram Shandy*, and not with *A Sentimental Journey*, it is clear that *A Political Romance* is essential reading for anyone who wishes to understand Sterne's strange development. If the reader questions its inclusion in an edition of *A Sentimental Journey*, the editor may perhaps be permitted to adapt Sterne's own words in the postscript of his letter to the unfortunate Dr. Topham: 'I beg Pardon for *clapping* this upon the *Back* of the [*Sentimental Journey*],—which is done out of no Disrespect to you.—But the *Vehicle* stood ready at the Door,—and as . . . there was Room enough behind it,—it was the cheapest and readiest Conveyance I could think of.'

Only the briefest account of the 'squabble . . . at York' need be given here, as the interested reader can always turn to the account by Arthur H. Cash in *Laurence Sterne: The Early & Middle Years*. It is sufficient for our purpose to recall that differences between the Archbishop of York, Dr. Matthew Hutton, and the Dean of York, John Fountayne, were deliberately fomented by Dr. Francis Topham, whom some may remember as Didius, the great church-lawyer, in *Tristram Shandy*. This clerical Pooh-bah was to combine in his own person, at a slightly later time, the posts of Commissary and Keeper-General of the Exchequer and Prerogative Courts of the Archbishop of York, 'Official to the Archdeacon of York, Official to the Archdeacon of the East Riding, Official to the Archdeacon of Cleveland, Official to the Precentor, Official to the Chancellor, and Official to several of the prebendaries'. When our story begins, Dr. Topham had his eye on two further offices: the Commissaryship of the Peculiar Court of Pickering and Pocklington, and the Commissaryship of the Dean and Chapter of York. Initially the Dean had favoured his aspirations, but on learning more of Topham's character he did not in fact use his interest in his favour. A certain William Stables was appointed to the second office, while Sterne himself, who had helped the Dean by writing for him an eloquent Latin sermon for the Cambridge Commencement, was appointed to Pickering and Pocklington.

Dr. Topham, who had felt so certain of the latter appointment that he had had the patent for it made out, with his own name inserted, was furious. He and his friends spread a damaging rumour that the Dean had promised him both appointments, and had simply broken his word. Incensed by this charge, the Dean took the opportunity of a 'public sessions dinner' at York to accuse Topham of spreading the story, and then gave his own version of the affair. At first Topham denied the accusation; but when pressed by Sterne he 'did at last acknowledge it; adding, as his Reason or Excuse for so doing, That he apprehended . . . he had a *Promise* under the *Dean's own hand*, of the *Dean and Chapter's Commissaryship*'. Whatever the rights and wrongs of the affair it seems clear that Topham emerged from a dinner which was destined to provide material for *Tristram Shandy** with the appearance of a man who had been badly defeated.

This he neither forgot nor forgave. When a new Archbishop of York succeeded Dr. Hutton, six years later, Topham went out of his way to make himself indispensable to him. Having succeeded in this endeavour, he asked a favour: having discovered that his best-paid office, that of Commissary of the Exchequer and Prerogative Courts, had formerly been granted for two lives, he asked for permission (in effect) to ensure that his son should succeed him in this lucrative position. To this neither the Archbishop (in spite of some initial wavering) nor the Dean would give his agreement.

In December 1758, accordingly, Dr. Topham published *A LETTER Address'd to the Reverend the DEAN of York; In which is given A full Detail of some very extraordinary Behaviour of his, in relation to his Denial of a Promise made by him to Dr. TOPHAM.*

* Vol. IV, chs. xxvi–xxix.

Although this dealt primarily with the appointment which had gone to Sterne, it touched on the whole complication of quarrels. A fortnight later the Dean or his party published *An ANSWER To A LETTER Address'd to the DEAN of YORK, In the NAME of Dr. TOPHAM* containing (among other things) a declaration of what had happened at the dinner, signed by Sterne and other J.P.s. As those who are versed in the ways of eighteenth-century controversy will have anticipated, this *ANSWER* called forth *A REPLY*. Among other matters, this claimed that the Dean's *ANSWER* had been a collaborative performance, 'the Child and Offspring of many Parents': Sterne and others were said to have given their assistance in 'Correcting, Revising, Ornamenting, and Embellishing' the Dean's nerveless prose.*

The immediate reception of *A Political Romance*, which was printed towards the end of January 1759, might perhaps have been predicted. Topham sent word that he would 'quit his pretensions' if the satire was suppressed, and it was felt even by his enemies that the publication was hardly calculated to uphold the dignity of the Church. In his exasperation, Sterne is said to have expressed his regret that he had ever praised a 'weak and ignorant' Dean so highly, and even to have doubted whether Dr. Topham had really deserved such severe treatment. The book was burnt, however: Sterne and the Dean were somehow reconciled 'beyond the power of any future breach': and one of the great English comic writers had come into his inheritance.

A Political Romance is a most skilful burlesque. In a letter written in 1759 we find Sterne telling an unknown correspondent that 'the happiness of the Cervantic humour arises from . . . describing silly and trifling Events, with the Circumstantial Pomp of great Ones'. In this satire he takes the opposite course and reduces the diocese of York to a country parish, the Archbishop to an ordinary parson, and the Dean

* On the composition of the *Romance* see *Tristram Shandy*, ed. Melvin and Joan New (Florida, 1978), ii. 815–17.

to his parish clerk. The aim is clearly to reduce the scale of the events he is describing without offending either of these potentates. Dr. Topham, on the other hand, who was a man of some importance (particularly, but by no means exclusively, in his own eyes), becomes the sexton and dog-whipper of the parish, Trim. His plea that he had served the Archbishop well is translated as follows:

> He had black'd the Parson's Shoes without Count, and greased his Boots above fifty Times:—. . . He had run for Eggs into the Town upon all Occasions;—whetted the Knives at all Hours;—catched his Horse and rubbed him down.

The unfortunate Mrs. Topham comes in for her share of the satire:

> She had been ready upon all Occasions to charr for them;—and neither he nor she, to the best of his Remembrance, ever took a Farthing, or any thing beyond a Mug of Ale.——

Later in the story Trim is asked if he is not ashamed of himself:

> Are you not Sexton and Dog-Whipper, worth Three Pounds a Year?—Then you begg'd the Church-Wardens to let your Wife have the Washing and Darning of the Surplice and Church-Linen, which brings you in Thirteen Shillings and Four Pence.—Then you have Six Shillings and Eight Pence for oiling and winding up the Clock. . . . The Pinder's Place, which is worth Forty Shillings a Year,—you have got that too.—You are the Bailiff, which the late Parson got you, which brings you in Forty Shillings more.—Besides all this, you have Six Pounds a Year . . . for being Mole-Catcher to the Parish. . . . You catch STRAY CONIES too in the Dark. . . . You catch Conies! cries a toothless old Woman, who was just passing by.——

The Commissaryship of Pickering and Pocklington becomes an old pair of breeches, 'not much the worse for wearing', and that of the Dean and Chapter of York a 'great Green Pulpit-Cloth and old Velvet Cushion'.

A Political Romance is further evidence, if such should be required, that Sterne was an admirer of *A Tale of a Tub*, and it is interesting to find him insisting—in the satirical *Key*, in which he introduces a number of friends arguing about the sense of the pamphlet—that

as great a Variety of Personages, Opinions, Transactions, and Truths, [were] found to lay hid under the dark Veil of its Allegory, as ever were discovered in the thrice-renowned History of the Acts of *Gargantua* and *Pantagruel*.

The introduction of another cause of quarrel between the Archbishop and the Dean—a dispute over the appointment of preachers in the cathedral, in which Dr. Topham had again played his part—allows Sterne to reveal a debt to yet another master of satire, and there is a clear reminiscence of *Le Lutrin*. Yet most interesting of all (perhaps) is the anticipation of *Tristram Shandy*, which he was so shortly to begin, that is particularly evident in the discussion among the members of the club about the meaning of the allegory: each disputant rides his own preposterous hobby-horse, and none shows any interest in the views advanced by his fellows.

A POLITICAL ROMANCE, &c.

SIR,

IN my last, for want of something better to write about, I told you what a World of Fending and Proving[1] we have had of late, in this little Village of ours, about an *old-cast-Pair-of-black-Plush-Breeches,* which *John,* our Parish-Clerk, about ten Years ago, it seems, had made a Promise of to one *Trim,* who is our Sexton and Dog-Whipper.——To this you write me Word, that you have had more than either one or two Occasions to know a good deal of the shifty Behaviour of this said Master *Trim,*—and that you are astonished, nor can you for your Soul conceive, how so worthless a Fellow, and so worthless a Thing into the Bargain, could become the Occasion of such a Racket as I have represented.

Now, though you do not say expressly, you could wish to hear any more about it, yet I see plain enough that I have raised your Curiosity; and therefore, from the same Motive, that I slightly mentioned it at all in my last Letter, I will, in this, give you a full and very circumstantial Account of the whole Affair.

But, before I begin, I must first set you right in one very material Point, in which I have missled you, as to the true Cause of all this Uproar amongst us;——which does not take its Rise, as I then told you, from the Affair of the *Breeches*[2];— but, on the contrary, the whole Affair of the *Breeches* has taken its Rise from it:——To understand which, you must know, that the first Beginning of the Squabble was not between *John* the Parish-Clerk and *Trim* the Sexton, but betwixt the Parson of the Parish and the said Master *Trim,* about an old

Watch-Coat, which had many Years hung up in the Church, which *Trim* had set his Heart upon; and nothing would serve *Trim* but he must take it home, in order to have it converted into a *warm Under-Petticoat* for his Wife, and a *Jerkin* for himself, against Winter; which, in a plaintive Tone, he most humbly begg'd his Reverence would consent to.

I need not tell you, Sir, who have so often felt it, that a Principle of strong Compassion transports a generous Mind sometimes beyond what is strictly right,—the Parson was within an Ace of being an honourable Example of this very Crime;—for no sooner did the distinct Words—*Petticoat——poor Wife——warm——Winter* strike upon his Ear,——but his Heart warmed,—and, before *Trim* had well got to the End of his Petition, (being a Gentleman of a frank and open Temper) he told him he was welcome to it, with all his Heart and Soul. But, *Trim*, says he, as you see I am but just got down to my Living, and am an utter Stranger to all Parish-Matters, know nothing about this old Watch-Coat you beg of me, having never seen it in my Life, and therefore cannot be a Judge whether 'tis fit for such a Purpose; or, if it is, in Truth, know not whether 'tis mine to bestow upon you or not;—— you must have a Week or ten Days Patience, till I can make some Inquiries about it;—and, if I find it is in my Power, I tell you again, Man, your Wife is heartily welcome to an Under-Petticoat out of it, and you to a Jerkin, was the Thing as good again as you represent it.

It is necessary to inform you, Sir, in this Place, That the Parson was earnestly bent to serve *Trim* in this Affair, not only from the Motive of Generosity, which I have justly ascribed to him, but likewise from another Motive; and that was by way of making some Sort of Recompence for a Multitude of small Services which *Trim* had occasionally done, and indeed was continually doing, (as he was much about the House) when his own Man was out of the Way. For all these Reasons together, I say, the Parson of the Parish intended to serve

Trim in this Matter to the utmost of his Power: All that was wanting was previously to inquire, if any one had a *Claim* to it;—or whether, as it had, Time immemorial, hung up in the Church, the taking it down might not raise a Clamour in the Parish. These Inquiries were the very Thing that *Trim* dreaded in his Heart.—He knew very well that if the Parson should but say one Word to the Church-Wardens about it, there would be an End of the whole Affair. For this, and some other Reasons not necessary to be told you, at present, *Trim* was for allowing no Time in this Matter;—but, on the contrary, doubled his Diligence and Importunity at the Vicarage-House;—plagued the whole Family to Death;—pressed his Suit Morning, Noon, and Night; and, to shorten my Story, teazed the poor Gentleman, who was but in an ill State of Health, almost out of his Life about it.

You will not wonder, when I tell you, that all this Hurry and Precipitation, on the Side of Master *Trim*, produced its natural Effect on the Side of the Parson, and that was, a Suspicion that all was not right at the Bottom.

He was one Evening sitting alone in his Study, weighing and turning this Doubt every Way in his Mind; and, after an Hour and a half's serious Deliberation upon the Affair, and running over *Trim*'s Behaviour throughout,—he was just saying to himself, *It must be so*;—when a sudden Rap at the Door put an End to his Soliloquy,—and, in a few Minutes, to his Doubts too; for a Labourer in the Town, who deem'd himself past his fifty-second Year, had been returned by the Constable in the Militia-List,—and he had come, with a Groat in his Hand, to search the Parish Register for his Age.— The Parson bid the poor Fellow put the Groat into his Pocket, and go into the Kitchen:—Then shutting the Study Door, and taking down the Parish Register,—*Who knows*, says he, *but I may find something here about this self-same Watch-Coat?* —He had scarce unclasped the Book, in saying this, when he popp'd upon the very Thing he wanted, fairly wrote on the first Page, pasted to the Inside of one of the Covers, whereon was a Memorandum about the very Thing in Question, in these express Words:

MEMORANDUM

The great Watch-Coat was purchased and given above two hundred Years ago, by the Lord of the Manor, to this Parish-Church, to the sole Use and Behoof of the poor Sertons thereof, and their Successors, for ever, to be worn by them respectively in winterly cold Nights, in ringing Complines, Passing-Bells, &c. which the said Lord of the Manor had done, in Piety, to keep the poor Wretches warm, and for the Good of his own Soul, for which they were directed to pray, &c. &c. &c. &c. *Just Heaven!* said the Parson to himself, looking upwards, *What an Escape have I had! Give this for an Under-Petticoat to* Trim's *Wife! I would not have consented to such a Desecration to be Primate of all* England; *nay, I would not have disturb'd a single Button of it for half my Tythes!*

Scarce were the Words out of his Mouth, when in pops *Trim* with the whole Subject of the Exclamation under both his Arms.—I say, under both his Arms;—for he had actually got it ripp'd and cut out ready, his own Jerkin under one Arm, and the Petticoat under the other, in order to be carried to the Taylor to be made up,—and had just stepp'd in, in high Spirits, to shew the Parson how cleverly it had held out.

There are many good Similies now subsisting in the World, but which I have neither Time to recollect or look for, which would give you a strong Conception of the Astonishment and honest Indignation which this unexpected Stroke of *Trim's* Impudence impress'd upon the Parson's Looks.—Let it suffice to say, That it exceeded all fair Description,—as well as all Power of proper Resentment,——except this, that *Trim* was ordered, in a stern Voice, to lay the Bundles down upon the Table,—to go about his Business, and wait upon him, at his Peril, the next Morning at Eleven precisely:—Against this Hour, like a wise Man, the Parson had sent to desire *John* the Parish-Clerk, who bore an exceeding good Character as a Man of Truth, and who having, moreover, a pretty Freehold of about eighteen Pounds a Year in the Township, was a leading Man in it; and, upon the whole, was such a one of whom it might be said,—That he rather did Honour to his Office,—than that his Office did Honour to him.—Him he sends for, with the Church-Wardens, and one of the Sides-Men, a grave, knowing, old Man, to be present:—For as *Trim* had with-held the whole Truth from the Parson, touching the Watch-Coat, he thought it probable he would as certainly do the same Thing to others; though this, I said, was wise, the Trouble of the Precaution might have been spared,—because the Parson's Character was unblemish'd,—and he had ever been held by the World in the Estimation of a Man of Honour and Integrity.—*Trim*'s Character, on the contrary, was as well known, if not in the World, yet, at least, in all the Parish, to be that of a little, dirty, pimping, pettifogging, ambidextrous[1] Fellow,—who neither cared what he did or said of any, provided he could get a Penny by it.—This might, I say, have made any Precaution needless;—but you must know, as the Parson had in a Manner but just got down to his Living, he dreaded the Consequences of the least ill Impression on his first Entrance amongst his Parishioners, which would have disabled him from doing them the Good he wished;—so that, out of Regard to his Flock, more than the necessary Care due to himself,—he was resolv'd not to lie at the Mercy of what Resentment might vent, or Malice lend an Ear to.—Accordingly the whole Matter was rehearsed from first to last by the Parson, in the Manner I've told you, in the Hearing of *John* the Parish-Clerk, and in the Presence of *Trim*.

Trim had little to say for himself, except 'That the Parson had absolutely promised to befriend him and his Wife in the Affair, to the utmost of his Power: That the Watch-Coat was certainly in his Power, and that he might still give it him if he pleased.'

To this, the Parson's Reply was short, but strong, 'That nothing was in his *Power* to do, but what he could do *honestly*: —That in giving the Coat to him and his Wife, he should do a manifest Wrong to the *next* Sexton; the great Watch-Coat being the most comfortable Part of the Place:—That he should, moreover, injure the Right of his own Successor, who would be just so much a worse Patron, as the Worth of the Coat amounted to;—and, in a Word, he declared, that his whole Intent in promising that Coat, was Charity to *Trim*; but *Wrong* to no Man; that was a Reserve, he said, made in all Cases of this Kind:—and he declared solemnly, *in Verbo Sacerdotis*, That this was his Meaning, and was so understood by *Trim* himself.'

With the Weight of this Truth, and the great good Sense and strong Reason which accompanied all the Parson said upon the Subject,—poor *Trim* was driven to his last Shift,—and begg'd he might be suffered to plead his Right and Title to the Watch-Coat, if not by *Promise*, at least by *Services*.—It was well known how much he was entitled to it upon these Scores: That he had black'd the Parson's Shoes without Count, and greased his Boots above fifty Times:—That he had run for Eggs into the Town upon all Occasions;—— whetted the Knives at all Hours;—catched his Horse and rubbed him down:——That for his Wife she had been ready upon all Occasions to charr for them;—and neither he nor she, to the best of his Remembrance, ever took a Farthing, or any thing beyond a Mug of Ale.—To this Account of his Services he begg'd Leave to add those of his Wishes, which, he said, had been equally great.—He affirmed, and was ready, he said, to make it appear, by Numbers of Witnesses, 'He had drank his Reverence's Health a thousand Times, (by the bye, he did not add out of the Parson's own Ale): That he not only drank his Health, but wish'd it; and never came to the House, but ask'd his Man kindly how he did; that in particular, about half a Year ago, when his Reverence cut his Finger in paring an Apple, he went half a Mile to ask a cunning Woman, what was good to stanch Blood, and actually returned with a Cobweb in his Breeches Pocket:——Nay, says *Trim*, it was not a Fortnight ago, when your Reverence took that violent Purge, that I went to the far End of the whole Town to borrow you a Close-stool,—and came back, as my Neighbours, who flouted me, will all bear witness, with the Pan upon my Head, and never thought it too much.'

Trim concluded his pathetick Remonstrance with saying, 'He hoped his Reverence's Heart would not suffer him to requite so many faithful Services by so unkind a Return:— That if it was so, as he was the first, so he hoped he should be the last, Example of a Man of his Condition so treated.'—— This Plan of *Trim*'s Defence, which *Trim* had put himself upon,—could admit of no other Reply but a general Smile.

Upon the whole, let me inform you, That all that could be said, *pro* and *con*, on both Sides, being fairly heard, it was plain, That *Trim*, in every Part of this Affair, had behaved very ill;——and *one* Thing, which was never expected to be known of him, happening in the Course of this Debate to come out against him;—namely, That he had gone and told the Parson, before he had ever set Foot in his Parish, That *John* his Parish-Clerk,—his Church-Wardens, and some of the Heads of the Parish, were a Parcel of Scoundrels.—Upon the Upshot, *Trim* was kick'd out of Doors; and told, at his Peril, never to come there again.

At first *Trim* huff'd and bounced most terribly;—swore he would get a Warrant;—then nothing would serve him but he would call a Bye-Law[1], and tell the whole Parish how the Parson had misused him;—but cooling of that, as fearing the Parson might possibly bind him over to his good Behaviour, and, for aught he knew, might send him to the House of Correction,—he let the Parson alone; and, to revenge himself, falls foul upon his Clerk, who had no more to do in the Quarrel than you or I;—rips up the Promise of the old-cast-Pair-of-black-Plush-Breeches, and raises an Uproar in the Town about it, notwithstanding it had slept ten Years.—But all this, you must know, is look'd upon in no other Light, but as an artful Stroke of Generalship in *Trim*, to raise a Dust, and cover himself under the disgraceful Chastisement he has undergone.

If your Curiosity is not yet satisfied,—I will now proceed to relate the *Battle* of the Breeches, in the same exact Manner I have done *that* of the Watch-Coat.

Be it known then, that, about ten Years ago, when *John* was appointed Parish-Clerk of this Church, this said Master *Trim* took no small Pains to get into *John's* good Graces; in order, as it afterwards appeared, to coax a Promise out of him of a Pair of Breeches, which *John* had then by him, of black Plush, not much the worse for wearing;—*Trim* only begging for God's Sake to have them bestowed upon him when *John* should think fit to cast them.

Trim was one of those kind of Men who loved a Bit of Finery in his Heart, and would rather have a tatter'd Rag of a Better Body's, than the best plain whole Thing his Wife could spin him.

John, who was naturally unsuspicious, made no more Difficulty of promising the Breeches, than the Parson had done in promising the Great Coat; and, indeed, with something less Reserve,——because the Breeches were *John's* *own*, and he could give them, without Wrong, to whom he thought fit.

It happened, I was going to say unluckily, but, I should rather say, most luckily, for *Trim*, for he was the only Gainer by it,—that a Quarrel, about some six or eight Weeks after this, broke out between *the late* Parson of the Parish and *John* the Clerk. Somebody (and it was thought to be Nobody but

Trim) had put it into the Parson's Head, 'That *John*'s Desk[1] in the Church was, at the least, four Inches higher than it should be:——That the Thing gave Offence, and was indecorous, inasmuch as it approach'd too near upon a Level with the Parson's Desk itself. This Hardship the Parson complained of loudly,—and told *John* one Day after Prayers,— 'He could bear it no longer:—And would have it alter'd and brought down as it should be.' *John* made no other Reply, but, 'That the Desk was not of his raising:——That 'twas not one Hair Breadth higher than he found it;—and that as he found it, so would he leave it:——In short, he would neither make an Encroachment, nor would he suffer one.'

The *late* Parson might have his Virtues, but the leading Part of his Character was not *Humility*; so that *John*'s Stiffness in this Point was not likely to reconcile Matters.—This was *Trim*'s Harvest.

After a friendly Hint to *John* to stand his Ground,—away hies *Trim* to make his Market[2] at the Vicarage:——What pass'd there, I will not say, intending not to be uncharitable; so shall content myself with only guessing at it, from the sudden Change that appeared in *Trim*'s Dress for the better; —for he had left his old ragged Coat, Hat and Wig, in the Stable, and was come forth strutting across the Church-yard, y'clad in a good creditable cast Coat[3], large Hat and Wig, which the Parson had just given him.——Ho! Ho! Hollo! *John!* cries *Trim*, in an insolent Bravo, as loud as ever he could bawl—See here, my Lad! how fine I am.——The more Shame for you, answered *John*, seriously.—Do you think, *Trim*, says he, such Finery, gain'd by such Services, becomes you, or can wear well?—Fye upon it, *Trim*;—I could not have expected this from you, considering what Friendship you pretended, and how kind I have ever been to you:—How many Shillings and Sixpences I have generously lent you in your Distresses? —Nay, it was but t'other Day that I promised you these black Plush Breeches I have on.——Rot your Breeches, quoth

Trim; for *Trim*'s Brain was half turn'd with his new Finery:
—Rot your Breeches, says he,—I would not take them up,
were they laid at my Door;—give 'em, and be d——d to you,
to whom you like;——I would have you to know I can have a
better Pair at the Parson's any Day in the Week:——*John* told
him plainly, as his Word had once pass'd him, he had a Spirit
above taking Advantage of his Insolence, in giving them away
to another:—But, to tell him his Mind freely, he thought he
had got so many Favours of that Kind, and was so likely to get
many more for the same Services, of the Parson, that he had
better give up the Breeches, with good Nature, to some one
who would be more thankful for them.

Here *John* mentioned *Mark Slender*[1], (who, it seems, the
Day before, had ask'd *John* for 'em) not knowing they were
under Promise to *Trim*.——'Come, *Trim*, says he, let poor
Mark have 'em,——You know he has not a Pair to his A——:
Besides, you see he is just of my Size, and they will fit him to
a T; whereas, if I give 'em to you,—look ye, they are not worth
much; and, besides, you could not get your Backside into
them, if you had them, without tearing them all to Pieces.'

Every Tittle of this was most undoubtedly true; for *Trim*,
you must know, by foul Feeding, and playing the good Fellow
at the Parson's, was grown somewhat gross about the lower
Parts, *if not higher:* So that, as all *John* said upon the Occasion
was fact, *Trim*, with much ado, and after a hundred Hum's
and Hah's, at last, out of mere Compassion to *Mark*, *signs,
seals, and delivers up* 𝔞𝔩𝔩 𝔚𝔦𝔤𝔥𝔱, 𝔍𝔫𝔱𝔢𝔯𝔢𝔰𝔱, 𝔞𝔫𝔡 𝔓𝔯𝔢𝔱𝔢𝔫=
𝔰𝔦𝔬𝔫𝔰 𝔴𝔥𝔞𝔱𝔰𝔬𝔢𝔳𝔢𝔯, 𝔦𝔫 𝔞𝔫𝔡 𝔱𝔬 𝔱𝔥𝔢 𝔰𝔞𝔦𝔡 𝔚𝔯𝔢𝔢𝔠𝔥𝔢𝔰;
𝔱𝔥𝔢𝔯𝔢𝔟𝔶 𝔟𝔦𝔫𝔡𝔦𝔫𝔤 𝔥𝔦𝔰 𝔥𝔢𝔦𝔯𝔰, 𝔈𝔯𝔢𝔠𝔲𝔱𝔬𝔯𝔰, 𝔞𝔡𝔪𝔦𝔫𝔦𝔰𝔱𝔯𝔞=
𝔱𝔬𝔯𝔰, 𝔞𝔫𝔡 𝔞𝔰𝔰𝔦𝔤𝔫𝔢𝔰, 𝔫𝔢𝔳𝔢𝔯 𝔪𝔬𝔯𝔢 𝔱𝔬 𝔠𝔞𝔩𝔩 𝔱𝔥𝔢 𝔰𝔞𝔦𝔡
𝔠𝔩𝔞𝔦𝔪 𝔦𝔫 𝔔𝔲𝔢𝔰𝔱𝔦𝔬𝔫.

All this Renunciation was set forth in an ample Manner, to
be in pure Pity to *Mark*'s Nakedness;—but the Secret was,
Trim had an Eye to, and firmly expected in his own Mind, the
great Green Pulpit-Cloth and old Velvet Cushion, which were

that very Year to be taken down;—which, by the Bye, could he have wheedled *John* a second Time out of 'em, as he hoped, he had made up the Loss of his Breeches Seven-fold.

Now, you must know, this Pulpit-Cloth and Cushion were not in *John*'s Gift, but in the Church-Wardens, *&c.*— However, as I said above, that *John* was a leading Man in the Parish, *Trim* knew he could help him to them if he would:—But *John* had got a Surfeit of him;—so, when the Pulpit-Cloth, *&c.* were taken down, they were immediately given (*John* having a great Say in it) to *William Doe*[1], who understood very well what Use to make of them.

As for the old Breeches, poor *Mark Slender* lived to wear them but a short Time, and they got into the Possession of *Lorry Slim*[2], an unlucky Wight, by whom they are still worn; ——in Truth, as you will guess, they are very thin by this Time:—But *Lorry* has a light Heart; and what recommends them to him, is this, that, as thin as they are, he knows that *Trim*, let him say what he will to the contrary, still envies the *Possessor* of them,—and, with all his Pride, would be very glad to wear them after *him*.

Upon this Footing have these Affairs slept quietly for near ten Years,——and would have slept for ever, but for the unlucky Kicking-Bout; which, as I said, has ripp'd this Squabble up afresh: So that it was no longer ago than last Week, that *Trim* met and insulted *John* in the public Town-Way, before a hundred People;—tax'd him with the Promise of the old-cast-Pair-of-black-Breeches, notwithstanding *Trim*'s solemn Renunciation; twitted him with the Pulpit-Cloth and Velvet Cushion[3],—as good as told him, he was ignorant of the common Duties of his Clerkship; adding, very insolently, That he knew not so much as to give out a common Psalm in Tune.——

John contented himself with giving a plain Answer to every Article that *Trim* had laid to his Charge, and appealed to his Neighbours who remembered the whole Affair;—and as he knew there was never any Thing to be got in wrestling with a

Chimney-Sweeper,—he was going to take Leave of *Trim* for ever.———But, hold,—the Mob by this Time had got round them, and their High Mightinesses insisted upon having *Trim* tried upon the Spot.—*Trim* was accordingly tried; and, after a full Hearing, was convicted a second Time, and handled more roughly by one or more of them, than even at the Parson's.

Trim, says one, are you not ashamed of yourself, to make all this Rout and Disturbance in the Town, and set Neighbours together by the Ears, about an old-worn-out-Pair-of-cast-Breeches, not worth Half a Crown?———Is there a cast-Coat, or a Place in the whole Town, that will bring you in a Shilling, but what you have snapp'd up, like a greedy Hound as you are?

In the first Place, are you not Sexton and Dog-Whipper, worth Three Pounds a Year?———Then you begg'd the Church-Wardens to let your Wife have the Washing and Darning of the Surplice and Church-Linen, which brings you in Thirteen Shillings and Four Pence.—Then you have Six Shillings and Eight Pence for oiling and winding up the Clock, both paid you at *Easter*.—The Pinder's Place[1], which is worth Forty Shillings a Year,—you have got that too.—You are the Bailiff, which the late Parson got you, which brings you in Forty Shillings more.—Besides all this, you have Six Pounds a Year, paid you Quarterly for being Mole-Catcher to the Parish.—Aye, says the luckless Wight above-mentioned, (who was standing close to him with his Plush Breeches on) 'You are not only Mole-Catcher, *Trim*, but you catch STRAY CONIES[2] too in the *Dark*; and you pretend a *Licence* for it, which, I trow, will be look'd into at the next Quarter Sessions.' I maintain it, I have a Licence, says *Trim*, blushing as red as Scarlet:———I have a Licence,—and as I farm a Warren in the next Parish, I will catch Conies every Hour of the Night.——— *You catch Conies!* cries a toothless old Woman, who was just passing by.———

This set the Mob a laughing, and sent every Man home in

perfect good Humour, except *Trim*, who waddled very slowly off with that Kind of inflexible Gravity only to be equalled by one Animal in the whole Creation,—and surpassed by none. I am,

SIR,

Yours, &c. &c.

FINIS.

POSTSCRIPT.

I HAVE broke open my Letter to inform you, that I miss'd the Opportunity of sending it by the Messenger, who I expected would have called upon me in his Return through this Village to *York*, so it has laid a Week or ten Days by me.

——I am not sorry for the Disappointment, because something has since happened, in Continuation of this Affair, which I am thereby enabled to transmit to you, all under one Trouble.

When I finished the above Account, I thought (as did every Soul in the Parish) *Trim* had met with so thorough a Rebuff from *John* the Parish-Clerk and the Town's Folks, who all took against him, that *Trim* would be glad to be quiet, and let the Matter rest.

But, it seems, it is not half an Hour ago since *Trim* sallied forth again; and, having borrowed a Sow-Gelder's Horn[1], with hard Blowing he got the whole Town round him, and endeavoured to raise a Disturbance, and fight the whole Battle over again:—That he had been used in the last Fray worse than a Dog;—not by *John* the Parish-Clerk,—for I shou'd not, quoth *Trim*, have valued him a Rush single Hands:—But all the Town sided with him, and twelve Men in *Buckram* set upon me all at once, and kept me in Play at Sword's Point for three Hours together.—Besides, quoth *Trim*, there were two misbegotten Knaves in *Kendal Green*[2], who lay all the while in Ambush in *John*'s own House, and they all *sixteen* came upon my Back, and let drive at me together.—A Plague, says *Trim*, of all Cowards!—*Trim* repeated this Story above a Dozen Times;—which made some of the Neighbours pity him, thinking the poor Fellow crack-brain'd, and that he actually believed what he said. After this *Trim* dropp'd the Affair of the *Breeches*, and begun a fresh Dispute about the *Reading-Desk*, which I told you had occasioned some small Dispute between the *late* Parson and *John*, some Years ago.

This *Reading-Desk*, as you will observe, was but an Episode wove into the main Story by the Bye;—for the main Affair was the *Battle of the Breeches* and *Great Watch-Coat*.—— However, *Trim* being at last driven out of these two Citadels, —he has seized hold, in his Retreat, of this *Reading-Desk*, with a View, as it seems, to take Shelter behind it.

I cannot say but the Man has fought it out obstinately enough;——and, had his Cause been good, I should have really pitied him. For when he was driven out of the *Great Watch-Coat*,——you see, he did not run away;—no,—he retreated behind the *Breeches*;—and, when he could make nothing of it behind the *Breeches*,—he got behind the *Reading-Desk*.—To what other Hold[1] *Trim* will next retreat, the Politicians of this Village are not agreed.—Some think his next Move will be towards the Rear of the Parson's Boot;— but, as it is thought he cannot make a long Stand there,— others are of Opinion, That *Trim* will once more in his Life get hold of the Parson's Horse, and charge upon him, or perhaps behind him.——But as the Horse is not easy to be caught, the more general Opinion is, That, when he is driven out of the *Reading-Desk*, he will make his last Retreat in such a Manner, as, if possible, to gain the *Close-Stool*, and defend himself behind it to the very last Drop. If *Trim* should make this Movement, by my Advice he should be left besides his Citadel, in full Possession of the Field of Battle;—where, 'tis certain, he will keep every Body a League off, and may pop by himself till he is weary: Besides, as *Trim* seems bent upon *purging* himself, and may have Abundance of foul Humours to work off, I think he cannot be better placed.

But this is all Matter of Speculation.—Let me carry you back to Matter of Fact, and tell you what Kind of a Stand *Trim* has actually made behind the said *Desk*.

'Neighbours and Townsmen all, I will be sworn before my Lord Mayor, That *John* and his nineteen Men in *Buckram*, have abused me worse than a Dog; for they told you that I play'd fast and go-loose with the *late* Parson and him, in that old Dispute of theirs about the *Reading-Desk*; and that I made Matters worse between them, and not better.'

Of this Charge, *Trim* declared he was as innocent as the Child that was unborn: That he would be Book-sworn[1] he had no Hand in it. He produced a strong Witness;—and, moreover, insinuated, that *John* himself, instead of being angry for what he had done in it, had actually thank'd him. Aye, *Trim*, says the Wight in the Plush Breeches, but that was, *Trim*, the Day before *John* found thee out.—Besides, *Trim*, there is nothing in that:——For, the very Year that thou wast made Town's Pinder, thou knowest well, that I both thank'd thee myself; and, moreover, gave thee a good warm Supper for turning *John Lund*'s Cows and Horses out of my Hard-Corn Close; which if thou had'st not done, (as thou told'st me) I should have lost my whole Crop: Whereas, *John Lund* and *Thomas Patt*, who are both here to testify, and will take their Oaths on't, That thou thyself wast the very Man who set the Gate open; and, after all,—it was not thee, *Trim*,—'twas the Blacksmith's poor Lad who turn'd them out: So that a Man may be thank'd and rewarded too for a good Turn which he never did, nor ever did intend.

Trim could not sustain this unexpected Stroke;—so *Trim* march'd off the Field, without Colours flying, or his Horn sounding, or any other Ensigns of Honour whatever.

Whether after this *Trim* intends to rally a second Time, ——or whether *Trim* may not take it into his Head to claim the Victory,—no one but *Trim* himself can inform you:—However, the general Opinion, upon the whole, is this,——That, in three several pitch'd Battles, *Trim* has been so *trimm'd*,[1] as never disastrous Hero was trimm'd before him.

The KEY.

This *Romance* was, by some Mischance or other, dropp'd in the *Minster-Yard*, *York*, and pick'd up by a Member of a small Political Club[1] in that City; where it was carried, and publickly read to the Members the last Club Night.

It was instantly agreed to, by a great Majority, That it was a *Political Romance*; but concerning what State or Potentate, could not so easily be settled amongst them.

The President of the Night, who is thought to be as clear and quick-sighted as any one of the whole Club in Things of this Nature, discovered plainly, That the Disturbances therein set forth, related to those on the *Continent*:—That *Trim* could be Nobody but the King of *France*, by whose shifting and intriguing Behaviour, all *Europe* was set together by the Ears:—That *Trim*'s Wife was certainly the *Empress*, who are as kind together, says he, as any Man and Wife can be for their Lives.—The more Shame for 'em, says an Alderman, low to himself.—Agreeable to this Key, continues the President,—The *Parson*, who I think is a most excellent Character,—is His Most Excellent Majesty King *George*;——*John*, the Parish-Clerk, is the King of *Prussia*; who, by the Manner of his first entering *Saxony*, shew'd the World most evidently,—That he did know how to lead out the Psalm, and in Tune and Time too, notwithstanding *Trim*'s vile Insult upon him in that Particular.—But who do you think, says a Surgeon and Man-Midwife, who sat next him, (whose Coat-Button the President, in the Earnestness of this Explanation, had got fast hold of, and had thereby partly drawn him over to his Opinion) Who do you think, Mr. President, says he, are meant by the

Church-Wardens, Sides-Men, Mark Slender, Lorry Slim, &c.
—Who do I think? says he, Why,—Why, Sir, as I take the
Thing,——the *Church-Wardens* and *Sides-Men,* are the
Electors and the other *Princes* who form the *Germanick Body.*
—And as for the other subordinate Characters of *Mark Slim,*
—the *unlucky Wight* in the Plush Breeches,—the *Parson*'s
Man who was so often out of the Way, &c. &c.—these, to be
sure, are the several *Marshals* and *Generals,* who fought, or
should have fought, under them the last Campaign.—The
Men in *Buckram,* continued the President, are the Gross[1] of
the King of *Prussia*'s Army, who are as *stiff* a Body of Men as
are in the World:—And *Trim*'s saying they were twelve, and
then nineteen, is a Wipe[2] for the *Brussels Gazetteer,* who, to
my Knowledge, was never two Weeks in the same Story,
about that or any thing else.

As for the rest of the *Romance,* continued the President, it
sufficiently explains itself,—*The Old-cast-Pair-of-Black-
Plush-Breeches* must be *Saxony,* which the *Elector,* you see,
has left off wearing:—And as for the *Great Watch-Coat,* which,
you know, covers all, it signifies all *Europe*; comprehending,
at least, so many of its different States and Dominions, as we
have any Concern with in the present War.

I protest, says a Gentleman who sat next but one to the
President, and who, it seems, was the Parson of the Parish, a
Member not only of the Political, but also of a Musical Club
in the next Street;——I protest, says he, if this Explanation is
right, which I think it is,——That the whole makes a very fine
Symbol.—You have always some Musical Instrument or
other in your Head, I think, says the Alderman.——Musical
Instrument! replies the Parson, in Astonishment,—Mr.
Alderman, I mean an Allegory; and I think the greedy Disposition of *Trim* and his Wife, in ripping the *Great Watch-
Coat* to Pieces, in order to convert it into a Petticoat for the
one, and a Jerkin for the other, is one of the most beautiful of
the Kind I ever met with; and will shew all the World what

have been the true Views and Intentions of the Houses of *Bourbon* and *Austria* in this abominable Coalition,—I might have called it Whoredom:—Nay, says the Alderman, 'tis downright Adulterydom, or nothing.

This Hypothesis of the President's explain'd every Thing in the *Romance* extreamly well; and, withall, was delivered with so much Readiness and Air of Certainty, as begot an Opinion in two Thirds of the Club, that Mr. President was actually the Author of the *Romance* himself: But a Gentleman who sat on the opposite Side of the Table, who had come piping-hot from reading the History of King *William*'s and Queen *Anne*'s Wars, and who was thought, at the Bottom, to envy the President the Honour both of the *Romance* and Explanation too, gave an entire new Turn to it all. He acquainted the Club, That Mr. President was altogether wrong in every Supposition he had made, except that one, where the *Great Watch-Coat* was said by him to represent *Europe*, or at least a great Part of it:—So far he acknowledged he was pretty right; but that he had not gone far enough back-wards into our History to come at the Truth. He then acquainted them, that the dividing the *Great Watch-Coat* did, and could, allude to nothing else in the World but the *Partition-Treaty*[1]; which, by the Bye, he told them, was the most un-happy and scandalous Transaction in all King *William*'s Life: It was that false Step, and that only, says he, rising from his Chair, and striking his Hand upon the Table with great Violence; it was that false Step, says he, knitting his Brows and throwing his Pipe down upon the Ground, that has laid the Foundation of all the Disturbances and Sorrows we feel and lament at this very Hour; and as for *Trim*'s giving up the *Breeches*, look ye, it is almost Word for Word copied from the *French* King and *Dauphin*'s Renunciation of *Spain* and the *West-Indies*, which all the World knew (as was the very Case of the *Breeches*) were renounced by them on purpose to be reclaim'd when Time should serve.

This Explanation had too much Ingenuity in it to be altogether slighted; and, in Truth, the worst Fault it had, seem'd to be the prodigious Heat of it; which (as an Apothecary, who sat next the Fire, observ'd, in a very low Whisper to his next Neighbour) was so much incorporated into every Particle of it, that it was impossible, under such Fermentation, it should work its desired Effect.

This, however, no way intimidated a little valiant Gentleman, though he sat the very next Man, from giving an Opinion as diametrically opposite as *East* is from *West*.

This Gentleman, who was by much the best Geographer in the whole Club, and, moreover, second Cousin to an Engineer, was positive the *Breeches* meant *Gibraltar*; for, if you remember, Gentlemen, says he, tho' possibly you don't, the Ichnography[1] and Plan of that Town and Fortress, it exactly resembles a Pair of Trunk-Hose, the two Promontories forming the two Slops[2], *&c. &c.*—Now we all know, continued he, that King *George* the First made a Promise of that important Pass to the King of *Spain*:——So that the whole Drift of the *Romance*, according to my Sense of Things, is merely to vindicate the King and the Parliament in that Transaction, which made so much Noise in the World.

A Wholesale Taylor, who from the Beginning had resolved not to speak at all in the Debate,—was at last drawn into it, by something very unexpected in the last Person's Argument.

He told the Company, frankly, he did not understand what *Ichnography* meant:——But as for the Shape of a *Pair of Breeches*, as he had had the Advantage of cutting out so many hundred Pairs in his Life-Time, he hoped he might be allowed to know as much of the Matter as another Man.

Now, to my Mind, says he, there is nothing in all the Terraqueous Globe (a Map of which, it seems, hung up in his Work-Shop) so like a *Pair of Breeches* unmade up, as the Island of *Sicily*:—Nor is there any thing, if you go to that, quoth an honest Shoe-maker, who had the Honour to be a Member of the Club, so much like a *Jack-Boot*, to my Fancy, as the Kingdom of *Italy*.—What the Duce has either *Italy* or *Sicily* to do in the Affair? cries the President, who, by this Time, began to tremble for his Hypothesis,——What have they to do?—Why, answered the *Partition-Treaty* Gentleman, with great Spirit and Joy sparkling in his Eyes,—They have just so much, Sir, to do in the Debate as to overthrow your Suppositions, and to establish the Certainty of mine beyond the Possibility of a Doubt: For, says he, (with an Air of Sovereign Triumph over the President's Politicks)——By the *Partition-Treaty*, Sir, both *Naples* and *Sicily* were the very Kingdoms made to devolve upon the *Dauphin*;—and *Trim's greasing the Parson's Boots*, is a Devilish Satyrical Stroke;—for it exposes the Corruption and Bribery made Use of at that Juncture, in bringing over the several States and Princes of *Italy* to use their Interests at *Rome*, to stop the Pope from giving the Investitures of those Kingdoms to any Body else.—The Pope has not the Investiture[1] of *Sicily*, cries another Gentleman.— I care not, says he, for that.

Almost every one apprehended the Debate to be now ended, and that no one Member would venture any new Conjecture upon the *Romance*, after so many clear and decisive Interpretations had been given. But, hold,——Close to the Fire, and opposite to where the Apothecary sat, there sat also a Gentleman of the Law, who, from the Beginning to the End of the Hearing of this Cause, seem'd no way satisfied in his Conscience with any one Proceeding in it. This Gentleman had not yet opened his Mouth, but had waited patiently till they had all gone thro' their several Evidences on the other Side;—reserving himself, like an expert Practitioner, for the last Word in the Debate. When the *Partition-Treaty*-Gentleman had finish'd what he had to say,——He got up,—and, advancing towards the Table, told them, That the Error they had all gone upon thus far, in making out the several Facts in the *Romance*,—was in looking too high; which, with great

Candor, he said, was a very natural Thing, and very excusable withall, in such a Political Club as theirs: For Instance, continues he, you have been searching the *Registers*, and looking into the *Deeds* of *Kings* and *Emperors*,——as if Nobody had any *Deeds* to shew or compare the *Romance* to but themselves. ——This, continued the Attorney, is just as much out of the Way of good Practice, as if I should carry a Thing slap-dash into the House of Lords, which was under forty Shillings, and might be decided in the next County-Court for six Shillings and Eight-pence.—He then took the *Romance* in his Left Hand, and pointing with the Fore-Finger of his Right towards the second Page, he humbly begg'd Leave to observe, (and, to do him Justice, he did it in somewhat of a *forensic Air*) That the *Parson*, *John*, and *Sexton*, shewed incontestably the Thing to be *Tripartite*; now, if you will take Notice, Gentlemen, says he, these several Persons, who are Parties to this Instrument, are merely Ecclesiastical; that the *Reading-Desk*, *Pulpit-Cloth*, and *Velvet Cushion*, are tripartite too; and are, by Intendment of Law, Goods and Chattles merely of an Ecclesiastick Nature, belonging and appertaining 'only unto them,' *and to them only*. —So that it appears very plain to me, That the *Romance*, neither directly nor indirectly, goes upon Temporal, but altogether upon Church-Matters.—And do not you think, says he, softening his Voice a little, and addressing himself to the Parson with a forced Smile,——Do not you think Doctor, says he, That the Dispute in the *Romance*, between the *Parson* of the Parish and *John*, about the Height of *John*'s Desk, is a very fine Panegyrick upon the *Humility* of *Church-Men?*—— I think, says the Parson, it is much of the same Fineness with that which your Profession is complimented with, in the pimping, dirty, pettyfogging Character of *Trim*,—which, in my Opinion, Sir, is just such another Panegyrick upon the *Honesty* of *Attornies*.

Nothing whets the Spirits like an Insult:—Therefore the Parson went on with a visible Superiority and an uncommon

Acuteness.——As you are so happy, Sir, continues he, in making Applications,—pray turn over a Page or two to the black Law-Letters in the *Romance*.—What do you think of them, Sir?——Nay,—pray read the Grant of the *Great Watch-Coat*—and *Trim*'s Renunciation of the *Breeches*.— Why, there is downright **Leaſe** and **Releaſe** for you,— 'tis the very Thing, Man;——only with this small Difference, —and in which consists the whole Strength of the Panegyric, ——That the Author of the *Romance* has convey'd and re-convey'd, in about ten Lines,—what you, with the glorious Prolixity of the Law, could not have crowded into as many Skins of Parchment.

The Apothecary, who had paid the Attorney, the same Afternoon, a Demand of Three Pounds Six Shillings and Eight-Pence, for much such another Jobb,——was so highly tickled with the Parson's Repartee in that particular Point, —that he rubb'd his Hands together most fervently,—and laugh'd most triumphantly thereupon.

This could not escape the Attorney's Notice, any more than the Cause of it did escape his Penetration.

I think, Sir, says he, (dropping his Voice a Third) you might well have spared this immoderate Mirth, since you and your Profession have the least Reason to triumph here of any of us.——I beg, quoth he, that you would reflect a Moment upon the *Cob-Web* which *Trim* went so far for, and brought back with an Air of so much Importance, in his Breeches Pocket, to lay upon the Parson's cut Finger.——This said Cob-Web, Sir, is a fine-spun Satyre, upon the flimsy Nature of one Half of the Shop-Medicines, with which you make a Property of the Sick, the Ignorant, and the Unsuspecting.—— And as for the Moral of the *Close-Stool-Pan*, Sir, 'tis too plain,——Does not nine Parts in ten of the whole Practice, and of all you vend under *its Colours*, pass into and concenter in that one nasty Utensil?——And let me tell you, Sir, says he, raising his Voice,—had not your unseasonable Mirth blinded you, you might have seen that *Trim*'s carrying the Close-Stool-Pan upon his Head the whole Length of the Town, without blushing, is a pointed Raillery, —and one of the sharpest Sarcasms, Sir, that ever was thrown out upon you;—for it unveils the solemn Impudence of the whole Profession, who, I see, are ashamed of nothing which brings in Money.

There were two Apothecaries in the Club, besides the Surgeon mentioned before, with a Chemist and an Undertaker, who all felt themselves equally hurt and aggrieved by this discourteous Retort:—And they were all five rising up together from their Chairs, with full Intent of Heart, as it was thought, to return the *Reproof Valiant*[1] thereupon. —But the President, fearing it would end in a general Engagement, he instantly call'd out, *To Order*;—and gave Notice, That if there was any Member in the Club, who had not yet spoke, and yet did desire to speak upon the main Subject of the Debate, —that he should immediately be heard.

This was a happy Invitation for a stammering Member, who, it seems, had but a weak Voice at the best, and having often attempted to speak in the Debate, but to no Purpose, had sat down in utter Despair of an Opportunity.

This Member, you must know, had got a sad Crush upon his Hip, in the late *Election*, which gave him intolerable Anguish;—so that, in short, he could think of nothing else: For which Cause, and others, he was strongly of Opinion, That the whole *Romance* was a just Gird at the late *York* Election; and I think, says he, that the *Promise* of the *Breeches* broke, may well and truly signify *Somebody's else Promise* which was broke, and occasion'd so much Disturbance amongst us.

——Thus every Man turn'd the Story to what was swimming uppermost in his own Brain; so that, before all was over, there were full as many Satyres spun out of it, —and as great a Variety of Personages, Opinions, Transactions, and

Truths, found to lay hid under the dark Veil of its Allegory, as ever were discovered in the thrice-renowned History of the Acts of *Gargantua* and *Pantagruel*.

At the Close of all, and just before the Club was going to break up,—Mr. President rose from his Chair, and begg'd Leave to make the two following Motions, which were instantly agreed to, without any Division.

First, Gentlemen, says he, as *Trim*'s Character in the *Romance*, of a shuffling intriguing Fellow,—whoever it was drawn for, is, in Truth, as like the *French King* as it can stare, --—I move, That the *Romance* be forthwith *printed*:—For, continues he, if we can but once turn the Laugh against him, and make him asham'd of what he has done, it may be a great Means, with the Blessing of God upon our Fleets and Armies, to save the Liberties of *Europe*.

In the *second* Place, I move, That Mr. Attorney, our worthy Member, be desired to take Minutes, upon the Spot, of every Conjecture which has been made upon the *Romance*, by the several Members who have spoke; which, I think, says he, will answer two good Ends:

1*st*, It will establish the Political Knowledge of our Club for ever, and place it in a respectable Light to all the World.

In the *next* Place, it will furnish what will be wanted; that is, a *Key* to the *Romance*.——In troth you might have said a whole Bunch of *Keys*, quoth a Whitesmith[1], who was the only Member in the Club who had not said something in the Debate: But let me tell you, Mr. President, says he, That the *Right Key*, if it could but be found, would be worth the whole Bunch put together.

$$To \text{———} \text{———}, Esq;$$
$$of \text{ YORK.}^{1}$$

SIR,

YOU write me Word that the Letter I wrote to you, and now stiled *The Political Romance* is printing; and that, as it was drop'd by Carelessness, to make some Amends, you will overlook the Printing of it yourself, and take Care to see that it comes right into the World.

I was just going to return you Thanks, and to beg, withal, you would take Care That the Child be not laid at my Door.—But having, this Moment, perused the *Reply* to the *Dean* of *York*'s *Answer*,—it has made me alter my Mind in that respect; so that, instead of making you the Request I intended, I do here desire That the Child be filiated upon me, *Laurence Sterne*, Prebendary of *York*, &c. &c. And I do, accordingly, own it for my own true and lawful Offspring.

My Reason for this is plain;——for as, you see, the *Writer* of that *Reply*, has taken upon him to invade this *incontested Right* of another Man's in a Thing of this Kind, it is high Time for every Man to look to his own—Since, upon the *same Grounds*, and with half the Degree of Anger, that he affirms the Production of that very Reverend Gentleman's, to be the Child of many Fathers, some one in his Spight (for I am not without my Friends of that Stamp) may run headlong into the other Extream, and swear, That mine had no Father at all:—And therefore, to make use of *Bays*'s Plea in the *Rehearsal*², for *Prince Pretty-Man*; I merely do it, as he says, 'for fear it should be said to be no Body's Child at all.'

I have only to add two Things:—First, That, at your Peril, you do not presume to alter or transpose one Word, nor rectify one false Spelling, nor so much as add or diminish one Comma or Tittle, in or to my *Romance*:—For if you do, —In case any of the Descendents of *Curl* should think fit to invade my Copy-Right, and print it over again in my Teeth, I may not be able, in a Court of Justice, to swear strictly to my own Child, after you had *so large a Share* in the begetting it.

In the next Place, I do not approve of your *quaint Conceit*[1] at the Foot of the Title Page of my *Romance*,——It would only set People on smiling a Page or two before I give them Leave;—and besides, all Attempts either at Wit or Humour, in that Place, are a Forestalling of what slender Entertainment of those Kinds are prepared within: Therefore I would have it stand thus:

YORK:

Printed in the Year 1759.

(*Price One Shilling.*)

I know you will tell me, That it is set too high; and as a Proof, you will say, That this last *Reply* to the *Dean's Answer* does consist of near as many Pages as mine; and yet is all sold for Six-pence.——But mine, my dear Friend, is quite a *different Story:*—It is a Web wrought out of my own Brain, of twice the Fineness of this which he has spun out of his; and besides, I maintain it, it is of a more curious Pattern, and could not be afforded at the Price that his is sold at, by any *honest* Workman in *Great-Britain*.

Moreover, Sir, you do not consider, That the Writer is interested in his *Story*, and that it is his Business to set it a-going at *any Price:* And indeed, from the Information of Persons conversant in Paper and Print, I have very good Reason to believe, if he should sell every Pamphlet of them, he would inevitably be a *Great Loser* by it. This I believe verily, and am,

Dear Sir,

Your obliged Friend

Sutton on the Forest,
Jan. 20, 1759.

and humble Servant,

LAURENCE STERNE.

To Dr. TOPHAM.

SIR,

THOUGH the *Reply* to the *Dean* of *York* is not declared, in the *Title-Page*, or elsewhere, to be wrote by you,—Yet I take that Point for granted; and therefore beg Leave, in this public Manner, to write to you in Behalf of myself; with Intent to set you right in two Points where I stand concerned in this Affair; and which I find you have misapprehended, and consequently (as I hope) misrepresented.

The *First* is, in respect of some Words, made use of in the Instrument, signed by Dr. *Herring*, Mr. *Berdmore*[1] and myself. —Namely, *to the best of our Remembrance and Belief*, which Words you have caught hold of, as implying some Abatement of our Certainty as to the Facts therein attested. Whether it was so with the other two Gentlemen who signed that Attestation with me, it is not for me to say; they are able to answer for themselves, and I desire to do so for myself; and therefore I declare to you, and to all Mankind, 'That the Words in the first Paragraph, *to the best of our Remembrance and Belief*, implied no Doubt remaining upon my Mind, nor any Distrust whatever of my Memory, from the Distance of Time;—Nor, in short, was it my Intention to attest the several Facts therein, as Matters of Belief——But as Matters of as much Certainty as a Man was capable of having, or giving Evidence to. In Consequence of this Explanation of myself, I do declare myself ready to attest the same Instrument over again, striking out the Words *to the best of our Remembrance and Belief*, which I see, have raised this Exception to it.

Whether I was mistaken or no, I leave to better Judges; but I understood those Words were a very common Preamble to Attestations of Things, to which we bore the clearest Evidence:——However, Dr. *Topham*, as you have claimed just such another Indulgence yourself, in the Case of begging the *Dean*'s Authority to say, what, as you affirm, you had sufficient Authority to say without, as a modest and Gentleman-like Way of Affirmation;—I wish you had spared either the one or the other of your Remarks upon these two Passages:

——*Veniam petimus, demusque vicissim.*[1]

There is another Observation relating to this Instrument, which I perceive has escaped your Notice; which I take the Liberty to point out to you, namely, That the Words, *To the best of our Remembrance and Belief*, if they imply any Abatement of Certainty, seem only confined to that Paragraph, and to what is immediately attested after them in it:—For in the second Paragraph, wherein the main Points are minutely attested, and upon which the whole Dispute, and main Charge against the *Dean*, turns, it is introduced thus: '*We do particularly remember*, That as soon as Dinner was over, *&c.*'

In the second Place you affirm, 'That it is not said, That Mr. *Sterne* could affirm he had heard you charge the *Dean* with a Promise, in its own Nature so very extraordinary, as of the Commissaryship of the Dean and Chapter:'——To this I answer, That my true Intent in subscribing that very Instrument, and I suppose of others, was to attest this *very Thing*; and I have just now read that Part of the Instrument over; and cannot, for my Life, affirm it either more directly or expresly, than in the Words as they there stand;——therefore please to let me transcribe them.

——'But being press'd by Mr. *Sterne* with an undeniable Proof, That he, (Dr. *Topham*) did propagate the said Story, (viz. *of a Promise from the Dean to Dr.* Topham *of the Dean and Chapter's Commissaryship*)—Dr. *Topham* did at last acknowledge it; adding, as his Reason or Excuse for so doing, That he apprehended (or Words to that Effect) he had a *Promise* under the *Dean's own Hand*, of the *Dean and Chapter's Commissaryship.*'

This I have attested, and what Weight the Sanction of an Oath will add to it, I am willing and ready to give.

As for Mr. *Ricard's*[1] feeble Attestation, brought to shake the Credit of this firm and solemn one, I have nothing to say to it, as it is only an Attestation of Mr *Ricard's* Conjectures upon the Subject.—But this I can say, That I had the Honour to be at the Deanery with the learned Counsel, when Mr. *Ricard* underwent that *most formidable* Examination you speak of;——and I solemnly affirm, That he then said, He knew nothing at all about the Matter, one Way or the other; and the Reasons he gave for his utter Ignorance, were, first, That he was then so full of Concern, at the Difference which arose between two Gentlemen, both his Friends, that he did not attend to the Subject Matter of it,——and of which he declared again he knew nothing at all. And secondly, If he had understood it then, the Distance would have put it out of his Head by this Time.

He has since scower'd his Memory, I ween; for now he says, That he apprehended the Dispute regarded something in the Dean's Gift, as he could not *naturally* suppose, *&c.* 'Tis certain, at the Deanery, he had *naturally* no Suppositions in his Head about this Affair; so that I wish this may not prove one of the After-Thoughts you speak of, and not so much a *natural* as an *artificial* Supposition of my good Friend's.

As for the *formidable* Enquiry you represent him as undergoing,—let me intreat you to give me Credit in what I say upon it,——namely,——That it was as much the Reverse to every Idea that ever was couch'd under that Word, as Words can represent it to you. As for the learned Counsel and myself, who were in the Room all the Time, I do not remember that we, either of us, spoke ten Words. The Dean was the only one that ask'd Mr. *Ricard* what he remembered about the Affair of the Sessions Dinner; which he did in the most Gentleman-like and candid Manner,—and with an Air of as much Calmness and seeming Indifference, as if he had been questioning him about the News in the last *Brussels Gazette*.

What Mr. *Ricard* saw to terrify him so sadly, I cannot apprehend, unless the Dean's *Gothic* Book-Case,—which I own has an odd Appearance to a Stranger; so that if he came terrified in his Mind there, and with a Resolution not to *plead*, he might *naturally suppose* it to be a great Engine brought there on purpose to exercise the *Peine fort et dure*[1] upon him. ——But to be serious; if Mr. *Ricard* told you, That this Enquiry was *most formidable*, *He* was much to blame;—and if you have said it, without his express Information, then *You* are much to blame.

This is all, I think, in your *Reply*, which concerns me to answer:—As for the many coarse and unchristian Insinuations scatter'd throughout your *Reply*,—as it is my Duty to beg God to forgive you, so I do from my Heart: Believe me, Dr. *Topham*, they hurt yourself more than the Person they are aimed at; and when the *first Transport* of Rage is a little over, they will grieve you more too.

————*prima est hæc Ultio*.[2]

But these I hold to be no answerable Part of a Controversy;—and for the little that remains unanswered in yours,—I believe I could, in another half Hour, set it right in the Eyes of the World:——But this is not my Business.——And if it is thought worth the while, which I hope it never will, I know no one more able to do it than the very Reverend and Worthy Gentleman whom you have so unhandsomely insulted upon that Score.

As for the *supposed Compilers*, whom you have been so wrath and so unmerciful against, I'll be answerable for it, as they are Creatures of your own Fancy, they will bear you no Malice. However, I think the more positively any Charge is made, let it be against whom it will, the better it should be supported; and therefore I should be sorry, for your own Honour, if you have not some better Grounds for all you have thrown out about them, than the mere Heat of your Imagination or Anger. To tell you truly, your Suppositions on this Head oft put me in Mind of *Trim*'s twelve Men in *Buckram*, which his disordered Fancy represented as laying in Ambush in *John* the Clerk's House, and letting drive at him all together. I am,

SIR,

Your most obedient

Sutton on the Forest, }
Jan. 20, 1759. }

And most humble Servant,

LAWRENCE STERNE.

P.S. I beg Pardon for *clapping* this upon the *Back* of the *Romance,*—which is done out of no Disrespect to you.—But the *Vehicle* stood ready at the Door,—and as I was to pay the whole Fare, and there was Room enough behind it,—it was the cheapest and readiest Conveyance I could think of.

FINIS.

EXPLANATORY NOTES

Abbreviations

Letters   *Letters of Laurence Sterne*, edited by Lewis Perry Curtis (Oxford, 1935)

Life and   *The Life and Times of Laurence Sterne*, by Wilbur L. Cross
Times   (third edition, New Haven and London, 1929)

Work   *The Life and Opinions of Tristram Shandy, Gentleman*, edited by James Aiken Work (Odyssey Press, New York, 1940)

A SENTIMENTAL JOURNEY

VOLUME I

Page 3. (1) *this matter*: 'The subject in debate was the inconvenience of drinking healths whilst at meal, and toasts afterwards': *Yorick's Sentimental Journey Continued . . . By Eugenius* (1769), in the section 'The Post-Chaise'. While it is now considered unlikely that this inferior continuation is by John Hall-Stevenson, its explanation of the opening of Sterne's book seems convincing. See my letter in *TLS*, 4 Feb. 1977, p. 131.

(2) *my gentleman*: my manservant.

(3) note: i.e. such goods go by right to a person who pays a regular sum in return for the privilege. Cf. note on p. 110, below.

Page 4. (1) *for the accommodation*: as a result of settling the matter (in my own mind).

(2) *physical precieuse*: a lady with pretensions to being a (materialistic) philosopher.

Page 5. (1) *puissant*: potent.

(2) *Guido*: Guido Reni (1574-1642) specialized in religious painting of a melodramatic and sentimental type. Keats compares his painting to the portrayal of Father Nicholas in an essay by Henry Mackenzie, the author of *The Man of Feeling* (*Letters of John Keats*, ed. H. E. Rollins, ii. 19).

Page 6. (1) *a Bramin*: a Brahmin is a member of the highest or priestly caste among the Hindus. Cf. p. 130, above.

(2) *the attitude of Intreaty*: Sterne was keenly interested in painting, and in the attitudes conventionally associated with the various passions.

Page 7. the order of St. Francis: the Franciscans are a mendicant Order.

Page 9. a peripatetic philosopher: the phrase is normally used to describe the followers of Aristotle. Sterne himself is a 'peripatetic philosopher' in the sense that he travels about and makes philosophic observations.

Page 10. *with the benefit of the clergy*: accompanied by clerical tutors, as was common for young 'milords' on the Grand Tour. Sterne is glancing humorously at the usual meaning of the phrase 'benefit of clergy'— exemption from the jurisdiction of the ordinary courts of law.

Page 11. *Idle Traveller*: Sterne may mean 'Idle Travellers' as a general category which includes 'Inquisitive Travellers', 'Lying Travellers', etc., just as 'the Travellers of Necessity' is a general category which includes 'The delinquent and felonious Traveller', etc.

Page 12. (1) *by discovering his nakedness*: possibly a reminiscence of the drunkenness of Noah: Genesis 9: 20-23.

(2) *as Sancho Pança said to Don Quixote*: In fact he was speaking to his wife. See *Don Quixote*, trans. Motteux (rev. Ozell), Part II, ch. v ('Of the wise and pleasant Discourse which passed between Sancho Panza and his Wife . . .').

Page 13. *where art is encouraged, and will so soon rise high*: the Royal Academy was founded in the year in which *A Sentimental Journey* was published.

(2) *effectually*: *en effet*, in fact.

Page 14. *Remise*: coach-house. On p. 74 below, however, 'remise' means a hired carriage.

Page 17. (1) *as if she had dived into the Tiber for it*: Sterne must have heard a good deal about archaeological discoveries in the Tiber and elsewhere when he was in Italy in 1766. In Naples he was kindly treated by the Hon. William Hamilton, who was a passionate collector.

(2) *as in the days of Esdras*: 2 Esdras 10: 31 (Apocrypha). Cf. Psalms 42: 5.

Page 23. *tartufish*: hypocritical: a reference to *Le Tartuffe* (1664), by Molière.

Page 28. (1) *from Dan to Beersheba*: cf. Judges 20: 1 and other Biblical texts.

(2) *SMELFUNGUS*: cf. Introduction, pp. xii-xiii.

Page 29. (1) *of moving accidents . . . Anthropophagi*: *Othello*, I. iii. 134 ff.

(2) *Mundungus*: traditionally, Dr. Samuel Sharp, whose *Letters from Italy* were published in 1766.

(3) note: *Travels through France and Italy* (1766), Letter no. xxxi.

Page 30. (1) *Mad^lle Janatone*: cf. *Tristram Shandy*, VII. ix.

(2) *Mr. H——*: John Home the poet, celebrated in his day for the tragedy of *Douglas* (1756), and David Hume, the philosopher and historian. As their names were pronounced in the same way, the two men were frequently confused.

Page 31. *the mood I am in . . . the person I am to govern*: Sterne is here playing with the terminology of grammar.

Page 32. *spatterdashes*: long gaiters or leggings worn in riding, to keep the trousers or stockings from being spattered.

Page 33. *complexional*: constitutional.

Page 34. (1) *I was making not so much La Fleur's eloge, as my own*: I was not so much praising La Fleur, as myself. (The word 'eloge' occurs occasionally in English in the eighteenth century).

(2) A FRAGMENT: Sterne took the idea of 'A Fragment' from Burton's *Anatomy of Melancholy*, Pt. 3, Sect. 2, Mem. 2, Subs. 4. Burton's source was Lucian's letter, 'How to Write History'.

(3) *the Andromeda of Euripides*: only fragments of the play have survived.

(4) *the whole orchestra*: the 'orchestra' in a Greek theatre was the semicircular space in front of the stage, where the chorus danced and sang. In the Roman theatre seats in the orchestra were reserved for senators and other people of distinction.

Page 36. *the whole parterre*: the whole audience in the pit of a theatre.

Page 38. *doublets*: throwing the same number with both dice.

Page 40. (1) *Sancho's lamentation*: *Don Quixote*, Part I, Book III, ch. ix. ('Of what befel Don Quixote in the Sierra Morena . . .').

(2) *pannel*: a piece of cloth placed under the saddle to prevent the horse's back from being galled.

Page 42. *the clue*: the thread (the original sense of the word).

Page 43. (1) *from what* penchant *she had not considered*: the meaning seems to be that her inclination (to the author) had prevented her from telling him her story.

(2) *reprobate*: severe, appropriate to reprobates.

Page 45. (1) *hôtel*: town house.

(2) *prevenancy*: disposition to be obliging. The French form of the word, 'prevenance', occasionally occurs in eighteenth-century English.

Page 46. *fob*: a small pocket in the waistband of a pair of breeches, for carrying a watch or other valuables.

Page 47. *L'amour n'est rien sans sentiment*: 'I am glad that you are in love', Sterne wrote to a friend one day in 1765: '—'twill cure you (at least) of the spleen. . . . I myself must ever have some dulcinea in my head—it harmonises the soul . . . but I carry on my affairs quite in the French way, sentimentally—"*L'amour* (say they) *n'est rien sans sentiment*" . . . .' *Letters*, p. 256.

Page 48. *running at the ring of pleasure*: running at the ring is a sport of medieval origin in which a number of riders compete to carry off a circle of metal suspended from a post. Cf. *Letters*, p. 294.

Page 49. (1) *tourniquet*: turnstile.

(2) *grisset*: a working girl of easy virtue. The French spelling is of course *grisette*.

Page 52. *temperature*: temperament.

Page 53. *Eugenius*: John Hall-Stevenson (1718-85), the Eugenius of *Tristram Shandy*, Sterne's close friend and the leader of the 'Demoniacs', who gathered at his house, Skelton Castle, to talk, drink, and look into the curious collection of books in the library.

Page 54. (1) *thrum*: made of waste threads of yarn, or of very coarse material.

(2) *salique*: the salic law was the law by which succession to the French crown was barred to women.

(3) *it is not good for thee to sit alone*: 'And the LORD God said, It is not good that the man should be alone; I will make him an help meet for him': Genesis 2: 18.

Page 55. *reins*: the seat of the feelings or affections (Biblical).

Page 56. *THE TRANSLATION*: the 'translation' of the language of gestures and the nuances of behaviour is referred to. The Traveller has gone to the Opera.

Page 57. (1) *Martini's concert*: Giovanni Battista Martini (1706-84) was one of the most prominent musicians of the time.

(2) *the Marquesina di F****: Wilbur Cross's identification of the lady as the Marchesa Fagniani (*Life and Times*, p. 400) is now seriously questioned.

Page 58. (1) *chicheshee: cavaliere servente*.

(2) *parterre*: pit.

Page 59. *Mr. Shandy the elder*: the views of Mr. Walter Shandy on the begetting, rearing, and education of children form one of the main comic themes of *Tristram Shandy*.

Page 61. *queue*: pigtail.

Page 62. *loges*: boxes, seats.

Page 63. (1) *Madame de Rambouliet*: Sterne mischievously uses the name of the celebrated Marquise de Rambouillet in this story—the hostess of the celebrated seventeenth-century *salon* where men like Malesherbes, Voiture, and La Rochefoucauld were in the habit of meeting. The ladies of this circle came to be known as the 'précieuses'.

(2) *CASTALIA*: a fountain of Parnassus sacred to the Muses.

VOLUME II

Page 64. Les Égarements du Cœur & de l'Esprit: by Claude-Prosper Jolyot de Crébillon ('Crébillon fils'), a tale of amorous adventure spiced with social satire and literary criticism (1736). Crébillon proposed to Sterne that each of them should write a pamphlet expostulating on the indecorums in the work of the other, and that the two pamphlets should be published together as a joke (*Letters*, p. 162). No such pamphlets are known.

Page 68. (1) *we were at war with France*: Sterne left London for Paris during the first week of 1762, while war was still going on between England and France. A preliminary peace treaty was signed on 3 November, and then the definitive treaty on 10 February 1763. Two letters refer to Sterne's waiting on Count Choiseul to solicit passports for his wife and daughter (*Letters*, pp. 163–4).

(2) *the packet*: packet-boat.

Page 71. (1) *the sombre pencil!*: dark colours (a reference to the terminology of art criticism).

(2) *the starling*: 'The more learned of the family evidently associated their name with the old English word *stearn*, dialectal *starn* to this day, signifying a *starling*; for as soon as they rose to rank and wealth, their arms appeared, with some variation, as "gold, a chevron engrailed between three crosses flory sable, surmounted with a starling in proper colours for a crest". That starling, made captive, . . . was long afterwards brought into the *Sentimental Journey* as the motif for a pathetic discourse on the bitterness of slavery': *Life and Times*, pp. 2–3.

Page 73. (1) *hope deferr'd*: Proverbs 13 : 12.

(2) *the iron enter into his soul*: Psalm 105 : 18 (Psalter version).

(3) *remise*: a carriage. Cf. note on p. 14 above.

Page 75. to get in: to get on socially, climb the social ladder.

Page 76. (1) *the field . . . the cabinet*: the field of battle and the cabinet where political and other business is transacted. Cf. *Tristram Shandy*, III. xxv, para 1.

(2) *succours*: safety (?)

Page 77. to meet it: i.e. life.

Page 78. hotels: town houses (as on p. 54).

Page 81. the mounting: equipment, or here perhaps in general the expenses of keeping up the station of a man of honour.

Pages 85-6. (1) '*He could not bear . . . sermons wrote by the king of Denmark's jester*': the same objection was made by the *Monthly Review* (*Life and Times*, pp. 238-9).

(2) *Horwendillus*: in the *Historia Danica* of Saxo Grammaticus, Horwendillus, King of Denmark, is the father of Amlethus, Shakespeare's Hamlet. Cf. *Tristram Shandy*, I. xi (*Work*, p. 24).

(3) *Alexander the Great*: cf. *Hamlet*, v. i. 218.

(4) *translated*: a bishop is translated from one see to another.

Page 87. (1) *the elysian fields*: *Aeneid* vi. 635.

(2) *walking in a vain shadow*: Psalm 39: 6 (adapted).

(3) *beating up . . . for some kindly and gentle sensation*: 'to beat up for recruits' (or game) was a common phrase in the eighteenth century.

Page 88. *Bevoriskius*: Johan van Beverwyck (or Beverovicius), the Dutch theologian.

Page 93. *hussive*: a pocket-case for needle and thread, etc.

Page 97. (1) *cullibility*: this form of the word is also to be found in Swift (*Correspondence*, ed. Sherburn, iii, p. 294).

(2) *If I had not had more than four Louis d'ors . . .*: even if I had only had four louis d'or, I could not have sent her away until I had given her three of them.

Page 98. *took away*: cleared away the supper-things.

Page 99. *the king of Babylon*: for Nebuchadnezzar's dreams see Daniel 2.

Page 100. *a new bag and a solitaire*: a bag was a small silk pouch to contain the back hair of a wig, a solitaire a ring with a single stone (perhaps here over the neck of the bag). Cf. p. 112 below.

Page 101. (1) *Behold, I am thy servant*: 2 Samuel 9: 6.

(2) *print of butter*: pat of butter (moulded to a shape).

Page 102. (1) *I at it again*: i.e. I went at it again.

(2) *Gruter or Jacob Spon*: Jan Gruter or Gruytère published *Inscriptiones antiquae totius orbis Romanorum* in 1603. Jacques Spon, the French archaeologist, was a pioneer in the study of Greek monuments and antiquities.

Page 103. (1) *a little fume of a woman*: i.e. a woman who readily got into a 'fume' or fury.

(2) *garde d'eau*: the warning called out from upper windows before pouring out the slops, in France and in Edinburgh.

Page 104. (1) *being a gascon*: Gascons were famous braggarts. A harquebus was a type of heavy portable gun which rested on a tripod.

(2) *castor*: a hat made of beaver or other fur.

(3) *pontific*: pertaining to a bridge (a facetious use of the word).

Page 105. *bandoleer*: a broad belt, worn over the shoulder and across the breast.

Page 107. *Capadosia, Pontus and Asia*: Acts 2: 9-10.

Page 109. *concentre*: concentrate.

Page 110. *farmer-general*: Alexandre-Jean-Joseph le Riche de la Popelinière, the wealthy tax-collector who entertained Sterne in 1762 (Arthur Cash). 'Mons. D***' is presumably Diderot.

Page 111. *the door of my lips*: perhaps a humorous reminiscence of the Homeric phrase ἕρκος ὀδόντων, the barrier of the teeth.

Page 112. (1) *their Encyclopedia*: the *Encyclopédie* of Diderot and others. 'The Abbe M——' is presumably l'Abbé André Morellet (1727-1819), one of the few churchmen to contribute largely to the *Encyclopédie*.

(2) *the young Count de Faineant*: the literal meaning of the name is 'Do-Nothing', 'Idler'.

(3) *solitaire*: ring used for the neck-tie. Cf. note to p. 100 above.

Page 113. (1) *poor Maria*: *Tristram Shandy*, vol. ix, ch. 24.

(2) *the Knight of the Woeful Countenance*: Don Quixote.

Page 115. *God tempers the wind*: Sterne's felicitous translation of the French proverb, '*Dieu mesure le froid à la brebis tondue*'. George Herbert's earlier version is much less striking: 'To a close-shorn sheep, God gives wind by measure' (*Outlandish Proverbs*, no. 867).

Page 116. *eat of my bread*: cf. 2 Samuel 9: 7.

Page 117. '*my soul shrinks back . . .*': Addison's *Cato*, v. i. 5-7. This soliloquy was well known throughout the century. Boswell repeated it by heart when he first came in sight of London: *James Boswell: The Earlier Years: 1740-1769*, by Frederick A. Pottle (1966), p. 96.

Page 118. *thill-horse*: the horse between the shafts which is drawing the chaise.

Page 119. *the vielle*: 'a musical instrument with four strings played by means of a small wheel; a hurdy-gurdy' (O.E.D.).

As the title-page makes clear, Sterne originally intended to take his traveller from France to Italy, perhaps producing a work in four volumes (*Letters*, p. 284). He was prevented by death.

THE JOURNAL TO ELIZA

Page 135. (1) *April 13*: as Curtis points out, Sunday fell on 12 April. The other entries for the week are also one day in advance.

(2) *Hall*: John Hall-Stevenson, on whom see note to page 53, above. He and his friends called themselves the 'Demoniacs', in imitation of the Rabelaisian Monks of Medmenham Abbey.

Page 136. (1) *Mrs James*: William James retired in 1759, after a most distinguished career in the East India Company. His London residence consisted of two adjoining houses on the south side of Gerrard Street, Soho. His wife, Anne Goddard, was a charming and sentimental lady well known as a hostess to the 'Anglo-Indians' of the time. To Sterne she proved a most kindly friend.

(2) *James's Powder*: a popular medicine, invented by a certain Dr. Robert James, which induced plentiful sweating. See *Notes and Queries*, 18 January 1941.

Page 138. (1) *Orm's account of India*: Robert Orme, *History of the Military Transactions of the British Nation in Indostan* (1763-78).

(2) Here and elsewhere in the *Journal* Sterne made a cross (x), no doubt for a kiss.

Page 139. *Corporal Trim's uneasy night*: *Tristram Shandy*, vol. viii, ch. xx.

Page 140. *the Newnhams*: as may be seen from the list of Subscribers to the first edition of *A Sentimental Journey*, 'the Newnhams' rallied round on that occasion, at least. They were a well-to-do family with strong commercial interests.

Page 143. *Gotham*: a village proverbial for the folly of its inhabitants. 'The wise men of Gotham' = fools.

Page 148. *Sheba*: uncertain: perhaps Lady Warkworth. As Curtis points out, Sterne had compared Mrs. Vesey to the Queen of Sheba some years previously (Letter 76).

Page 149. Job 2: 4.

Page 152. (1) *Soho Con[c]ert*: in the 1760s and '70s Mme Cornelys organized a fashionable Rout at Carlisle House, Soho. Apart from such entertainments as dancing and card-playing, there were concerts which were organized by J. C. Bach and Abel, the son and pupil respectively of Johann Sebastian Bach. Habitués included Sheridan, Garrick, Gainsborough, and Sir Joshua Reynolds—but not Samuel Johnson, who is reported to have asked: 'Pray, sir, who is this Bach? Is he a piper?'

Page 153. (1) *Lord and Lady Bellasis*: Henry, Lord Bellasis and his wife: Sterne knew a number of members of the family. Cf. note (1) to page 165 below.

(2) *Lady Spencer*: the wife of John Spencer (1734-83), created Baron Spencer of Althorp and Viscount Spencer of Althorp in 1761. Lord Spencer was a celebrated book-collector. Sterne dedicated to him the 5th and 6th volumes of *Tristram Shandy*, and to his wife the story of Le Fever.

(3) *Ranalagh*: Ranelagh was famous for its masquerades and concerts.

Page 155. *remember thee!*: *Hamlet*, I. v. 95-99.

Page 156. *as my uncle Toby did*: *Tristram Shandy*, vol. VIII. vi.

Page 163. *Cosway*: Richard Cosway (1740-1821).

Page 165. (1) *Lord ffauconberg's*: Thomas Belasyse (1699–1774), first Earl Fauconberg of Newburgh. He had presented Sterne to the perpetual curacy of Coxwold in March 1760. He had a famous house in George Street, Hanover Square.

(2) *so Crawford's like*: no doubt a reference to John Craufurd, a well-known wit and eccentric of the time. Craufurd was a generous man, who subscribed to vols. iii and iv of Sterne's *Sermons*, and told him the anecdote which became the basis of 'The Case of Delicacy' in *A Sentimental Journey*.

Page 167. *This last Sheet*: i.e. the prophecy that Sterne and Eliza would become free to marry.

Page 169. (1) *here*: at Skelton.

(2) *Bombay-Lascelles*: Peter Lascelles made three voyages to Bombay as Captain of the *York*, before retiring in August 1766. He was closely associated with William James as a director of the East India Company. 'Poor sorry soul' or not, he subscribed to *A Sentimental Journey*.

Page 173. *Dillon*: John Talbot Dillon (1734-1806).

Page 180. *Behold the Woman . . .*: cf. Genesis 3: 12.

Page 183. *M*r *Turner's*: Charles Turner (?1726-83), once described as 'one of the most eccentric men who ever sat in parliament', was none the less a man of parts with an expert knowledge of agriculture.

Page 184. (1) *our Archbishop*: Robert Hay Drummond (1711-76), Archbishop of York, was celebrated for his good manners, his liberality of mind, and his hospitality to his friends.

(2) *a Chamber in the Wall*: 2 Kings 4: 10.

Page 185. (1) *Iago*: i.e. Santiago.

(2) *Ill love thee . . .*: *Othello*. I. iii. 167.

Page 186. *The Bishop of Cork and Ross*: Dr. Jemmett Browne (? 1703–82), once described by Mrs. Elizabeth Carter as a 'perfectly anti-sublime . . . dignitary'. In September he was to entertain Sterne at Scarborough.

Page 187. (1) *but I will not*: in letter 224, as Curtis points out, Sterne reworked this passage and substituted his daughter Lydia for Eliza Draper.

(2) *August 4*: Sterne knew that his wife and daughter were not due for a further month: in fact they did not arrive until the end of September.

A POLITICAL ROMANCE

Page 189. Title-page motto: Horace, *Satires*, I. x. 14–15.

Page 197. (1) *Fending and Proving*: argument, wrangling.

(2) *Breeches*: the Commissaryship of the Peculiar Court of Pickering and Pocklington.

Page 201. *ambidextrous*: double-dealing.

Page 203. *call*: invoke.

Page 205. (1) *John's Desk*: cf. Boileau's mock-heroic poem, *Le Lutrin* ('The Lectern'). For a quarrel between Archbishop Hutton and Dr. Fountayne about the key to the cathedral pulpit see *Life and Times*, p. 176.

(2) *to make his Market*: to do some bargaining.

(3) *a good creditable cast Coat*: Dr. Topham had just secured the patent of the Prerogative Courts at York.

Page 206. *Dr. Mark Slender*: Mark Braithwaite, who enjoyed the fees of the Commissaryship of the Peculiar Court of Pickering and Pocklington and of the Commissaryship of the Dean and Chapter of York during the incapacity through illness of Dr. Ward.

Page 207. (1) *William Doe*: William Stables, who was appointed to the Commissaryship of the Dean and Chapter on the death of Dr. Ward.

(2) *Long Slim*: Laurence Sterne, who was appointed Commissary of the Peculiar Court of Pickering and Pocklington about the same time.

(3) *the Pulpit-Cloth and Velvet Cushion*: the Commissaryship of the Dean and Chapter of York.

Page 208. (1) *The Pinder's Place*: a pinder was 'an officer of a manor, having the duty of impounding stray beasts' (O.E.D.).

(2) *CONIES*: rabbits. The old woman is thinking of the slang use of the word for gullible people (or, conceivably, young girls).

Page 210. (1) *a Sow-Gelder's Horn*: cf. *Hudibras*, I. ii. 537–8:

> No *Sow-gelder* did blow his Horn
> To geld a Cat, but cry'd *Reform*.

(2) *Knaves in Kendal Green*: as with Falstaff: cf. *1 Henry IV*, II. iv. 189 ff.

Page 211. *Hold*: stronghold, place of refuge.

Page 212. *Book-sworn*: sworn on the Bible.

Page 213. *trimm'd*: beaten, thrashed, trounced.

Page 214. *a small Political Club*: cf. the 'Grand Committee' which recommends the writing of *A Tale of a Tub*. This 'KEY' was probably suggested by Pope's 'A Key to the Lock'.

Page 215. (1) *the Gross*: the body.
   (2) *a Wipe*: a hit at.

Page 216. *the Partition-Treaty*: there were in fact two treaties (dated 11 October 1698 and 11 October 1700) which attempted to settle the complicated question of the Spanish Succession on the death of the King, Charles II.

Page 217. (1) *Ichnography*: ground-plan, horizontal section.
   (2) *Slops*: legs.

Page 218. *Investiture*: 'a conveyance of the fee-simple, right, or interest in lands or tenements, . . . giving first the possession, and afterwards the interest in the estate conveyed' (O.E.D.).

Page 221. *the Reproof Valiant*: *As You Like It*, V. iv. 92.

Page 222. *a Whitesmith*: a locksmith and worker in metals.

Page 223. (1) *Heading*: probably addressed to Caesar Ward, who printed *A Political Romance*: see *Letters*, pp. 67-9.
   (2) *the Rehearsal*: *The Rehearsal* (1672), by the Duke of Buckingham and others.

Page 224. *your quaint Conceit*: perhaps a reference to the little vignette of two fighting cocks subsequently set at the end of the text of *A Political Romance*.

Page 226. *Dr. Herring; Mr. Berdmore*: Dr. William Herring, Chancellor of York, and William Berdmore, one of the two resident canons.

Page 227. *—Veniam petimus . . .*: Horace, *Ars Poetica*, line 11 (misquoted).

Page 228. *Mr. Ricard*: Arthur Ricard, father and son, were attorneys at York.

Page 229. *the Peine fort et dure*: pressing to death (a punishment inflicted on felons who refused to plead).
   (2) *—prima est hæc Ultio*: Juvenal, *Satires*, xiii. 2.

THE WORLD'S CLASSICS

A Select List

VIRGIL: The Aeneid
Translated by C. Day Lewis
Edited by Jasper Griffin

HORACE WALPOLE: The Castle of Otranto
Edited by W. S. Lewis

IZAAK WALTON and CHARLES COTTON:
The Compleat Angler
Edited by John Buxton
Introduction by John Buchan

OSCAR WILDE: Complete Shorter Fiction
Edited by Isobel Murray

The Picture of Dorian Gray
Edited by Isobel Murray

VIRGINIA WOOLF: Orlando
Edited by Rachel Bowlby

ÉMILE ZOLA:
The Attack on the Mill and other stories
Translated by Douglas Parmée

A complete list of Oxford Paperbacks, including The World's Classics, OPUS, Past Masters, Oxford Authors, Oxford Shakespeare, and Oxford Paperback Reference, is available in the UK from the Arts and Reference Publicity Department (BH), Oxford University Press, Walton Street, Oxford OX2 6DP.

In the USA, complete lists are available from the Paperbacks Marketing Manager, Oxford University Press, 200 Madison Avenue, New York, NY 10016.

Oxford Paperbacks are available from all good bookshops. In case of difficulty, customers in the UK can order direct from Oxford University Press Bookshop, Freepost, 116 High Street, Oxford, OX1 4BR, enclosing full payment. Please add 10 per cent of published price for postage and packing.